Wish Upon a K-Star

ALSO BY KAT CHO

Once Upon a K-Prom

Wicked Fox

Vicious Spirits

KAT CHO

HYPERION
Los Angeles   New York

First Edition, April 2025
1 3 5 7 9 10 8 6 4 2
FAC-004510-25044
Printed in the United States of America

This book is set in Caslon/Monotype
Designed by Marci Senders

Library of Congress Cataloging-in-Publication Data

Names: Cho, Kat, author.
Title: Wish upon a K-star / by Kat Cho.
Description: First edition. • Los Angeles : Hyperion, 2025. • Audience:
Ages 12–18. • Audience: Grades 7–9. • Summary: Told in alternating
voices, when rising K-drama star Shin Hyeri and K-pop idol Moon Minseok
are filmed having an argument, the two stars must participate in a fake
dating show to keep their careers on track.
Identifiers: LCCN 2024018396 • ISBN 9781368103015 (hardcover) •
ISBN 9781368103039 (ebook)
Subjects: CYAC: Celebrities—Fiction. • Dating—Fiction. •
Korean Americans—Fiction. • Romance stories. •
LCGFT: Romance fiction. • Novels.
Classification: LCC PZ7.2.C5312 Wj 2025 • DDC [Fic]—dc23
LC record available at https://lccn.loc.gov/2024018396

Reinforced binding

Visit www.HyperionTeens.com

SUSTAINABLE FORESTRY INITIATIVE — Certified Sourcing
www.forests.org
SFI-01681

Logo Applies to Text Stock Only

For Rebecca, an amazing friend and editor
who's helped me bring my K-Pop worlds to life!

K-Pop Fan Attic article:
"Netizens React as an Alleged Case of a
Celebrity's Trainee Bullying Is Brought into Light"

Netizens are abuzz about an anonymous post claiming that a big rookie celebrity (Celebrity A) may have bullied another (Celebrity B) during their trainee years!

Neither celebrity was named, but there's speculation that Celebrity A may be the rookie actress Shin Hyeri, who has been getting more attention for her audience-pleasing supporting role in one of the hottest K-dramas of the year, *Youthful Exchange*. If Celebrity A is Shin Hyeri, many are guessing that Celebrity B would be Kim Ana, who has been the nation's princess ever since she won first place in the wildly popular audition program *Citizen Producer*, the show that gave both Shin Hyeri and Kim Ana their start when they were chosen as two of the nine girls to debut as Helloglow under CDB Entertainment Group (the media company that produced *Citizen Producer* for HBS). The girl group released multiple hits, earning them many rookie-of-the-year awards—until their unfortunate early disbandment due to a voting scandal that hit HBS almost a year after Helloglow's debut.

Though Shin Hyeri finished in third place in *CiPro*, many allege that said voting scandal means she should never have debuted in Helloglow and that manipulation of the votes was specifically for her benefit. Even her casting in *CiPro* seemed to be a publicity stunt as she is the younger sister of Hyejun from the popular boy group AX1S (who are currently promoting their comeback single, which hit #1 on the Oricon, Melon, and Circle charts). This is one of many alleged scandals attached to Shin Hyeri in her short career, leading to netizens branding her as the "scandal princess."

The now-viral post claims that Celebrity A broke into Celebrity B's phone and texted a boy trainee inappropriate pictures from her photo roll.

But the reason many believe Celebrity A to be Shin Hyeri specifically is because of the allegations accusing Celebrity A of hiding Celebrity B's costume before an evaluation. Fans might remember that during one of the evaluations on *CiPro*, Kim Ana was late, claiming it was due to a lost costume. Though Shin Hyeri disputed it, many fans did blame her for hiding the costume, as she was roommates with Kim Ana at the time.

Though Shin Hyeri has found some success in her re-debut as an actress. These allegations of bullying could have a ripple effect as Korea takes bullying accusations seriously. Many celebrities have taken forced breaks after such allegations, with some even made to retire from the entertainment industry entirely. Netizens have started tagging Shin Hyeri's agency in criticisms against the rookie actress.

Meanwhile, Shin Hyeri is scheduled to be the cohost of the midsummer K-pop festival with fan favorite Moonster of the mega boy-group WDB.

WDB has had their share of scandals recently with the dating reveal of leader JD, as well as his injury during tour leading to his current break from all scheduled activities. Plus, maknae Robbie being spotted in public with his rumored non-celebrity girlfriend.

Whether these rumors about Shin Hyeri are true, netizens are already very curious to see what happens during the live-cast of the midsummer festival.

ONE
HYERI

Growing up, I hated when people lied.

Whether it was my brother laying the blame for a broken glass on me, or Mom telling our halmeoni we couldn't visit for the holidays because I had a nonexistent school event, or even a total stranger claiming they were ahead of you in line for the register. It always bothered me when others lied.

Which is why I probably shouldn't have debuted as an idol.

All we're taught is how to lie.

Lie that we're perfect role models who only know training and practice rooms.

Lie that we are naturally beautiful even when half of us have gotten some kind of procedure.

Lie that we all like one another, when I know many of the idols I debuted with hate each other's guts.

Everyone lies in this industry.

And even with all the rampant lies, people will still believe anything.

Which is why I'm in handroll mode, blanket tight around me.

The problem with the most recent gossip article about me is that it's not 100 percent lies. Which is how they get you. They tell a few known truths peppered in with the gossip and the rumors. And people assume, since they know one to be true, they all must be.

Yes, I am the unfortunate owner of the nickname "scandal princess." And it did all stem from my time on *Citizen Producer*. But I definitely did *not* text a boy from Kim Ana's phone when we were trainees. And I worked my ass off and earned my way into Helloglow fair and square.

But the worst things are the half-truths. The things that look bad because they don't have the full story. And I can never tell it, not now. Because I'll be accused of making it up to save face, even if all I tell is the truth. Finally.

I roll over to shove my face into my pillow and let out a strangled scream. Instead of releasing the tension it just brings my tears closer to the surface. So, I keep my face pressed tightly to the pillow to catch them so they don't fall on my face and make it all puffy. I still have an appearance today.

I hear the beep of the door lock a second before Min Sohee's singsong voice calls out. "Eonniii! Where are youuu?"

I don't reply. I know she'll find me anyway.

The trainee dorms are empty right now except for Sohee and me. And soon she will be gone too.

After Helloglow disbanded last year, Sohee and I moved back into Bright Star's trainee dorms. We commiserated over our time in the group, both good and bad. Well, Sohee had most of the good stuff and I had most of the bad. But we went through it together, and that's what counts. She's never asked me if any of the rumors or gossip are true.

Now Sohee is about to re-debut in Bright Star Entertainment's first girl group, Kastor. And they're starting to film their pre-debut show this week, so the company is making her move in with her members.

I'm not upset about it. Mostly.

It's just that she's my best . . . fine, only friend in the industry. Losing her is like losing my entire social life.

"Eonni!" Sohee calls again, her voice echoing down the long hallway.

It's strange—when we first met, Sohee's constant enthusiasm and positivity kind of annoyed me. And now, it's what makes me love her so much. Except when I'm in the mood to metaphorically burn everything down. Like right now.

So, I'm hiding in my cocoon of depression. I'd stay here all day except I'm supposed to cohost HBS's midsummer K-pop festival today. I wish I could just tell my manager I'm sick and can't do it. But I know that won't fly. I am expected to make my scheduled appearances unless I'm bleeding on the floor or I'm literally puking my guts out (and even that's not always an accepted excuse).

And, now more than ever, I can't afford to miss things. The message will be too obvious. That I'm bothered by the article. That the article must be true if I'm skipping appearances after its release.

The bedroom door opens, and I hear the shuffle of her house slippers move across the floor.

"I know you're in there, Eonni."

She pushes my privacy curtain aside. It's strung across the bunk bed I call home. There are three bunks shoved into each of the two rooms in this apartment. This place was probably intended to house a young couple, maybe a new family like the one that lives across the hall. But Bright Star rents it out as a dorm for the trainees. And at capacity it can house twelve hopefuls with dreams of stardom.

When it was full, there were girls everywhere at all times. A bunk curtain was as good as a closed door, indicating the occupant wants to be left alone. Of course, Sohee doesn't follow that rule when it comes to me.

She's too used to my depression cycles.

"Eonni, come on."

Sohee pulls on the covers. But my blanket handroll holds fast. I am an expert at it at this point, having made so many in the last two years.

"I have tteokbokki."

My mouth waters at the mention of it.

"I'm not hungry," I lie.

"Really?" I can feel her leaning forward and then the delicious spicy scent wafts through my blanket barrier.

My stomach grumbles loudly.

"Fine." I fling the blanket off to reveal Sohee's grinning face. I squint in defense against the bright room lights. Then I see the takeout bag and snatch it from her.

Without asking, Sohee reaches under my bed and pulls out the tray I keep there for secret bed eating. I didn't eat in here when the dorm was more full—some girls were sensitive to food smells, so we usually ate in the kitchen or the tiled living room. But now that it's just Sohee and me, we eat in our rooms sometimes when the situation warrants it. And wallowing in self-pity definitely warrants.

At 163 centimeters and with her sweet oval face and large doe eyes, Sohee is the epitome of adorable. And Bright Star has played into it with her new style, a shoulder-length bob with blunt ends and straight bangs.

Without even getting out of bed, I reach around the side into a small open shelf and pull out a crumpled bag of Honey Butter Chips. My favorite. There's barely any left. I pour the last of the crushed crumbs over the steaming spicy rice cakes.

Sohee rolls her eyes affectionately. "I can't believe you eat it that way."

"I like the crunch." I take a huge bite and close my eyes. It's heaven. And a billion calories. But I don't care. Because I'm depressed and I can't show it during the broadcast today. So, I've earned bad-for-me snack food. I'll eat five short tubules and that's it, I promise myself.

I tune back in to hear Sohee say, "So I came right over after practice."

"Oh?" I say vaguely, not quite sure what she was talking about.

"You spaced out again, didn't you?" Sohee shakes her head, but there's no malice in it.

It's a bad habit of mine. When I have a lot on my mind, I tend to get lost in my thoughts. Even mid-conversation.

"Sorry."

Sohee lifts a knowing brow. "You read the article, didn't you?"

I ignore her and pluck up my second tube of rice cake, shoving it in my mouth. Hoping that it'll discourage her from demanding an answer. Instead, she crosses her arms and waits.

Sometimes I hate how stubborn Sohee is. Most think she's so sweet and bubbly and carefree. But I've never met someone more headstrong than Min Sohee. Once she has a goal in mind, nothing will stop her from achieving it. And if she wants something from you, she won't stop pestering until you give in.

It's why she's successful, I'm sure of it.

"Maybe I shouldn't go to the festival today. What if it just makes things worse after that article?"

"Eonni, you're not supposed to read those things," Sohee says, wagging her chopsticks at me.

"Isn't the polite thing to pretend you didn't read it either?" I ask through my third rice cake. Savoring it because I only have two more allotted.

I should have known that Sohee wouldn't pretend, at least between us. Sohee is the kind of girl who faces things head-on. Probably because her sweet face makes everyone want to fawn over her. Didn't hurt that as the maknae of Helloglow, she was babied by every member and manager. Even our fans.

"Maybe I should stay in the dorm another day," she says with a pout.

Immediately, I feel guilty. I know she put off moving into her new dorm because she worried about me being alone. I'm the older one, I should be the one taking care of her. But it's the other way around.

"Nah, I'm good." I take a small bite of my fourth tteok.

"Are you sure? You're not faking it, are you?" She jabs her chopsticks at me.

"Of course not." I use my chopsticks to push hers down. "And be careful, what if you poke my eye out? Hongjoo-eonni will be angry at you for making me wear an eyepatch on live TV."

"Hongjoo-eonni never gets mad at me," Sohee says with a confident grin as she plucks up another tteokbokki.

"You know, you're not the youngest of your new group," I grumble. "You're going to have to learn that you won't always get your way."

"No, I'm the leader," Sohee says with a saucy wiggle of her brows. "So, I get unrestrained power!"

"Really?" For a moment, I forget my problems as Sohee's excitement becomes infectious. "They officially announced?"

Sohee nods. "We filmed the reveal video today with the group! It's going to go live on the Kastor channel next week."

"Congratulations, Sohee-yah. You're going to be great," I say. And I mean it. I know that Sohee was really worried about the possibility of being chosen as leader; it's a huge responsibility, but she also secretly wanted it. I could tell.

And she's perfect for the role. Everyone listens to her. She never gets into fights. And she already has experience from being in Helloglow. Not that anyone asked me, but I would've told them to choose Sohee as leader, hands down.

Maybe I missed my calling behind the scenes. Maybe I should've become a manager or producer instead of an actress. Then I'd be less in the spotlight. And have less chances for the public to judge every move I make.

But I know if I stop pursuing a celebrity career, Mom will nag me about it for the rest of my life. Which will be severely shortened from being annoyed to death by Mom's aforementioned nagging.

That's why I debuted as an actress.

What sucks about it, though, is I kind of like it.

I can even see myself loving it someday. And that scares the ever-living snot out of me.

Because, if I let myself like it and then I lose it, it'll be so much more painful. And every day, there are people who'd love to see me lose it all.

Part of me feels like I *have* to succeed if only to stick it to those people. And part of me feels like those people have way more energy and drive than I do and I'll never overtake them.

Well, today certainly is another test. Who will come out on top?

Honestly, I have no idea.

Sohee indiscriminately shoves like five tteoks into her mouth. A warning almost falls from my lips. She's about to debut, she's probably on a diet. But I hold it in. We get criticism from enough places in our lives, she doesn't need to hear that stuff from me too.

My phone buzzes with a text from my manager, Hongjoo.

"I gotta go." I stare longingly at the half container left of tteokbokki. "Thanks for the pick-me-up, even if it's going to add a kilogram to me on camera today."

"You're too skinny anyway," Sohee says. "People won't like that."

"People never like anything about me," I point out.

"Not true, they love you after your drama. Don't let one article get you down, it doesn't mean anything. It'll all pass soon," she says with a bright smile. I want to roll my eyes at her unwavering optimism, but I smile back at her instead.

On the elevator I can't stop myself from reading the article again. I glare at the title. I hate that it's trending. But of course it is.

At least my name isn't in the headline. A small gift in this whole situation. But I still hate this article far more than most of the others. Even the ones that exclaim "Shin Hyeri Accused of Being a Bully!" in bold letters at the top.

And that's because of what's in the last paragraphs. A name that sticks out and mocks me.

Because what bothers me the most, somehow, is that they mentioned Moonster in the article. Of all the people to be flagged in my current humiliation cycle, it had to be my nemesis.

SHIN HYERI PROFILE

STAGE NAME: Hyeri
NAME: Shin Hyeri (신혜리)
GROUP: Helloglow (헬로글로우) (disbanded)
GROUP POSITION: Lead vocal
CURRENT PROFESSION: Actress
BIRTHDAY: November 20
SIGN: Scorpio
HEIGHT: 167 cm (5'5.75")
BLOOD TYPE: O
MBTI: INTJ
BIRTHPLACE: Los Angeles, California, USA
FAMILY: Mom, Dad, brother (older by 2 years)
HOBBIES: Drawing
EDUCATION: Chung-Ang University, department of theater and film creation
NATIONALITY: Korean American

HYERI FACTS:

• Hyejun, member of AX1S, is her older brother.
• She is currently attending Chung-Ang University.
• She was recruited by Bright Star Entertainment at a Korean festival with her brother. Her parents made her wait two more years before allowing her to become a trainee.
• She used to be a member of Helloglow, formed in 2020 on the show *Citizen Producer*, disbanded in 2021.
• While filming *Welcome to Helloglow* she said she doesn't like being the center of attention.
• Debuted in 2022 as an actress with a supporting role in teen drama *Youthful Exchange*.

HYERI DRAMA SERIES

Youthful Exchange (나의 청춘)—HBS/2022, Lee Soojung.

TWO
MINSEOK

Moon Minseok, better known by his stage name Moonster, is good at being a celebrity. In fact, he's amazing at it.

His ability to pick up things quickly has served him well in his chosen profession. Naturally a good singer and rapper, he quickly learned dance from the age of five when he convinced his parents to sign him up for lessons at a local hip-hop studio during his family's tenure in Westminster, London. Yes, that Westminster. The one close to the famous Abbey Road Studios. Some might imagine this proximity to rock and roll history was a factor in Minseok's love of music. And whether it's true or not, it is indeed included on his official idol profile.

In addition to his talent in singing, dancing, and rapping, Minseok is fluent in three languages and proficient in a fourth.

But Minseok knows his true skill as a celebrity, in fact, lies in his power to be liked. He is liked by nearly everyone in the industry. Friends with many fellow celebrities of his same year. Respected by most others as part of the world-famous group WDB, not in small part due to the group's knack for breaking records again and again.

Moonster is found charming and easygoing by any who've had the pleasure of being on a variety or reality show alongside him. His easy rapport with fellow celebrities means he's often asked to guest host music shows and festival events as well.

To Minseok this is both a blessing and a curse. He still remembers a time when WDB was struggling to gain recognition. When they weren't asked on any shows or to do any events. They were from a small label with limited connections. So, he is grateful for the boom in popularity and requests over the last two years. Truly he is. But, despite Minseok's proclivity for entertaining, he's in fact an introvert (an ISTP the last time WDB was given the MBTI test for a show).

In his off-time, he prefers to be alone with his music or his books or his shows. In fact, he rarely leaves his bed on days off.

Which makes his intense summer schedule that much more annoying.

He is now suddenly the de facto face of what he has come to think of as the "WDB rehabilitation plan," made necessary after a couple of not-so-simple scandals featuring the two most popular members of the group. (Note: ranking of popularity based on unverified polls on *K-Pop Fan Attic* forums. Moon Minseok does not personally validate such rankings.)

He reminds himself that's why he's at the midsummer K-pop festival. So he can pretend like everything is okay in the Wonder-verse. And that no one need worry about the group breaking up (a rumor going around) or that their leader, JD, is hiding out on a cabbage farm in shame from his recent dating scandal (a funny image to Minseok as he knows Jongdae would never be caught dead on a farm).

"Moonster-ssi, the next question is for you," says the assistant PD conducting the behind-the-scenes interview.

Moonster gives her a polite smile and a nod.

"We heard you were involved in writing the lyrics for this song. What inspired you to write something so romantic? Perhaps your beautiful duet partner?"

Minseok glances at the girl beside him. Kim Ana is gorgeous. No one can deny that. But when she smiles, it does nothing for him. Ana is talented. She's polite and says all the right things at the right time. But, for some reason, Minseok feels like he's looking at a photograph instead of a person.

Still, he plasters on an easygoing smile. "She definitely would have helped. But I wrote the lyrics before I got the pleasure of meeting Ana-ssi. The producers sent me a scene from the drama, and Robbie and I wrote the lyrics based on that."

"Fans were really excited about the surprise self-produced song Robbie released on YouTube at the beginning of summer. Are the rumors of new solo music from him true?"

Minseok gives a shrug and a sly smile. "Robbie has always been a great songwriter. I've heard some of his recent songs he's working on and they sound amazing, maybe he'll share something new soon."

It is a lie. Minseok hasn't heard any of the tracks Robbie is working on. He has barely had time to see the other guys this summer outside of the few times they see each other in the dorm. But he knows how to promote things, and he knows what would best help the group. The company only let Robbie drop a surprise solo track to help everyone forget that the next WDB group album is delayed due to JD's scandal.

"And, Kim Ana, how did it feel working with Moonster?"

Ana sends Moonster another empty smile. "It was amazing and

nerve-racking. I was a huge fan of Oppa before. Definitely a total Constellation! So, I was very starstruck. But Oppa made me feel so comfortable during the entire recording session."

Kim Ana knows it's a lie. Moonster barely said a passing hello to her as he left the recording studio when she arrived for her session. And this is the first time she's ever called him Oppa. But she is experienced enough to know that Moonster isn't going to expose her in front of a camera. It would make him look bad as well. Plus, this lie is for both of their benefits. Pretending to have a close treasured memory from the recording session will help keep the song on the charts.

As expected, Moonster grins, sending her a little wink. "It was easy with such a talented hoobae."

"Great!" the interviewer says, clapping her hands.

She's delighted by how perfect Moonster and Kim Ana look on camera together. This will almost definitely fuel the fledgling rumors that they're secretly dating. Two of the hottest idols right now and she gets to interview them. She begged the head PD for the opportunity.

"That was great! Thank you, Moonster-ssi, Ana-ssi."

Moonster nods and turns to Ana to say goodbye. But she's already walking away. It doesn't bother him. Some idols don't like making small talk. He returns to his dressing room. He had been pulled away from his lunch for the interview. But when he walks in, there's another camera crew there.

"Ah, here he is," says Hanbin, Minseok's manager. "You can capture some content while he finishes getting ready for sound check. Minseok-ah, this is a behind-the-scenes crew hoping to get vlog content for the HBS YouTube channel." Hanbin looks like he's in his late thirties rather than his late twenties with a receding hairline and worry lines around his mouth. Minseok knows he and his members gave Hanbin the majority of those wrinkles.

As he's hurried into the makeup chair, Minseok sends a sad look at his cooling pasta. All he wants is to eat and nap, in that order.

The stylist immediately starts fixing Minseok's concealer. She's been fighting with the dark bags under his eyes all day. Ones created by three hours of sleep as Minseok's scheduled appearances last night ended at three a.m.

For someone who loves lying down, Minseok has barely done that in the last forty-eight hours.

Minseok's phone rings with a call from WDB's maknae, Robbie (birth name: Choi Jiseok).

He holds the caller ID up, knowing they will blur out the actual details in post and only show Robbie's name.

"Robiya," Minseok answers. Tone lightly teasing.

"Hey, you getting ready for the show?"

"Of course. Do you miss me, jagi-ya?" Minseok says. Playful voice still attached. He's well aware that the fans like when the boys are lovey-dovey with each other.

Which is hard to accomplish these days, all alone.

Still, Minseok thinks, not for the first time, that it is probably for the best that his summer has shifted to solo activities. He was originally scheduled for a sub-unit debut with JD.

The duo of Moon Minseok and Lee Jongdae (endearingly known as MinDae by fans) have been linked together since trainee days. They both gained a small fandom even before debut due to their time as young street buskers. The moment the two met, they bonded over a love of American '90s hip-hop, sushi, and Korean melodramas (though Jongdae denies the third and Minseok loyally keeps that secret).

Despite being the son of the CEO, Jongdae never used that fact to get out of training or make things easier on himself. And in return, Minseok built an honest respect for Jongdae. He's always believed his best friend had a baseline of integrity. Something not all celebrities possess. Which is why he is currently in a state of disillusionment when it comes to Jongdae.

This past spring brought many changes for WDB. They had their first world tour. And their first big stage accident. And first huge scandal.

An accident backstage at KFest-Chicago had landed Jongdae with a broken leg. When Nam Sooyeon was caught visiting him in the hospital, it came out that she and Jongdae had been secretly dating. Sooyeon was a K-pop darling once deemed the "nation's girl next door," and her reputation had taken a beating due to the dating reveal. She'd lost her contract with one of the biggest K-pop companies because of it.

Some of her loyal fans blamed Jongdae for her fall from grace.

And, if he was being honest, Minseok sometimes felt the same way. Granted, he's always thought the archaic dating clauses that the bigger companies insisted on went too far. But how could Jongdae make such a huge mistake that risked Sooyeon's career and the careers of the other WDB members?

"JD-hyeong says he's worried about the article," Robbie says.

As if JD has a right to be worried about scandals, Minseok thinks. But aloud he says, "Of course, I miss you too."

"What?" Robbie says, then lets out a knowing sigh. "Are there cameras there?"

"Yup, want to say hello to the fans?" Minseok lets an easy grin spread over his face, effortlessly hiding his discordant thoughts. A female crew member sighs behind the assistant PD in charge of the shoot.

"Yeah." Robbie groans. He's good on camera, but he's also painfully shy.

Minseok turns the phone on speaker and says, "What are you doing, jagi-ya?"

Robbie replies in an equally joking voice. "Waiting for you to get home, jagi."

Their maknae might be shy, but his showmanship is always good.

Minseok laughs. "What are you really doing?"

"Deciding on what we want to order for dinner, so we can watch the live broadcast."

"Good. Thanks for monitoring, Robiya."

"Yup. Drink lots of water and have fun!"

"I always do," Minseok says before hanging up cheerfully.

The assistant PD calls for the cameras to cut, pleased with the footage. It is kismet timing he caught the conversation. Fans are thirsting for interactions between the WDB members after they had to abruptly end their tour. This clip will definitely go viral and he will get credit.

"Thanks, Moonster-ssi. That was perfect."

"Anything for HBS," Minseok says, lowering his head in a bow as the crew leaves.

It isn't until they are gone that Minseok finally lets himself relax. As part of the biggest K-pop group in the world, Minseok long ago learned the need for control in front of the public, which includes production crews and cameras by extension. Even though fans love the "real" moments between the boys, the bigger they've become, the more he finds a need to keep some things private. Just for himself, even if it's small, meaningless things. It helps Minseok feel like a person instead of a product.

His phone buzzes, and he finds a text from Robbie.

Robbie: *Hyeong is still asking if you saw the article?*

Minseok knows exactly what article Robbie is referencing. Yet he doesn't reply immediately. It annoys him that JD continues to monitor these things when he is supposed to be on hiatus. And that is compounded by the fact that he is getting Robbie to do his dirty work right now.

Minseok calls foul on using the maknae to get him to respond. But these days, Minseok and JD don't really talk that much.

Robbie: *Hyeong says to be on alert during today's festival.*

Robbie: *He says he's going to call Hyejun-hyeong about it.*

This gets Minseok to type furiously back

Minseok: *Tell him not to call Hyejun. Hyeri will freak out if we send her older brother to bother her over this.*

He watches the three typing dots float at the bottom of his screen.

Robbie: *Okay, got Hyeong to hold off on calling.*

Minseok feels misgivings about the broadcast, but he knows better than to let bad feelings or superstitions stop him from doing his job. He chalks it up to the cracked relationship between him and his best friend. His hand hovers over his phone—perhaps he should call JD? But he stops himself. If they're going to have it out, it should be in person and not before he's about to go on live TV. He must focus on his job. Even JD would agree.

At least today he'll have something to distract himself with. Because the one person in this world who doesn't seem to like Minseok is Shin Hyeri. Which makes it impossible for him not to poke at her. It is one of his favorite pastimes, and it always makes him feel better.

MOONSTER PROFILE

STAGE NAME: Moonster
NAME: Moon Minseok (문민석)
GROUP: WDB (원더별)
GROUP POSITION: Subvocal, lead rapper
BIRTHDAY: February 18
SIGN: Aquarius
HEIGHT: 176 cm (5'9.5")
BLOOD TYPE: B
MBTI: ISTP
BIRTHPLACE: Paris, France
FAMILY: Mom, Dad, brother (older by five years)
HOBBIES: Watching movies
EDUCATION: Seoul School of Performing Arts; Global Cyber University
LIGHTSTICK COLOR: Yellow

MOONSTER FACTS:

• He was born in Paris but moved to England with his family when he was only three (Westminster, London) and then to Shanghai when he was seven. They finally moved to South Korea when he entered middle school (equivalent of seventh grade).
• Is friends with AX1S's Hyejun, SF9's Chani, Stray Kids' Han, Stray Kids' Felix, The Boyz's Sunwoo, Itzy's Yeji, (G)I-DLE's Shuhua.
• Speaks English, French, Korean, and Mandarin.
• Spends most of his free time in his bed in the dorm.
• Can sleep anywhere.
• The commercial he'd most like to be cast for is for fried chicken.
• Role model is Block B's Zico.

THREE
HYERI

t's strange being back at a concert venue.

I haven't been to one since Helloglow disbanded.

Before then, I practically lived on stages. It was a whirlwind of broadcast stations, college festivals, music shows, and arenas. I'd experienced almost everything you could as an idol in just one short year.

I know it's something I should be grateful for.

No, I *am* grateful for it. But that gratitude is overlaid with a vibrating anxiety every time I think of that part of my life.

My hair is yanked and I hide a flinch as my roots protest.

"Sorry," the assistant stylist mutters. He's young, barely older than me. He's new and clearly nervous. Which wouldn't usually bother me, except he keeps sneaking timid peeks at my face in the mirror. I can recognize those curious looks by now. He's probably waiting to see if I yell at the hair and makeup team, or throw a tantrum about the temperature of my coffee. Because of course someone with my reputation would be a total nightmare to work with.

As if to prove him wrong, I don't even move as he keeps pulling at my hair.

But when he tries to pin some of it back, he jabs me in the ear.

This time I can't hide the wince of pain and I notice his slight frown. Like he's already telling himself that's proof that I'm difficult. Darn it.

"Jeongho, stop before you take out her eye." David Reyes, the head stylist, comes over, curler in hand. He's tall with tan skin and a full, well-groomed beard. He moved to Korea over a decade ago.

His more skilled hands take over and I relax a bit. Other than Hongjoo, he's known me the longest, ever since he was assigned to do my hair for the first evaluation performance on *CiPro*. When I first debuted, he'd teach me Spanish and I'd help him with his Korean, though sometimes I think he speaks better Korean than I do.

He's my favorite stylist, even if he's always yelling at me when I neglect my hair.

As if on cue, David frowns. "Hyeri, honey. Are you using the serum I gave you?"

"I keep forgetting," I admit, and he gives me a disappointed look in the mirror. "I'll use it, I swear."

"Hmm." He shakes some of his own serum into his palms and warms it before running it through my hair.

I pull out my phone, knowing styling can sometimes take a while. And when I open SNS, a post about the article is the first on my feed. I shouldn't, but I expand the comments.

Bullies should go to jail.

Why protect the identity of a bully? We KNOW Celebrity A is Shin Hyeri!

Can't wait for her agency to deny all allegations and continue to protect a bully!

Shin Hyeri is shameless for continuing to promote when she used to be such a bully.

Shin Hyeri = yeombyeong idol!

Shin Hyeri should be sent to hell to burn for her sins against an angel like Kim Ana!

That last one sends a chill down my spine. I'm used to angry commenters, and this one is from a handle I recognize, HyeriTopAnti.

They regularly comment on articles about my scandals. I know Hongjoo is going to yell at me when I tell her I was reading the comments, but I flag it to show to my manager. There is a file for them now, another sad reality of my life. Will this happen the rest of my career? Having to collect the worst of the worst to make sure they don't actually follow through with their promises? I shiver just thinking of it.

The movement pulls on my hair, still in David's hands.

"If you don't sit still, I might accidentally give you a mullet," he warns.

"Sorry," I mutter, staring at the phone.

"Sweetie, you're not reading forbidden things, are you?"

"Not anymore," I promise, lowering the phone to my lap.

I finally look up and his eyes capture mine in the mirror. Soft and understanding. He's been around for the worst of it. I've cried too many times to count while he's cut or dyed my hair.

"You shouldn't do anything to mess with your own head before a broadcast," David says in a knowing voice.

He's right. I'm on edge as it is. Being back at one of the big arenas makes me remember my year in Helloglow and how I'd get horrible stomachaches before performances. As it is, I'm regretting the tteokbokki with Sohee before coming here. It's rolling around in my stomach right now.

It doesn't help that every time the door opens, I jump in anticipation of a camera. Hongjoo told me there's a behind-the-scenes crew coming by today.

But instead of cameras it's Hongjoo. She's short, probably only 155 centimeters. She has a sweet round face and always wears her hair back in a ponytail. She looks like she could be a kindergarten teacher. But she's fierce. I've seen her put men two times her size in their place.

She hurries in, a tray of coffee drinks sloshing in her hands. Even as she jumps over a fallen paper takeout bag, she doesn't spill them. Hongjoo would never let coffee spill.

"David," Hongjoo says, handing him a latte.

He grins and gives her a smacking kiss on the lips in thanks. "When can we finally register our marriage, Hongjoo-yah?"

She rolls her eyes. "If you were interested in women, I would do it in a heartbeat."

"Oh, what could have been," David muses, then winks at me in the mirror. I can't help smiling. Hongjoo and David love to pretend to flirt to pass the time.

Hongjoo hands me my iced Americano before pulling out a vanilla latte for herself. I can practically see the calories swimming in it, and it makes my mouth water.

You had your cheat snack, I remind myself. One that would give Hongjoo a heart attack if she heard about it.

To slightly appease myself, I take a sip of my Americano. No sugar added. The bitter drink does the opposite of what I hoped.

"And then sound check in thirty, okay?" Hongjoo is saying.

Shoot, I did it again. Got lost in my own meandering thoughts. I chirp out a quick reply. "Okay."

"Hyeri, you have to pay attention." Hongjoo knows me too well for me to hide anything from her.

"Sorry, Eonni."

She shakes her head before continuing to read off the schedule. "After sound check you can come back here and finish your hair and makeup. Did you tell them what you wanted to order for lunch?"

"Salad with a side of salad," I say obediently. If Hongjoo hears the sarcasm in my voice, she doesn't react to it. She's too used to my moods by now.

I'm lucky that Bright Star let Hongjoo remain as my manager when I moved from the idol division to the actor division in the company. Sometimes I worry she regrets agreeing to continue working with me. She's always having to put out fires as my manager.

I close my eyes, taking eight deep breaths. Something I learned from the dance instructor at Bright Star. With each successive breath I relax a different region of my body: hands, feet, arms, legs, shoulders, neck, stomach. By the end of the exercise, I feel looser, if not better.

"Done for now," David declares. My long hair is in careless waves. It still has pins holding my fringe in place, but I know those will stay in until right before I go out onstage. "I'll be back before the show for final touch-ups."

"Thanks, David-oppa."

"Anything for my favorite. But don't tell anyone I said that." He winks at me in the mirror before gesturing for Jeongho to follow. The assistant scurries after David, carrying a bulky bag of styling equipment. The bag bumps against my seat.

My Americano wobbles and I grip it tighter, causing it to spill over onto my sweatpants.

"Sorry!" Jeongho lowers into a deep bow.

I give him a smile. "It's okay, these sweats are old."

He bows again as David calls impatiently from the hallway. Jeongho looks back and forth between the spill and the closing door.

"You should go," I say, adding a kind smile. "I can take care of this."

"Yes, sorry, okay, thank you." He scurries out.

I lean back in my chair with a sigh.

This should be a lesson, I tell myself. *Not every person is out to get you, Shin Hyeri. Sometimes they're just going through their own stuff.*

"How long until sound check?" I ask Hongjoo.

"Twenty-five. Nope, twenty-three minutes," she says without even looking up from her phone.

I wonder if that's enough time for a short nap. It usually takes me a while to actually fall asleep; I'll probably have to wake up as soon as I do.

"Oh hey, also, I saw your brother—" Hongjoo is cut off by a knock on the door. When she opens it, I hear her say, "Speak of the devil."

Hyejun saunters in, only wearing ripped jeans and a graphic tee, but I know the outfit probably costs more than my phone. AX1S is the kind of group that gets their casual-wear sent to them by high-end brands. They sell out things almost as quickly as WDB whenever they wear them.

He's tall and muscular but not bulky. His hair is shaved close on the sides but longer on top right now.

We have similar facial features, an oval face with a pointed chin. A taller nose bridge that all the other trainees used to tell me I was lucky to have. Hyejun's lips are fuller than mine, but we have the same shape with a pronounced Cupid's bow. And we both have a single freckle right under our right eye.

He comfortably greets the staff, always easygoing with anyone.

A rush of contradicting emotions fills me at the sight of him. Relief that it's not the camera crew yet. Annoyance because I know he's probably here to bother me. And an awkward tension, because he's my brother, but we're not like normal siblings. Our parents let him leave home when I was twelve. And even when I followed him to Seoul almost two years later, we were separated because we were in different companies. Hyejun was scouted by HQ Entertainment and I entered Bright Star.

Whenever Hyejun did come around BSE, he never really hung out with me. He was always there to see Jongdae and Minseok. He'd already made his friends and he didn't want his little sister shadowing him everywhere. But he was the only person I knew in Seoul.

"What's up, Riri?" he asks, using my childhood nickname. One he knows annoys me.

I sneer at him. "What do you want?"

"Just checking in with you. Eomma gave me an earful to keep an eye on you today." He lifts his hand to ruffle my hair, but a stern look from Hongjoo stops him.

I'm not surprised our mother called Hyejun instead of me. Just call the perfect son to rein in the problem child.

But I'm also a little relieved. My calls with Mom always leave me feeling inadequate. My mom likes to give me her notes on all the things I'm doing wrong. Her favorite is to tell me that I should be more personable like Hyejun. That people have an instant dislike for me because I'm so standoffish. It doesn't work to tell her it's because I still feel stiff and awkward in interviews. She'll just tell me that's not an excuse from a girl who was part of such a successful idol group.

"Hey, Hyeri-yah, did you hear me?"

"Huh?"

He rolls his eyes as he perches on the couch and opens one of the bags of Honey Butter Chips.

"Oppa, you know those are my favorite!" I complain. I'd been hoping to hoard them away for my stash after I was done with promotions and off diet.

"You want?" He holds the bag out to me, and I stare longingly at the delicious chips inside. But guilt over my morning snack still weighs on me both figuratively and literally. He shakes the bag encouragingly, but there's a smirk on his face. He's teasing me because he knows I'm on a diet.

"You need to be careful today." Hyejun shovels up another mouthful of chips. "People are going to be all over your performance after that ridiculous article."

"If you agree it's ridiculous, then why should I care about it?" I mutter.

He gives me a look that speaks volumes. It says, "You should know the answer to that." Because anything that could affect my reputation in this industry weighs much heavier since I'm already mired in controversy. I walk a thin line always.

"You know, Eomma sounded upset on the phone. She gets really worried about us. It took a lot for her to let us come here alone."

Now I want to lift a disbelieving brow. Because Hyejun and I both know that our mom *loves* having famous kids. She's constantly posting glamour shots of herself on her social media with captions like *Hyejun's eomma missing her son while he's on tour* or *Celebrating my son's most recent music show win. AX1S fighting!*

I can count on one hand the number of times she's posted about me: when I got first place on the first episode of *CiPro*, when I debuted with Helloglow, and when my drama ratings hit twenty-five.

I hated how happy that last one made me. Because it meant I really did still need her approval.

But now this article is out and I feel like I've reverted to where I was a year ago.

"Maybe you should call her. She mentioned you never call her anymore," Hyejun says.

I don't call my mother unscheduled anymore, because every time I do, she tells me I'm interrupting her day and immediately hangs up on me. Things always have to be done on Han Jooyoung's schedule or not at all. I can guarantee if I picked up the phone right now she'd be annoyed. But then she complains to Hyejun that I should call her more. I feel like the narrative of my life always shifts around me. The only consistency is that it's whatever makes me look the worst.

"Just go, Oppa. I need to get ready and so do you." I pretend to look through the apps on my phone.

"I can't." He leans back, crossing his legs comfortably. "I want to say hello to Minseok-ah first."

"Why would you wait here to say hi to him?"

"Because I told him to come here."

I spin to stare at him. "You what?"

Hyejun doesn't seem to hear the surprised anger in my voice. Or, more likely, doesn't care.

"I told him to meet me in your dressing room," he repeats, and I let out an annoyed huff. He *knows* that's not why I asked.

There's a quick rap on the door as it opens. He doesn't even wait for an answer. Just like Minseok to do whatever he wants.

"Hey!" He greets Hyejun with a handshake half hug. Then he sends me a grin. "What's up, Hyeri?"

He speaks in English. His accent skews British due to going to some fancy prep school in Westminster as a kid. Of course, it's another thing the fangirls swoon over.

It annoys me just thinking of it. So, I refuse to look at him. Instead, I stare at the mirror in front of me.

Minseok is undeniably handsome. He isn't as tall as Hyejun, but he has a presence that can't be denied. It's not so much about his looks as how he holds himself. There's an aura like he was born to be a celebrity.

Even though his hair is back to a more natural brown color instead of the bright magenta it was a few months ago and his makeup is subtle, he could take to the stage and everyone would know he's a performer.

"Any of the other guys coming?" Hyejun asks.

"Nah, I'm solo again today." Minseok shrugs.

I'm confused. Every time I've ever seen WDB, they've been in one another's pockets. Not all groups get along—it's bound to happen when you gather multiple big personalities and shove them into a group together—but WDB is notorious for being closer than family. Which is why it feels so strange that Minseok seems completely fine with going solo this summer.

Minseok plucks the last bag of Honey Butter Chips off the table. I know it's irrational, but it annoys me. He doesn't have the courtesy to ask, even if I can't eat them right now.

Thankfully, he puts the bag back down.

"I talked to Jongdae-hyeong. He seems to be doing much better. Enough to be bored." Hyejun laughs, snatching up the chips that Minseok discarded and tearing them open.

"Wait—" I start to say, but it's too late, he's already shoved a handful in his mouth. So much for saving them for later.

I sigh and tell myself to calm down. I can buy more. But I know I won't. It's one thing to hoard a free bag of chips. It's another to go out and buy them. I can't justify spending the money on the calories.

Minseok starts to fiddle with the brushes David left behind on the counter. "Yeah, well you know him." He picks up my script, lying open to the last page I was reviewing. "Did you read through all of this?"

"Of course." I grab the script from him. Maybe a little harder than necessary as I'm still annoyed about my lost chips. "Shouldn't you be getting ready?"

He shrugs. "I just have to change outfits later."

Lucky, I think. It takes me hours to get ready. But at least my current look doesn't involve dyeing my hair. I remember when I had icy-blue hair for the Helloglow summer album. I had to wake up hours before the other girls to get it re-toned before every performance.

"You'll take care of Woori-Riri. Mat-ji, Minseok-ah?" Hyejun asks in a mix of English and Korean. His default when it's just the three of us. I used to love it when it was the three of us. When I was younger, Minseok always convinced Hyejun to let me hang around. Something I used to mistake as affection. I've learned better since.

Seeing him now always makes me annoyed and on edge. He just loves to press my buttons for no reason. And I can't have that today. Not when I have to be careful after the article.

"Don't I always take care of Riri?" He gives a mischievous grin that I definitely do not trust. Then, he lunges and I find myself in a headlock.

"Let go!" I demand.

"Not until you say it."

I scowl because I know exactly what he wants, and I'll die before I give in. "No way!"

"Come on, Riri."

"I'd rather cut off my own tongue!" I claim, a little hyperbolic, but he pisses me off so much.

"Minseok-ssi, keumanhae," Hongjoo says sternly from the corner, her hand over the mouthpiece of her phone. She must be really annoyed to interrupt a phone call.

Minseok stops like she says and releases me. I carefully extract myself, patting the clips in my hair and turning to the mirror to check that no damage was done to the 'do.

"Geez, Hyeri, just call him Oppa. What's the big deal?" Hyejun asks, finishing the chips and crumpling the bag between his hands. "You used to call him that all the time."

"When I was thirteen and I didn't know better." I try to tuck a loosened strand behind a clip to hide it.

Hyejun laughs as he lobs the chip bag into the trash. "You act like you're so much older now. It's only been a few years."

"I'm hurt, Hyeri-ya. I thought we were close," Minseok says, catching my eyes in the mirror. And I can see the mocking in them.

Before I can retort, Hyejun's manager opens the door. "Hyejun-ah! What are you doing here? We're next for sound check!"

"Coming, Hyeong." Hyejun holds out his hand, which Minseok promptly slaps in one of those lazy-yet-complicated handshakes. I almost laugh. It's like two kids on the playground. But I feel a buzz of envy too. Hyejun and Minseok are allowed to play around like they're kids. Even be messy or unprofessional.

It's different for girl groups.

You're not an idol anymore, I remind myself. I shouldn't have to be as worried. But I still am. It's a hard thing to shake once it's been an every-waking-hour part of your life.

Hyejun hurries out after his manager, but, for some reason, Minseok lingers.

"Don't you have to go too?" I ask pointedly.

"We have sound check together. I can wait here with you for it." He flops onto the couch, folding his hands behind his head and closing his eyes. Like he's lying on a beach instead of invading my dressing room. Within moments, his breathing evens out and I swear he's already dozing off.

I consider poking at his feet to wake him, but Hongjoo hangs up and from her expression, I know it's not good.

I hurry over to her. "What is it, Eonni?"

"That was the director for *Idol Academy*."

"Oh, what did he say?" I ask, trying to keep my voice down so Minseok can't hear. *Idol Academy* is a new drama considering me for a leading role. I don't have the heart to admit to Hongjoo that I'm not sure if I even want the part. It's a drama about kids going to an elite art school to train as singers. Everyone around me says I'm tailor-made for the role. But just thinking about it makes me nervous. It reminds me too much of my past and all the scandals that come with it.

But it would be such a huge deal to book a lead role so soon, and Hongjoo worked so hard to get my name in for consideration. I tell myself that if I get it, I'll do my very best so I can make her proud.

Plus, I'll definitely get a Mom SNS post if I land this role.

"Did they decide on casting?" I ask anxiously.

Hongjoo slowly shakes her head. "They're going to need more time because they're also considering another rookie actress."

"Oh," I say slowly, keeping my voice low because then it won't waver as much. "I see. Well, I knew it was a long shot. It would only be my second full-length drama. I can't expect to get such a big part so soon."

"Yes, plus it's not official yet! They could still choose you over Ana."

"Ana?" It could be another Ana. I shouldn't jump to conclusions. But Hongjoo winces, and I know I'm right. It seems the universe is dead set on pitting me against Kim Ana.

FOUR
SIX YEARS AGO

Hyeri waited impatiently in the lobby of the Bright Star building.

It was Chuseok. Which meant the trainees had the long weekend off. Most of them were going home to visit their families. The rest were international trainees or had families who lived too far away to visit on a quick weekend trip.

Hyeri's mom and dad were still in LA, but Hyejun-oppa's company was also giving them today off. And when she'd seen him last month, he'd promised he'd take her to Everland. She'd only been in Seoul for a few months, and she was still too nervous to go all the way out to the amusement park alone. So, she had to depend on Hyejun to take her.

She glanced at the last message exchange with Hyejun.

Hyeri: *Are you coming to Bright Star today?*

Hyejun: *yup.*

Hyejun still refused to hang out with her most of the time. But he'd promised to come on Chuseok. She'd made him pinkie swear it—even though pinkie swears were a little immature for her at the ripe old age of thirteen-almost-fourteen, but it seemed to have worked, since he was on his way.

Hyeri spotted him coming through the large revolving doors and sprinted over before he could even make it to the security desk.

"Oppa, I'm ready! We can go."

"Hyeri? What?" He frowned at her before moving past toward the security desk.

"Oppa, what are you doing? You don't need to go inside. I came out to meet you. Let's go." She started pulling on his arm.

"I don't have time for this."

His phone dinged and he read the message before turning away from the security desk.

Hyeri thought that meant he was finally ready to go. Then she heard a familiar voice call out behind her. "Junie! Waseo?"

Hyeri blinked in disbelief as she turned to see Minseok and Jongdae striding over.

Immediately she started to blush, shifting to hide herself halfway behind her older brother. But Hyejun didn't seem to care about protecting her and her major crush from Minseok. He stepped forward and clasped hands with his friend, pulling him in for a one-armed hug before repeating the gesture with Jongdae.

"You ready?" Jongdae asked, slapping Hyejun on the back.

"Ye, Hyeong. Is it really okay?"

"Yeah, my uncle says that no one is using the studio today. We can record the guide track with the high-end equipment."

"Amazing." Hyejun grinned. "Let's go."

"Hey, Hyeri, I didn't see you there," Minseok said, the only one to acknowledge her so far. He spoke English, since her Korean wasn't that great, and she swooned a bit over his light British accent. "Did you come to see your oppas record?"

"Huh?" She blinked up at him. He was so vibrant. Most would argue that Jongdae was more conventionally attractive, but there was just some spark in Minseok that made it so Hyeri couldn't look away. She knew when he debuted he was going to be a huge star. "Oh, no. Oppa said he'd take me to Everland today."

"Ugh, Riri, seriously?" Hyejun rolled his eyes.

The childish nickname made Hyeri blush. She'd asked her brother to stop using it now that they were both trainees. She glanced at Minseok to see if he was laughing at her, but he was just glancing at his phone.

"I can't take you today, okay?" Hyejun said. "Let's just do it another time. Or you can wait until Eomma comes to visit."

"What?" Hyeri's whole body slumped in disappointment. "But you promised!"

"I'm busy today," Hyejun said, turning to go through the security turnstiles with Jongdae.

Hyeri rushed after them, the turnstiles slamming into her hips before she remembered to scan her ID card. She caught up with Hyejun just as the elevator arrived and grabbed his arm. "You pinkie swore!"

"That's kid shit, Hyeri. You're too old to believe in that." Hyejun pulled his arm away so hard that she stumbled back.

"Junie, come on," Minseok said, then turned to Hyeri with a smile. "You okay?"

He was satisfied when she nodded and gave a shy smile back. The kid was adorable and she always laughed at his jokes. To sixteen-year-old Minseok, that's all he needed to like a person. "Can you wait just an hour?

Oppas need to record this track and then we'll all take you to Everland."

"We will?" Jongdae said, eyebrows rising in surprise. "It's Chuseok."

"Is your family doing something?" Minseok asked in Korean.

Jongdae scowled and glanced at Hyejun's kid sister. But he remembered her grasp of Korean wasn't that good yet. And it wasn't really a secret that Jongdae's dad worked so much he never had time for family things, even on Chuseok. He sighed. "Fine, you're right. I don't have anywhere to be."

Hyejun interjected with a whine. "It's going to be so crowded."

"Be a good oppa." Minseok punched Hyejun on the arm, but it was soft and playful. "Plus, it might be nice to get an outsider perspective on the track."

"What could she know about music composition? She's a kid," Hyejun said. And Hyeri sent him a glare. Why did he constantly need to treat her like she was a child when she was only two years younger than him?

"Bright Star doesn't admit dud trainees," Minseok said. "She's training in music production just like the rest of us, right, Hyeri-ya?"

He grinned at her and she smiled back, heart racing from being the focus of his attention. He really was so handsome. "Yeah, my teacher says I'm doing great in my lessons. I'll give my honest opinion if you want."

"Fine." Hyejun sighed. Then he sent Hyeri a hard glare. "But you have to be completely silent while we're recording! Or I'm not taking you."

"You won't even know I'm there!" she promised, crossing her heart.

Hyejun scoffed at the motion, and she thought she heard him mutter that she was such a baby before turning to go into the waiting elevator with Jongdae.

"Come on, Hyeri-ya." Minseok held out his hand for her, and she felt a deep blush rise up before she took his hand, letting him pull her into the elevators.

FIVE
HYERI

Hosting is not as bad as I thought it would be. I can barely see the faces of the audience past the stage lights during the show, so that helps. I don't have to see any judging eyes, or anti-fan hatred.

I do spot the dozens of signs for Minseok. I don't see any for me. And it does sting a little. It shouldn't, but the glaring difference is so obvious. I'm sure Minseok notices it too.

Annoyingly, he's charming and charismatic and professional onstage. Delivering the jokes in the script perfectly and even ad-libbing a few of his own. Smiling down at me with a grin meant to charm. But I've had practice at being apathetic toward him.

Instead, I focus on pulling out all the charm of my own I can muster. It's not easy when I'm in direct comparison to Minseok and his easygoing persona. To compensate, I smile so hard that my cheeks hurt.

We get through half the show without any incidents.

The dressing rooms are too far for us to constantly go back and forth between our segments, so backstage there are a couple of chairs set up for us to sit in during performances. I make a beeline for them. The heels my stylist gave me are pinching my feet.

"You don't have to try so hard," Minseok says, pulling off his jacket and tie to change outfits.

He's performing a duet next. It's from the OST of the biggest fantasy K-drama of the summer. So, it's being played everywhere these days.

"What?" I frown at him.

"You're talking in that high voice you use when you're trying to sound like an announcer. And you're smiling so hard you look like a doll."

"What? No, I'm not." But I'm trying to remember what my voice sounded like just now onstage—was it too high? What does he know about the voices I use? He doesn't know anything about my appearances.

"You're too tense. You missed a line in that last segment."

I should have known he'd bring up the missed line. Why does he always have to needle me? "The lines weren't important," I say defensively. "And it didn't affect the show."

"Where's your manager?" He looks around even as his own team hurries over to attend to him, holding up mini fans and dabbing the sweat from his brow.

What is he going to do? Tell on me to Hongjoo?

"Shouldn't you go get ready for your stage?" I say. I don't want him standing here nitpicking my performance anymore.

"Are you—"

"Moonster-ssi, you've got three minutes for costume change," one of the stage managers says, tablet in hand. "Hyeri-ssi, just wait here for your next cue."

"Got it," I say, taking another sip of water, but not too much. Wouldn't do to have to pee in the middle of the show.

"Aren't you at least going to wish me luck?" Minseok asks, pulling off his lapel mic and pack to hand to the assistant hovering behind him.

"Do I have to?" It comes out before I can stop it.

He lifts a brow. I internally cringe. I shouldn't let my annoyance show so clearly. With my luck someone in the crew will post about how unfriendly I was to Minseok backstage.

"I mean . . ." I start to say.

"Nah, you're right." Minseok grins and winks. "I'm always good. I don't need luck."

I roll my eyes at his arrogance. Of course, he gets to act like it's confidence and charisma. It would be labeled something completely different on me.

I wonder, as I do sometimes, what it would be like to be seen as chic instead of cold. Adorable instead of awkward. Acerbic instead of rude.

There are two performances and a commercial before I have to introduce Minseok's duet, enough time to relax a moment. I start to sit back when colorful sequins catch my eye.

I recognize the group of girls coming off the stage and my whole body stiffens.

It's one of the hottest rookie groups, Pink Petal. Two of the girls, Mika and Yunseo, used to be in Helloglow with me. They were both tight with Kim Ana. Which means they were never very friendly to me. Still, I plaster a smile on my face, knowing that usually others play polite in these public situations.

"Hyeri-ssi," Yunseo says, her smile a little too derisive, but her voice butter smooth. "I can't believe I'm seeing you at a show again." Interpretation: *You don't belong here anymore.* "I feel like it's been forever." Interpretation: *We liked it better when you had disappeared.*

For a second, my intrusive thoughts take over and I wonder what it would be like if I told her to cut the fake crap. But my training quickly squashes the urge.

"I know, it's great to see you again," I say, mirroring her sickly-sweet tone.

"We were just talking to Ana about how this is like a mini reunion," Mika interjects. Her voice a bit more neutral, but her smile still reserved. "Maybe we should try to get together soon. Catch up?"

I can't tell if she really means it. A part of me wants to believe she does. That they're all ready to let the past be the past. But I can see from Yunseo's face that she does not want to get together.

"That would be nice. But I'm sure you're all very busy with your promotion schedules," I say, and see Yunseo nod, like I should definitely not assume they'll have time for me.

"And I'm sure you're busy too, with your little drama cameos."

I feel my cheek muscles waver as I try my hardest to keep my polite smile in place.

She's just trying to push your buttons, I tell myself. *Don't fall for it.*

"At first we were shocked you got into acting," Yunseo says. "But I heard it wasn't that hard since your oppa is close to the director, isn't he?"

Now my smile does fall despite my best efforts, and I bite the insides of my cheeks to hold myself back.

That was barely a rumor when I was cast. Hyejun was an ambassador for a brand when he debuted, and the director of my drama worked on a commercial for that same brand once. But the director and my oppa never overlapped or worked together. It was a tenuous connection at best, but one the antis used for a few days to try to mark me as benefiting from nepotism yet again.

I hate that it makes me immediately defensive. I don't need to defend myself against this kind of stuff anymore. I proved that I earned that role with my talent.

"The drama world is definitely different," I say slowly. "People aren't as into online gossip."

Her gaze turns caustic and I immediately regret my choice of words. Maybe being away from the K-pop scene has made me too careless.

"Gossip?" Yunseo laughs. "Your scandal rumors hurt the whole group. And doesn't the fact that you ran away prove some of them were true?"

I shake my head. I don't want to get into this, I shouldn't have even started this conversation. "I just want to do my job in peace."

"Are you saying that I'm *bothering* you?" Yunseo's voice rises. "Eonni, come on." Mika is pulling on Yunseo's arm. She clearly doesn't think this is the best thing to do here.

I try one last time to fix things. "I'm just saying we should try to move past things so it doesn't have to be so uncomfortable between us."

Yunseo finally lets her smile fall away to fully sneer at me. "You don't even know how uncomfortable I can make things for you."

My hands itch to push her away, but I grip my skirt to hold them in place. "Eonni!" Mika finally succeeds in pulling Yunseo back now.

Yunseo replaces her sweet smile for any passersby. "It was great seeing you again, Hyeri-ssi!" She blows a fake-ass kiss at me before striding away. Mika sends me a disappointed head shake before following.

And, more than anything, that bothers me. Does Mika really think this was my fault?

I sigh. Maybe she's right. Despite my best efforts, the wrong thing so often comes out of my mouth. I'm horrible at being quick on my feet with that stuff. It's why I'm not great at interviews and variety shows. And was flagged as one of my biggest weaknesses by my company. I let myself fall into my seat, closing my eyes. I feel completely drained now.

I focus on relaxing my body by zones. First my shoulders, then arms, then hands before I relax my legs and feet.

Move past it. It doesn't matter right now. Focus on your performance.

The mild meditation is sort of working; I can pull in full breaths again. And I no longer feel like I want to cry. Just another minute of careful breathing and I should be back to normal.

"Hyeri-ssi?"

I open my eyes to see a crew member standing in front of me. The monitor behind them shows that the commercial break is just starting, so there's no way I need to go onstage yet.

I worry for a moment that Yunseo complained about me. Would they kick me out as MC just because of her complaints? But then the crew member nervously says, "We need a favor."

"Oh?" My anxiety abates a bit. If they're asking for a favor, then that means I'm not in trouble. Still, I take a long breath to help steady myself.

"We need you to delay for five minutes," the crew says.

"Delay?" I ask, nerves building.

"Yeah, here's the script. It'll be a quick interview with AX1S."

"Why?" I ask, my head spinning as I glance down at the new cards. Something I haven't memorized yet. What if I mess up?

"The next act is having a wardrobe malfunction. Some part of her outfit just went missing, so they need some time to look for it."

"Missing?" I repeat, my brain mush right now as I try to process everything. Then I remember who sings the duet with Moonster, Kim Ana. *Her* outfit. So, it's Kim Ana who has the wardrobe malfunction.

"Oh," I say again, my heart dropping. But for a different reason than performance anxiety. Because of course it's Kim Ana. The very person that article claims I bullied. And one of the ways was allegedly hiding her costume.

Now it's happening again. At an event I'm cohosting.

Great, this day couldn't get any worse.

SIX
HYERI

The thing is Kim Ana and I were friends at first. Or I thought so, at least. But it's hard to keep friendships when it's a competition.

Originally, we bonded over being Korean American, staying up late gossiping in Konglish. Ana's Korean was better than mine since she came to Seoul when she was eight, but my English vocabulary was more advanced. So, we'd teach each other new slang phrases to use.

I grew attached to her quickly the way kids at summer camp do. Making promises to visit each other in the States the next time we were allowed to go, completely ignoring that she was from New York and I was from Los Angeles. To two teenagers, a few thousand miles didn't matter when friendship was on the line.

I don't blame her for distancing herself when the first wave of negative comments about me appeared, when it became clear the show was painting me as the villain. Many people already hated me because they thought I got a slot because of my famous older brother, and the producers of *CiPro* decided to capitalize on the drama.

And somehow Kim Ana became the favorite tool netizens used to beat at me and my reputation.

I know Ana was just as new as me, was fighting to debut just like me. I know she had nothing to do with the producers and the evil editing of my scenes. But sometimes I wonder why she didn't do anything to help me.

If she'd just spoken out to defend me at first, maybe it wouldn't have spiraled so quickly.

No, it's not worth wondering about what-ifs at this point.

I read the script for the last-minute interview. I hate things being sprung on me. I need time to mentally prepare for my appearances. It's why I did so badly at unscripted variety shows.

My cue comes as the commercial break ends and I enter the stage, stopping at the host podium. A Helloglow lightstick catches my eye. It's not that there aren't others with my old group's lightstick, but they're sparse enough that I've noticed each and every one. And I know the familiar frowning face. He's holding his lightstick beside his thin cheek, like he wants me to see him. I recognize his signature short-cropped, almost military haircut, which stands out from the shaggier styles that are more in fashion these days. An anti-fan named Kwak Dongha who used to follow Helloglow around. He's hated me since my *CiPro* era, and I'm half convinced he's the one behind the HyeriTopAnti account.

He probably wants me to screw up so he can post about it.

"Hyeri-yah!" Hyejun's greeting pulls me from my staring contest with Dongha. And I turn just as my big brother folds me into a half hug. I hear a bunch of squeals and giggles from the audience as the other members take their turns, giving me hugs and high fives. At least the AX1S fans still like me, probably because the group all collectively treats me like their sister, so I'm not a threat.

Still my nerves are so high that I stick only to the words on the page. I know I must seem stiff, but thankfully Hyejun and his members do most of the work, joking around and making the audience laugh.

After, I introduce Minseok and Ana, smiling wide at the cameras. Like I have no idea there is a rumor floating around that I bullied Kim Ana. Like I have no reason to feel awkward about introducing her.

It's the most difficult twenty seconds on camera of the year. But I get through it and let my shoulders fall when the lights dim around me and the center stage lights up.

Minseok walks out in his performance costume. No, he's not Minseok like this. He's Moonster. He wears a sparkling silver blazer accented by a red calla lily, a symbolic flower in the drama. He looks good, though I'd never tell him. He doesn't need me to tell him. He obviously knows it.

As Moonster finishes his verse, Ana's lifted from below the stage. Her dress is the same sparkling material as Moonster's blazer.

She looks absolutely stunning, just like she always does. From her shining raven hair framing her heart-shaped face in loose waves, to her full pouting lips, to her long legs that make her the tallest member from Helloglow. I linger at the edge of the stage, searching her costume for something that could be missing.

It's a futile task. How am I supposed to know what her original costume looked like? I turn back to the audience, searching for Dongha's angry leering face, but I can't find him again.

I give up and hurry backstage, looking for Hongjoo. I should tell her Dongha is here. He's never done anything to get banned from events or appearances. Which is why he scares me so much. He always walks right up to the line, but never crosses it. That doesn't mean he won't choose to one day.

I can't find Hongjoo right away, so I go back to my dressing room. There's time until I have to be onstage again with the back-to-back performances right now. But when I turn the corner, there's someone at the door. They have on a dark hoodie so I can't even see the color of their hair.

For a second, I'm convinced it's Kwak Dongha. They look tall enough to be him and every idol has heard horror stories of how sasaeng fans can even find a way into your hotel room. As they shift to get a better grip on the handle, I notice something bulging in their pocket. Did they steal something?

"Hello?" I call out.

Instead of replying they take off down the hall. Definitely suspicious.

"Hey!" Instinct and curiosity take over and I hurry after them.

They turn at the end of the hall squeezing around piles of crates. This part of the backstage area is mostly used to store sound and lighting equipment.

They stumble over a heap of heavy coiled wires before righting themselves, but in my heels, I can barely maneuver around the boxes and cords.

I bump into a cart holding the confetti guns for the finale and grab the stacked boxes to keep them from dropping. By the time I look up again, the person, whoever they were, is gone.

They were probably just in the wrong place, I tell myself. *Except, why did they run?*

Deciding there's nothing I can do but tell Hongjoo, I start back to my dressing room when I see a flash of color by the black wires.

It's a flower. The dark red petals so full and lush that it's as big as my hand. A pin sticking out the back pokes at my palm. Did it fall off someone's outfit?

And just at the thought of that, I feel like I've seen it somewhere. But where?

"What are you doing here?"

I spin around, forgetting about the wires piled around me, and I trip over a coil behind my foot.

My scream is cut short as Minseok lunges forward and catches me around the waist. My shoulder falls hard into his chest and he lets out a surprised grunt.

"Oh crap," I gasp out, forgetting my carefully controlled manners when I'm at an event.

"Shit, Hyeri, that fucking hurt." Minseok clearly isn't as worried with vulgarity as I am. Though the harsh English words sound posh in his light British accent. He always did have the habit of cursing in English instead of Korean.

"Stop groping me," I demand, pushing away from him. But as I do, I grab onto his lapel, where a flower is pinned. The red calla lily.

This is where I've seen it before.

Why would it be here when Minseok is already wearing his?

Then I realize that this isn't Minseok's flower. It's Kim Ana's. She wasn't wearing one onstage. This must be the missing part of her costume. Which means . . .

"Oh crap," I say again. This time, I don't care if someone catches me cursing. That's nothing compared to being caught with this flower.

"What is it?" Minseok asks, but I just shove the flower into his hands. Then fast walk back toward my dressing room.

"Wait, Hyeri!" Minseok calls after me.

Don't follow me, I think. *Just stay away and let me get to safety.*

But unfortunately, I'm not telepathic.

He continues after me. "Hyeri, what were you doing back there?"

"What were *you* doing back there?" I counter even though it sounds childish.

"I saw you running down the hall and thought something was wrong." He finally grabs my arm to stop me.

I eye his other hand, still holding the lily. "Keep that thing away from me."

"What? This?" And of course, he lifts the flower out toward me. Like a guy presenting a bouquet.

But I don't want it; it's probably poisonous for all my luck.

I can't let anyone see me with this flower. It would look like proof that I am actively sabotaging Kim Ana.

"I said keep away!" I grit out, smacking at the flower, and in the process slapping Minseok's hand too. The flower goes flying. But when I turn again to leave, he grabs my wrist.

"Wait."

No, I'm still too close to the evidence. I need to get out of here.

Minseok lets out a surprised shout as I push him away. There's a clatter that leads to a thud and then a crash. I turn in time to see him grabbing the cart holding the confetti guns before it tips completely over.

But I watch in slow-motion horror as a box slips off the top. A confetti shooter falls out, going off on impact with the floor.

Without the wide-open space of the stage, the confetti shoots into some of the stored equipment like paper shrapnel. It shatters a row of stage lights beside us.

Minseok tackles me as the glass rains down.

I'm crushed under him, my hand caught between our chests. One of his arms is shoved under my head—it's all that kept me from slamming my skull into the tile.

He's hovering low over me, his eyes scanning my face with concern.

"Did the glass cut you?" He's so close that he doesn't need to speak louder than a low murmur for me to hear.

Still, I'm disoriented from the fall and having him so close. "What?"

My reply is drowned out by approaching footsteps and shouts.

"Are you two okay?" A production assistant hurries over.

Another PA helps me up, making sure I don't touch the shattered glass all over the ground.

I can't stop myself from watching Minseok as his team gathers around him. When he turns towards his manager, I notice the smallest trail of blood on his neck. Why did he shield me like that? Was it just instinct?

Hongjoo calls my name, pushing through the crowd of people to get to my side.

"Did you get hurt? Let me see you." She grabs my chin, turning my head from side to side. I catch the glint of a lens out of the corner of my eye.

I've been trained to find cameras at this point. When you're performing, you always have to know where the camera is at all times.

And I find it. The HBS vlog team's camera, filming the whole thing.

KIM ANA PROFILE

STAGE NAME: Kim Ana
NAME: Anna Kim
KOREAN NAME: Kim Ayun (김아윤)
GROUP: Helloglow (헬로글로우) (disbanded)
GROUP POSITION: Lead vocal, center
CURRENT PROFESSION: soloist
BIRTHDAY: August 23
SIGN: Virgo
HEIGHT: 173 cm (5'8")
BLOOD TYPE: O
MBTI: ESTJ
BIRTHPLACE: New York, New York, USA
FAMILY: Mom, Dad, sister

KIM ANA FACTS:

• Came in first place in the survival show *Citizen Producer* and debuted with Helloglow.
• Favorite food is mala tang.
• Favorite ice cream flavor is mint chocolate chip.
• Signed with Fantazee Entertainment when she was fifteen.
• Born in New York City, moved to Seoul with her parents and older sister when she was eight.
• Friends with Pink Petal's Yunseo and Mika.
• The other girls called her Princess in *Citizen Producer* because she was such a light sleeper. This led to her nickname as "the nation's princess."

Citizen Producer raw footage

20200908.23:23

Testimonial0021

Contestant 52KAN

Property of Han Broadcasting Station (HBS)

APD: The first group challenge is over. How do you feel about the vote?

KIM ANA: Good. I'm grateful the judges chose to vote me through.

APD: Your group was almost at the bottom of the rank before voting. How did that make you feel?

KIM ANA: It's just the first challenge. I think we're all learning where we're lacking. With practice we can get better.

APD: How did you feel about the three girls in your group?

KIM ANA: They worked hard. I'm glad we all made it through.

APD: Two of the other girls got the worst feedback but were saved by Shin Hyeri. How did that make you feel?

KIM ANA: It was her benefit for coming in first in the prechallenge. She was allowed to save two teammates.

APD: But how did it make you feel that she chose those two over you?

[pause]

APD: Did you feel upset that she'd chosen them when they were the reason your team ranked so low? Min Sohee even forgot her lyrics. Did she deserve to be saved after that?

KIM ANA: Hyeri and Sohee are close.

APD: So, you think Hyeri showed her preferential treatment because they're in the same company?

KIM ANA: Maybe. Yeah, I guess she'd want to save Sohee because they're from the same company.

APD: Do you think the other two deserved to be saved over you when the judges ranked you so high?

[pause]

APD: Ana-ssi?

KIM ANA: What do you want me to say?

APD: I want you to tell us if Hyeri upset you.

KIM ANA: But she didn't.

APD: Are you sure?

KIM ANA: [shrug]

APD: Do you think Shin Hyeri chose them over you because she is intimidated by you? You were the only other girl who had a triple-digit score in the preliminary rankings.

KIM ANA: Yeah, I guess this is a competition.

APD: So, you think Shin Hyeri is trying to get rid of her competition?

KIM ANA: [shrugs] I dunno. It *is* a competition.

APD: Would you have voted for her if you were given the same benefit?

KIM ANA: Sure, she did a really good job.

[pause, sniffle]

APD: Are you okay? Do you need to stop?

KIM ANA: [sniffle] No, I'm okay. It's just . . . a lot. . . .

"Sohee, I'm almost there." I press the phone between my shoulder and ear as I adjust my grip on the bags of winter jackets and toiletries Sohee left behind. I should have used my earbuds, but I forgot them.

"Thank you, Eonni. I'm so sorry you have to do this. I could've just sent a manager to pick it up."

"No, it's fine, I'm already here. Buzz me in." I wrestle with the phone as I type into the building keypad to call Sohee's apartment and wait for the door to unlock.

I needed to get out of the dorm today, so when Sohee texted about her forgotten items, I offered to deliver them. I don't want to overthink what happened at the midsummer K-pop festival. Or, worse yet, dwell on the way it felt to have Minseok shielding me with his body, cradling me in his arms.

I can still feel his fingers brushing against my cheek to push back my hair.

I'm so distracted I almost slam into a couple of students as they hurry out of the elevators. And I lower myself into an awkward bow, limited by the heavy bags I'm dragging with me.

"Sorry," I mumble.

The girls stare at me curiously. And I remember too late that people in Korea don't usually apologize when they bump into each other, but it's a habit I never got rid of from growing up in the States.

I hope they don't recognize me. I'm wearing a hat and a face mask, but sometimes I feel like that just makes it way more obvious someone is trying to hide their identity.

They roll their eyes but seem to dismiss the incident as I press the floor for Sohee's new dorm with the other Kastor members.

The building is nice. New looking. Bright Star really doled out for a pre-debut group. Usually the rookies have to live in the most cramped and basic of apartments. But I suppose Bright Star can afford more luxury now, even for their debuts.

"Eonni," Sohee calls to me as I get off the elevator. She's waiting in front of her open door.

I hurry toward her.

"What are you doing? You can't just stand out here." I glance around nervously. Even though most residents of these buildings respect the privacy of celebrities, there's no knowing who's lurking or what sasaeng fans might have found a way inside.

And Sohee has to be even more cautious as she's already so widely known.

Thankfully, I don't spot anyone. I still urge her back into her apartment but stop short when I see the camera behind her.

Oh no, they're filming their vlogs right now? I immediately change course and stop outside the door, not even stepping into the foyer, which is already cluttered with dozens of shoes.

I'm sure the team won't use any footage with me in it. Better not mar the pristine image of their precious debut group with my bad reputation.

As if on cue, the crew lowers their cameras. The team leader whispers something to the two cameramen that has them retreating into the apartment.

It's something I'd expect. Any footage with me is useless. But still, it stings. If it had been another senior celebrity, they'd be ecstatic to have cross-interaction for the vlogs. But I'm tainted goods right now.

"Here you go." I drop the bags at her feet a little hastily, suddenly wishing I'd stayed home instead. But Sohee catches my hand to stop me.

"You're not going to come in? I want to show you the new place. Some of the girls are here; they'll want to greet you."

I highly doubt that.

I only know Sohee and another girl, Bomi, who's been a trainee for years with us. The other four joined Bright Star after Sohee and I were already on *CiPro*. After Helloglow disbanded and Sohee and I returned to Bright Star, I was worried the new trainees would assume all the rumors about me were true. I didn't want to deal with the sidelong glances or whispers behind my back. So, I kept my distance.

"I have a schedule," I lie. "Next time, okay?"

I squeeze her hand before pulling out of her grip and hurrying to the elevator.

Maybe I should have stayed, I think. *Did it look bad that I ran away so quickly?*

I almost turn to go back inside when I notice a small huddle of kids hovering next to the entrance. The same ones I almost ran into by the elevators. But now they have friends.

Their heads snap up, dirty looks aimed in my direction. And I have only two seconds to realize something bad is coming before the first attack.

One of the girls pulls her hand out from behind her back. Flour flies in my face, a cloud of dust blinding me for a second before it settles all over my hair, my face, my clothes.

The sting of the powder burns my eyes and I retreat a step. I try to blink it away as something hard cracks against my forehead. I don't know exactly what it is until I feel the slimy yolk run down my face.

"How could you *hurt* Oppa?!"

"What?" I ask as I feel another egg break against my shoulder. The cold yolk gets under my collar and runs down my back. I finally succeed in clearing my vision of the flour, fat tears clumping with it on my cheeks. But when I see the angry glares, I wonder if it was better when I couldn't see.

"Stay away from Moonster-oppa!"

"How dare you hit him!"

How could they know? Did HBS actually post their footage?

Another egg hits me in the chest and I stagger back like someone taking a bullet instead of raw baking ingredients. The scent is rancid. How did they find rotten eggs?

"Bully!" shouts one of the girls.

I vaguely register the irony of someone calling me a bully as they pelt me with eggs.

A strangled sound escapes me. I don't know if it's a cry or a laugh as I can't see past the futile resentment building in me.

"Eonni!" I hear Sohee calling my name, causing the teens to scatter.

I barely notice as I fall to my knees, the cold yolk of the egg running down my face. It seems the public knows about the accident at the midsummer festival.

KASTOR (카스토르) **GROUP PROFILE**

KASTOR: (카스토르) is a six-member girl group under Bright Star Entertainment. The members currently consist of Bomi, Sohee, Arin, Gem, Jo, and Minji.

FANDOM NAME: Pollux (폴룩스)

OFFICIAL COLOR: Starlight Gold

KASTOR FACTS:

• Kastor is named after Castor, the second-brightest star in the constellation Gemini. Although it appears as a single star in Earth's night sky to the naked eye, Castor is actually composed of six separate stars, thus the six members who make up Castor.

• Named their fandom Pollux after their twin star. Castor and Pollux asked to be together forever and were cast into the heavens as the two brightest stars of the Gemini constellation. Kastor hopes to walk down their path forever with their fans, Pollux.

• Debut concept teasers are a mermaid theme because the Gemini constellation guides sailors.

K-Pop Fan Attic article:
"Backstage Brawl at Midsummer K-Pop Festival"

An anonymous account posted a video from backstage at the midsummer K-pop festival showing cohost Moonster of WDB grabbing Shin Hyeri. A verbal fight seems to ensue. Then Shin Hyeri appears to push Moonster. He knocks over a confetti shooter, causing glass from a nearby lighting fixture to shatter. The video cuts off shortly after.

As both cohosts returned to the stage for the second half of the show, neither seemed to be injured.

Many comments claim Shin Hyeri overreacted as they point out that Moonster barely touched her. Perhaps Shin Hyeri was fueled by jealousy as Moonster has been romantically linked to his duet partner, Kim Ana, a rumored rival to Hyeri. Although many of WDB's ardent fans, also known as Constellations, are defending Moonster as the victim, there are some who believe he must have done something to Shin Hyeri to warrant such a reaction. Others are speculating that the charismatic Moonster may have harassed Hyeri. This could have horrible implications for Moonster and WDB, which is currently recovering from a huge dating scandal.

Bright Star has not released a statement yet addressing the video.

EIGHT
HYERI

hen I was younger, I used to always ask what-if questions.

"Appa, what if the road opens under our car and swallows it whole?"

"Oppa, what if all my hair fell out? Would you still tell people I was your sister?"

"Eomma, would you still love me if I was a worm?"

But now, all the what-ifs in the world wouldn't prepare me for what actually happens. My life is more improbable than any what-ifs I could come up with.

While I was busy wondering what if HBS released its backstage footage in the vlogs, it was actually an anonymous phone recording that outed us. Someone on the crew who thought it was worthwhile to film the disaster and post it online.

Hongjoo promises they're looking into who leaked the backstage footage, but I know better than anyone that it won't erase what is already out there.

It's not fair. But I've learned by now that wallowing in why it's not fair does nothing except make me feel worse. I try my best to snap out of it quickly, but today that's a hard task.

I hurry to the car idling in the parking garage. Bright Star wants an emergency meeting. My stomach is already twisted in knots.

But my plan to immediately ask Hongjoo for more details is ruined, since she's on the phone when I climb into the car.

"Yes, but it's a misunderstanding. Can't they take some more time to reconsider?" She's got that line on her brow that means she's holding in her anger. And even as it digs deeper, she keeps her professional voice. "Ye, ye. I understand. Thank you for calling personally. Let's have lunch sometime soon."

She hangs up and rubs at the bridge of her nose.

"Is it bad, Eonni?" I ask quietly.

"We'll recover," she says. "Buckle up."

"What did we lose?"

She sighs and closes her eyes for a moment. It must be bad if she can't say it right away. "They're going with Kim Ana for the drama."

I nod and let my chin drop to my chest. I'm good at keeping a straight face for bad news now, but Hongjoo is particularly good at seeing past my masks. And she knows better than anyone how sensitive I am when it comes to things involving Ana. Just her name has become a trigger for my anxiety by now.

I pull on the seat belt, but it locks up. I try again to no avail. By the third yank I'm pulling desperately at the belt with tears burning my eyes. Why is *nothing* going right?

"Ya, Shin Hyeri. Gentle. You always have issues with your seat belt. What are you, five?"

WISH UPON A K-STAR

I sigh and take a minute before pulling slowly on the belt. It finally extends so I can buckle it. "Let's just go, Eonni. We shouldn't be late, right?"

That would be the icing on the cake, showing up late to an emergency meeting about how I'm messing everything up.

The familiar streets zoom past the window. But still I read every sign to myself as we pass. A way to clear my head, to focus on something that doesn't dig up bad thoughts.

"This isn't that bad," Hongjoo says, glancing in the rearview mirror. "We've dealt with worse."

"That's not helping," I mutter, because it makes me think of all the worse things that have happened. Like when a rumor went around that I was dating one of the music producers on *CiPro*, a guy seventeen years older than me. Or the false plastic-surgery scandal that people still reference sometimes like it wasn't completely debunked. But, of course, the most hurtful ones are any time I'm painted as entitled or a bully.

People love to claim I'm a brat who doesn't deserve to be a celebrity. And the worst part of it, is, sometimes I worry they're right. What if I'm only here because of my famous brother?

But this time it's not just the fact that I'm in a scandal that upsets me. It's who the scandal is with. Of course it had to be Moon Minseok. Someone who can grate on my nerves just by being mentioned in the same sentence as me.

My phone buzzes with an incoming call. From my mother.

I don't want to answer it. But when I ignore her calls, my mom gets pissed. Once she called the CEO of my company looking for me. It was so embarrassing.

I answer. "Ye, Eomeoni?"

"Hyeri! What are you doing?" Her voice is high and angry.

"Eomma, please." I rub at my temples, a headache immediately brewing.

"People are *just* starting to forget your past mistakes and now you're ruining it all again! We've worked too hard for you to mess everything up."

Mistakes. Mess. That's how she sees me. She hasn't even asked me if I'm okay. Or made sure I wasn't actually hurt in the incident.

I tell myself that I should know better by now, but it still hurts. She's never once told me something isn't my fault. Even when the media publishes blatant lies.

I take a full deep breath. "Nothing happened. The video makes it look worse than it was."

"Well, that doesn't matter now, does it? Because the articles are out there. How could you let yourself get filmed hitting someone?"

I almost laugh. She's not actually mad that I hit someone, which would perhaps be valid. But that I did it in a place where I could get caught.

"Don't you care about why it happened?" I ask, laying my head back and closing my eyes.

"I care about what this is going to do for your already-tarnished image. What if it loses you the role in *Idol Academy*?"

I squirm because I know I have to tell her. But I really, really don't want to. "Well, you don't have to worry about that now, because I didn't get it."

Her voice gets low. "Are you telling me you lost the role?"

"There was no guarantee I was getting it—" I start to say.

"Oh, don't give me empty excuses, Hyeri." Mom cuts me off. "That's what people say when they're not trying hard enough."

"Sorry, Eomma," I say. It's almost an automatic reaction at this point. "But there will be other dramas."

"I already told half my friends about this role! Do you know how embarrassing it will be when I have to tell them I lied?" Her voice is so loud and shrill I have to pull the phone away from my ear. I'm sure Hongjoo hears it.

"I'm sorry, Eomma," I say again quietly. I don't have anything else I can say.

"Fine. We'll just find a way to recover. I've talked to one of your managers, told them that I think you should release a public apology for your actions."

"What about Minseok?" I blurt out. "He's the one who hit the confetti gun. Are you calling his manager to tell him to apologize?"

"Minseok is not my child. And as far as I'm concerned, he would never have hit it if you hadn't pushed him. There's no reason for you to have acted that way with a senior idol. And one as big as Moonster! You need to fix this, Hyeri. You can't let all our hard work go to waste."

"Yes, Mother." I barely have the words out before she hangs up. I let my hand drop into my lap but keep my head laid back, breathing slowly through gritted teeth. I count my inhales, relaxing myself slowly by zones until my jaw no longer clenches. Until I no longer want to throw my phone.

"Hyeri-ya?" Hongjoo says softly, and I flinch.

Then I slouch again. It's not like she hasn't seen all this before. "Did my mom call you?"

"She did."

"Do you think I should apologize?"

"We're going to discuss options with the company." A classic Hongjoo non-answer.

"But what do *you* think?" I need to know. I can feel tears threatening.

At a red light, Hongjoo turns in her seat so she can look me in the eye. "I think it's a misunderstanding. And we'll figure it out. Together." She reaches out to grip my hand, and I hold on to it a little tighter than I intended.

I nod, blinking hard, finally able to push away the tears. "Thank you, Eonni."

"Don't let your mom get to you, okay?" The light turns green, but she keeps herself turned toward me, waiting for my answer. A car behind us beeps impatiently, but she still doesn't move.

"I'll try." It's an empty promise because both of us know I won't keep it. It feels like we're constantly in crisis and cleanup mode. I wonder if Hongjoo and the rest of the team are as exhausted as I am.

"Don't worry too much, Hyeri-ya." Hongjoo steps on the gas again. "The marketing team has a potential solution for us."

There's something in her voice that rings alarm bells as we turn into the Bright Star building. "Is it something I'm going to hate?"

I see the reflection of her frown before she answers. "It's a variety show."

Immediately, I seize up at the suggestion. I hate going on variety shows. Too often I'm the butt of jokes and teasing by the hosts because I'm an easy target and that's what gets the most views. And I never have clever comebacks or replies. Without a script to lead me, I'm useless on-screen.

I put up with it while I was in Helloglow—it's all I could contribute to the promotions for the group and I felt like I'd been so lacking. So, I grinned and bore it. And if I had to cry, I knew how to save it for later, for the privacy of my own bed.

When I'd debuted as an actress, the company had promised going on the promo circuit wouldn't be necessary this time. I wasn't a main role. I could let the leads handle the variety shows and interviews.

But now, one mistake means I'm being thrown back into the fire.

I hate how often my entire life feels like it's at the whim of other people. Any small bits of control I think I have are so often taken away.

Hongjoo walks around the car to open my door. "You need a minute? I can tell them we're running late."

I shake my head. "I'm fine. Let's go see what the plan is."

NINE
MINSEOK

Minseok looks at the grim faces sitting across the conference room table. There's three of them: his manager, a senior marketing manager, and a creative director. It's the presence of the creative director that worries him.

Minseok has been in the industry long enough to know that this isn't an average meeting.

"Minseok-ah, here's your schedule for next week. There's been a few updates and tweaks." Hanbin hands him a printout of the schedule. Which is unnecessary, because Minseok's appointments are all synced onto his calendar by an assistant. Another reason why this meeting strikes him as odd.

"What's going on, Hyeong?" he asks Hanbin, but he looks at all three. Because all three are here for a reason. He's just not sure what that reason is yet.

The marketing manager clears his throat. "We just wanted to check in with you about a few things," he splutters. He's short and out of shape and in denial about his thinning hair. Sitting across from someone as casually attractive as Moonster is eroding his already flimsy self-esteem.

Despite being over a decade older than Minseok, he is intimidated by the global superstar. He also doesn't want to upset one of the highest earners in the company. And, per the manager, Moon Minseok is likely to be upset about what they're about to present to him.

"We need to discuss some things on your schedule next week," Hanbin says, taking over, to the gratitude of the nervous marketing manager.

"Minseok-ssi, we're really happy about everything you've recorded and attended so far this summer," adds the creative director. She's not nervous like the marketing manager. She's worked with many celebrities before joining Bright Star, and she will work with many more, she is sure. Her job here is to help maintain the strictly guarded image of the company's number one group. And she plans to do it by any means necessary.

"However," Minseok says, lifting an impatient brow. He might be affable, but he is also busy. And he knows when someone is taking their time getting to the point.

"Minseok-ah, we've been approached again about casting you in a variety show," Hanbin says.

"Again? Is it one I've heard of already?" Minseok asks, reading the apprehension on his manager's face.

Hanbin is not fazed. He's too used to Minseok and how he tends to ask blunt questions without batting an eye. "We *have* been approached for it before."

"Which means we've turned it down before," Minseok says, cutting to the heart of it quickly.

"Yes," Hanbin confirms calmly. He knows that this is a delicate dance.

"But at this time, we think it is now a unique opportunity to help people get over any bad feelings."

Minseok holds in a sigh and ignores the water bottle in front of him for a can of soda in the center of the table. The marketing manager jumps up, grabbing a cup and filling it with ice before Minseok can even open the can.

"Is it a show that erases baseless tabloid articles and hate comments?" Minseok asks wryly as he pours the soda into the offered cup.

"Minseok-ah," Hanbin admonishes him.

Minseok quickly dips his head in apology though he is not sorry. Everyone in the room knows about the issues surrounding WDB. A dating scandal alone might not have been bad. But Sooyeon had been the nation's girl next door, and Jongdae was blamed for tarnishing her innocent reputation.

There are some who even claim Jongdae took advantage of Sooyeon, since her reputation was so pure. And, like they'd been waiting for a chance to bring WDB down a peg, antis have started flooding forums with hate. The group's formerly pristine image has cracks in it now—and the company doesn't want any more to form.

"What's the show?" Minseok sips the soda before letting the fizz settle. The bubbles dance in his nose.

He glances across the table, locking eyes with the nervous marketing manager.

It's overwhelming for the man. He's never met someone so young who's so casually charismatic and confident like Moonster. He pushes nervously at the wispy bangs that don't do a good job of hiding his receding hairline, glancing at the creative director.

She just leans back in her chair, crossing her arms. "Why don't we wait for our other guests to arrive so we don't have to explain it twice."

Minseok glances at the empty seats with water bottles set in front of them. Perhaps the producers of the reality show are coming. That's happened before, so they can pitch the concept directly to the boys.

The privilege of being so sought after that producers will come to you. At least that hasn't changed yet.

Minseok realizes he can't rush this meeting. So, he might as well relax. He grabs one of the doughnuts in the center of the table. Hanbin gives a little cough of warning, ever vigilant of the calorie intake. So Minseok obediently breaks it in half.

Hanbin says, "Since we're waiting, it's a good time for me to get this conversation out of the way. Have you seen the article about you and Shin Hyeri?"

Minseok doesn't even pause in lifting the doughnut to his lips. He's been waiting for this. In fact, he assumed the last-minute meeting was about the article. That's why he was surprised to be told it was about his upcoming schedule.

He replies casually. "I skimmed it. Complete garbage. Not even worth addressing."

Hanbin frowns and Minseok lifts a brow. At least, it *wasn't* the type of article they'd ever address. But that was before JD's scandal.

Hanbin sighs. "Well, things are a bit different now. We've been shaken lately."

"Then we should say it's a misunderstanding. That it's not like that between me and Hyeri and it was an accident. That's the truth." *Mostly.*

The marketing manager clears his throat, and the room turns to him. The attention makes him sweat. But he knows he has to play his role. "Not all of the comments are negative. We've been monitoring them."

Minseok grins at that. "Good, then we're fine?"

"Most of them are not favorable," the creative director adds.

Minseok wonders if this was all scripted before he arrived. A kind of good cop, bad cop routine. And if so, what are they trying to get him to do?

"The issue is that, in the past something like this wouldn't have touched your reputation," the marketing manager says hesitantly, his eyes shifting imploringly to the creative director, looking for support. She gives none. The marketing manager gulps audibly. "However, recently with WDB's, well, issues, it seems some are quite happy to question your behavior and spread conjecture. And there are some who are alleging you were harassing Hyeri."

Minseok feels the first true stab of fear. There are many rumors one can easily ignore, but rumors about bullying and harassment aren't among them. He'd hoped that the few groundless comments about harassment would be easily dismissed since they were clearly false. "Are you saying we have to worry?" For the first time since their debut year, Minseok wonders if WDB's future is really in trouble.

"Well, most of the negative comments are about Shin Hyeri," he says slowly.

"Why are you saying that like it's a good thing?" Minseok scowls.

"Huh?" The marketing manager blinks rapidly in confusion.

"She is one of your artists too." His eyes sweep the table, landing on the director. "So, what are you going to do about it on her behalf?"

"Excuse me?" the creative director asks. She is not used to having artists question her so bluntly. She thought she'd be offended by such a thing, but instead it amuses her. Moon Minseok is clearly protective of Shin Hyeri. She wonders if they can use that to their advantage here.

Minseok turns to Hanbin. "You said that the article should be addressed. But I'm not the only one with a reputation to protect. You should be protecting Shin Hyeri's too. Are you going to do that?"

When no one answers, Minseok's responding laugh is filled with derision. "Of course not. Why put too much effort into someone like Hyeri, who is so clearly a lost cause?"

The door opens on his last sentence, and Shin Hyeri herself walks in.

TEN
HYERI

*S*omeone like Hyeri, *who is so clearly a lost cause.*

Is that really how Minseok thinks of me? A lost cause?

At least he has the good grace to look horrified to see me. Minseok wouldn't like to be caught talking about someone behind their back.

"Ah, Shin Hyeri, you're here." A man sitting at the table stands and ushers me toward a seat. I think I recognize him from the marketing team. Manager Jung? Manager Jang?

"Sorry we're late," Hongjoo says, bowing to the others in the room.

I'm still watching Minseok, who is staring at me like I'm a ghost.

"Hyeri-ssi?" the imposing woman at the table says.

"Ne?" I turn to blink at her. It takes me a second to recognize her as Director Yoon, an influential executive in the company.

I immediately lower into a bow. "Sorry."

"No need," Director Yoon says with a polite smile that curves her perfectly painted lips. "Would you like a drink?"

"Water is fine." I pick up one of the bottles of water. I try to avoid looking at Minseok.

He thinks I'm a lost cause, fine. I don't have to acknowledge someone who's already thrown me away.

"We can wait until you're done with your meeting." I smile at Director Yoon and Hanbin. I've seen him around enough times with the WDB boys. He's always been nice to me.

"Actually, this is the meeting," Hanbin says. "We were waiting for you."

"Us?" I frown. "Why would we be in this meeting with you?"

Now I can't help it—I glance at Minseok. But he's frowning at his manager. "Aren't we supposed to talk about some new show?"

"Yes, exactly. But you're both being cast," the creative director explains. "Hyeri-ssi, please sit."

I walk around the large conference table to one of the empty chairs. I'm having bad déjà vu flashbacks. The last time I was in this room was when I was told I'd been cast in *CiPro*.

"What do you mean about doing a show together?" I ask when I take my seat. I look at Hongjoo, who has suspiciously busied herself with pouring a soda. "I don't think that's a good idea."

Minseok nods. "Yeah, after the festival disaster are you sure it's smart for us to be seen together?" He sounds almost angry.

Does he hate the idea of working with me that much? Well, I don't want to work with him either.

The marketing manager clears his throat. I remember now that it's definitely Manager Jung. Like 99 percent certain. He looks sweaty and nervous. I wonder if he should drink water; he looks like he's about to pass out. "We reviewed the public reaction to the article. It seems that the majority fall into one of two camps. The ones who think you two fought . . ."

I close my eyes because it's better than letting them see how frustrated I am.

Minseok, though, sounds completely unaffected as he asks, "And the other camp?"

Manager Maybe-Jung continues. "The other camp thinks it's . . . romantic."

"What?" Minseok and I shout together. When I look at him now, Minseok's eyes are bulging and his mouth hangs open. Seems he is as put off by the idea as I am.

"Yeah, they think you were brave and cool for protecting Hyeri from the shattering glass. And they think that your visuals match well together." Manager Probably-Jung pulls up a post showing the ending of the video, as Minseok cradles me on the ground. It's an edited version, zooming in on us in the shadows. Hearts float around as the video plays out in slow motion with romantic music overlaid.

"What's the show?" I ask, my voice weak as I look away from the screen.

"Our Celebrity Marriage," the marketing manager answers.

"What? No!" I blurt out before I can stop myself.

Our Celebrity Marriage is a popular show where two celebrities pretend to get married, with challenges presented by the production team to play out the life of newlyweds. I've caught myself getting sucked into episodes sometimes. But never in a thousand years would I have considered doing it. And *definitely* not with Minseok.

How could they think this was a possible solution for us?

"You can't be serious." Minseok laughs. "We've turned that show down a dozen times already. Why are you even considering this?"

"We turned it down before because of your busy schedule and disinterest," Hanbin says. "But WDB's situation is different now. *Your* situation is different now. We need to convince people that you have an amicable relationship with Hyeri-ssi to squash the rumors about harassment before they get out of control."

Harassment? I think, eyeing Minseok, who refuses to look at me. I didn't see those comments. But then again, I was so focused on the hate parade aimed in my direction.

I slowly raise my hand like a student waiting to be called on. "Sorry to say this, but aren't WDB's problems due to dating scandals? Why go on a show that's all about marriage?"

I avoid meeting Minseok's eyes, knowing this could be a sensitive topic for him.

Director Yoon nods. "You're right, but it's not the same as actually dating. It's all for entertainment. And every celebrity who's appeared on it has seen a boost in public popularity right after."

"The show is already willing to change the opening format to fit the narrative that you've been friends since you were kids," Marketing Manager Probably-Jung adds.

Now I laugh. "Friends is pushing it."

Minseok gives me a glare. Probably mad that I'm not fawning all over him like everyone else always does.

"Either way. If we are able to change the narrative around you two into something we control, it'll be better for both of you."

It seems like I'm always asking the public for forgiveness, even when I've done nothing wrong. Except this time I can't completely claim that. I did lose my temper. I did make a mistake. So, I nod. "Fine, I'll do it."

I spare a glance at Minseok, who looks almost angry that I agreed. But I have no choice, and I've worked too hard to protect my career. If I have to submit to the torture of spending a few weeks with Moon Minseok, then so be it.

ELEVEN

HYERI

Two days later, I'm at my engagement photo shoot.

A part of me still has misgivings about this plan.

Working with a celebrity as big as Minseok, and on a show like *Our Celebrity Marriage*, sounds like a disaster waiting to happen.

I remember what it was like when rumors spread that I was dating a producer on *CiPro*—it was the most uncomfortable I'd been with any rumor. And now I have to be on a show where I literally pretend to marry someone? And Minseok of all people? I'd rather eat dirt.

Hongjoo seems tense too, though she's pretending really hard that it's another normal schedule. But I can tell she thinks this is important. So, I promise myself that I'll do my best; even if Minseok annoys me, I won't react to it. I'll be professional. I'll be perfect. I will make sure I don't waste this chance.

The shoot is being held at one of those engagement-photo studios, which sets off a swarm of butterflies in my stomach. They flutter angrily as I look at the different sets. One has an ivory upholstered settee in front of gold-embossed wallpaper, with bouquets spilling over stone planters on either side. Another set is designed to look like a gourmet chef's kitchen with rustic wooden accents. And still another is a dark and moody library study.

I vaguely remember engagement photos are a thing in the US, but they never seemed that big of a deal. In Korea, weddings and the trappings around them always seem so much more elaborate, so much more heightened. And I'm already nervous trying to emulate that amount of extra properly for the viewers.

"Shin Hyeri-ssi." A set assistant hurries up with a tablet in hand. "Let's get you in your first outfit."

She leads me to a back room. There's not much space to move because there's two racks of white and cream clothes in here. It looks so . . . bridal. And I feel my stomach churning more.

I turn to Hongjoo. "Are you sure this is okay? Won't people think I'm too young to be on this show?"

"You're nineteen," Hongjoo reminds me. "You started college this year."

"Started college" is a little generous. I've been on set more than I've been in class. But one thing fans always seemed to like about me was that I was a great student in high school, so my agency thought it would help my image to enroll.

I nod, knowing Hongjoo would never make me do something that was bad for me or my career. "Okay, I can do this."

"Why don't I go grab you something to drink, it'll help calm your nerves."

"No caffeine," I call after her as she steps out. Then I turn to the assistant. "What's the first outfit?"

She holds up a cream-colored skirt suit with a lace overlay design and a cropped jacket. It doesn't look *too* bridal. So, I take my deep breaths, relaxing myself zone by zone. This isn't that bad. I can't believe I'm so nervous; it's not like I haven't done a dozen photo shoots before.

I reach for the outfit when the assistant pulls back to press her finger to her earpiece. She's frowning as she listens. "Moonster is? When?" she asks, and my whole body tenses.

Ah, that's why this is all so uncomfortable. Of course I'd be stressed in anticipation of doing this with him. Pretending like we get along. Like we're more than happy to play pretend marriage together.

I press a finger to my temple, fighting back a headache.

"Sorry, looks like the order of the shoot is changing." The assistant puts the outfit back. "Moonster is running late, so we'll have to do your solo shoots first."

He's already being a nuisance and he's not even on set yet.

The assistant pulls out two options. One is a sweet sundress in a pastel pink, with a flowing skirt and spaghetti straps. It's something I'd pick to wear out with friends (if I had any). The other is another lacy number, but unlike the conservative skirt suit, it's skintight and so sheer I might as well be half-naked. It's way too wedding-night-lingerie style, and I immediately start to gesture to the pink sundress when the photographer comes in.

Mr. Lee has long limbs that jut out and weirdly remind me of the legs of a spider. His nose is sharp and his eyes large, almost bug-like, adding even more to the spider comparisons. And he leers. I'm not sure if he just does it with me, or with everyone, but it's always creeped me out a little. He did a few shoots for Helloglow, and even in that group setting he made me slide just a millimeter toward discomfort.

"Ah, Hyeri-ya, so good to see you again." He leans in and kisses both of my cheeks. Something he probably thinks makes him seem European.

But as he leaves a small trace of saliva, I resist the urge to wipe my face.

He smells like tobacco and cinnamon gum.

"It's good to see you again, Jakanim," I lie.

"So, we're doing your solo shoots." Mr. Lee reaches for the lacy number and holds it up. "This will go perfectly with the aesthetic we've set up for you."

I stare at the pseudo-lingerie. I can't wear this. We're trying to save my image, not completely demolish it. I'm all for sex-positive images of women, but I know that I will get immediate blowback if I'm the one trying it. I have to play it safe.

"Are you sure?" I ask. "Maybe we could try the dress first?"

But Mr. Lee yanks it out of my reach and throws it over his shoulder. It falls over the rack. He shoves the lingerie at me, the hanger poking into my chest.

"Go ahead and change so we can make sure it fits."

"What?" I glance at the flimsy changing screen. Usually, I'm not shy. But I'm most often only changing with my core team around. I don't want to get practically naked with this man in the room. "Jakanim, are you sure this is the right look?"

"We've already discussed a theme that revolves around this outfit." He leers at the lace number cradled in my arms. Which means he's also leering at my chest.

"Really?" I ask desperately. "What's the theme again?"

"Bridal chic," Mr. Lee says, spreading his palms out like he's presenting a grand idea.

I glance at the assistant, who clearly looks uncomfortable. She must also think that's a bunch of bull. This outfit is in no way chic.

"I just don't know. . . ." I trail off pathetically as the assistant and

Mr. Lee send me narrowed looks. Do they think I'm being difficult? "It's just that I'm not sure if this outfit gives that vibe."

"I personally vetted the outfits," Mr. Lee insists, his leer turning into a glower. "Are you saying you don't trust my creative vision here?"

"What?" I'm starting to sweat. Is it ruining my foundation? "Of course not, I was just hoping to discuss it more. . . ."

Mr. Lee shakes his head. "That will delay the schedule. We're already behind." He glances expectantly at his watch. "Go get changed." He crosses his arms and it's clear that he intends to wait here for me.

I start to turn toward the screen, my eyes shifting to the door. Where is Hongjoo? If she was here, I'd have backup. I look again at the assistant, who's doing everything she can to avoid my gaze. There will be no help there. I sigh and start to accept my fate when the door opens.

I turn desperately, hoping for Hongjoo.

Instead, Minseok bursts into the room. "I wasn't the one who made us late."

"You know how much he's dealing with right now, cut him some slack," Hanbin is saying. He looks harried and annoyed.

They both stop short as they look around. "Oh, sorry," Hanbin says, stepping forward to shake hands with the photographer. "We must be in the wrong dressing room."

"No, it's fine," Mr. Lee says. "You're right next door. We can shift back to the couple shoot, then, since Moonster-ssi is here." He calls for another assistant, directing them to reset the equipment.

"Do you have snacks here?" Minseok is asking, plopping down on a chair.

Minseok and his team are a whirlwind; everyone is paying attention to him. But for the first time in a long time, I'm relieved he's here. Because if everyone's paying attention to him, they're no longer focusing on me.

I take the hanger with the objectionable outfit and shove it into the middle of the clothing rack, trying to hide it in the folds of a voluminous gown.

Ten minutes later, I'm in a simple sundress layered with a loose thick-knit cardigan. It's a bit warm out for a sweater, but after the last clash over outfits, I refuse to bring up another objection.

We're led to a garden set and I'm directed to sit on a swing bench. A set assistant carefully arranges my skirt so it artfully splays out, while Minseok is placed behind like he's pushing me.

"Okay, grab onto the chain, Moonster-ssi."

Minseok does as directed, but he yanks the chain too hard, and I almost go toppling over. I clamp my teeth tight, a cage to hold in the angry words I want to snap at Minseok. Instead, I try to fix the lay of my dress again.

We feel so out of sync. Maybe this is a sign that this was a bad idea.

"Can we begin?" Mr. Lee calls out, annoyance clear in his voice.

I look up to realize he's staring at me, like the delays are all my fault even though Minseok was the one who was a half hour late. But I just nod meekly and try to settle back on the bench.

"No! Don't slouch!"

I straighten myself, embarrassed at being chastised twice in quick succession.

"Moonster-ssi, maybe try to soften your expression?" I try not to notice how much kinder the suggestions are when directed at Minseok.

"Okay, now Moonster-ssi, sit with Hyeri." He does, but he's all the way on the other side of the swing, a wide space between us.

"Hyeri, can you please try to act like you like him? Why are you so far away?"

I blink in disbelief. Minseok is the one who chose his position on the swing. I haven't even moved.

But I bite down on my lip and my complaints and scoot closer. Minseok is stiff as a board. When I try to lean into him, he just sits there. It feels like trying to pose with a statue.

"Hyeri, it still looks too unnatural. Can you try putting your head on his shoulder?"

It wouldn't be so unnatural if Minseok would pull the stick out of his a— No, I have to calm down. I can't let him get to me. I have no idea what's gotten into Minseok, but I refuse to let his attitude make me do any less than my best.

I lean in to rest my head on his shoulder. He doesn't even attempt to adjust his posture to accommodate me, so the extreme angle strains my neck. Even so, I am determined to obey every directive like I'm the most agreeable model in the world.

"Moonster-ssi, arm around Hyeri, please?"

He does, but so roughly that his hand disrupts the carefully placed curls along my collar.

I try to fluff them again, but he's crushing them with his closed fist.

"Can you relax?" I mutter.

"Just pose for the photo. We've wasted enough time already."

I gape up at him. "Are you serious?"

"This is not playtime, Hyeri. Can you save your conversations for after the shoot?" Mr. Lee says.

"Yeah, can we get this done?" Minseok says loudly enough for the entire crew to hear.

I'm shocked enough to lean away from him, but his arm is still tight around my shoulders, unyielding. And the motion instead pushes the swing out from under us. We both go toppling down into the dirt.

Hongjoo hurries over to help me up, but it's too late. Dirt and grass stains mar the soft pastel colors of my skirt.

"Great! Now we'll have to take a break for an outfit change." Mr. Lee shouts. He shoves his camera into the arms of his assistant. "Everyone, be back in fifteen exactly!" He storms off.

I start to ask Minseok what his issue is, but he's already striding quickly off set.

I chase after him to give him a piece of my mind.

He's already in his dressing room by the time I catch up, but I grab the door before it closes.

"What the hell is your problem?" I demand.

"Can you give me privacy to change?"

"Can *you* get over whatever has crawled up your—" I break off when he gives me a warning glare. But I still don't fully back down. "I don't know what's going on with you, but can you just suck it up for one hour?"

"I'm not in the mood today." He sounds exhausted. It breaks past my anger for a second, making me hesitate. I've never seen him look so defeated before. I almost ask what's wrong. But I stop myself. We don't have that kind of relationship.

"I don't *want* to be here right now," Minseok says. "So, let's just get this over with."

I can't help the laugh that bursts out of me. Dry and acrid. "And you think *I* want to be here?"

"I didn't say that. You're putting words in my mouth." He suddenly sounds so angry, but I know I haven't done anything to warrant this vitriol from him.

"Fine. You don't want to be here and neither do I." I can't believe I need to work so hard for his cooperation right now. If this plan doesn't help smooth over the latest scandal, I'm fairly certain Bright Star is ready to drop me. I can't let that happen, so I need Minseok to snap out of his mood. "We're both stuck. That doesn't mean we have to make it worse for each other. Even prisoners have social agreements between them, right?"

"Wow." Minseok sounds incredulous. "Things must be really bad for you to think of yourself as a prisoner."

"Like you care how bad things are." He's really starting to annoy me. Why can't he just agree to cooperate for a few hours? "Why did you even agree to do this if you were just going to complain the whole time?"

Minseok shrugs. "I'm here, aren't I? Ready to help fix your image."

"Kaeppul." I mutter the curse under my breath. "You don't care about my image. You're doing this because the festival accident made you look bad too, and WDB is no longer scandal-proof."

Minseok's eyes darken. Something I said must have struck a nerve. "I'm not the one constantly caught up in rumors. Maybe I should just leave. Maybe it'll force you to finally grow up and deal with your own shit instead of using it as an excuse to be a brat."

The way he says it sounds like he really does think all the scandals are my fault. Like he believes they could be true. It hurts more than anything the gossip articles or anti-fans could do or say to me.

"Wow, okay," I say slowly, my throat constricting so my voice barely scratches out. "I didn't know you felt that way." I move toward the door, but he shifts to block.

Minseok shakes his head. "I didn't mean it the way it sounded."

"No, you're totally right," I say. "I'll deal with my shit. But don't get in my way while I'm doing it."

"Hyeri, please."

In this moment, if he says anything else I might burst into tears. So, I forgo politeness and push past him to shove out the dressing room door.

TWELVE
HYERI

right Star Entertainment has grown since I became a trainee there.

When I arrived in Seoul six years ago, it was in a small four-story building in Cheongdamdong. But a year ago it moved to a building three times the size in Gangnam. And it's all thanks to the money WDB brings in.

It's still fresh enough that whenever an artist from Bright Star goes on a show, the classic joke often told is that WDB pays the rent. And everyone else helps pay for the toilet paper.

We all laugh and act like we're in on the joke. But I wonder if the other artists also feel like it's a reminder that we could disappear from Bright Star and they'd still be fine without us. Or maybe it's just me, the perpetual problem child.

I'm currently in the state-of-the-art salon in the company building.

Another new amenity. I hate that I'm dependent on this benefit. When I had to go to a shop before, there was always a chance of antis camping outside to shout and spit. And after the flour-and-egg situation, Hongjoo doesn't want to take any chances with security.

"Just remember the prewritten answers during the press junket today," Hongjoo is saying. She's pacing, which means she must be really nervous.

"All right, Eonni."

"You got a chance to memorize them?" she asks, glancing at her phone for the fifth time in the last minute.

"Yes, Eonni." I try to keep myself calm so I don't worry her more. It's a strange position swap. But oddly, it helps me. To be able to comfort Hongjoo. Maybe because it takes my mind off my own worries.

"Great, good. Maybe review them one last time?" Her phone dings before I can reply in the affirmative. And she nods. "Okay, they're here."

They? I almost ask, but she's already ushering me out the door.

"Eonni, maybe you should take something for your stomach? You seem really nervous," I say, handing her the bottle of water I'd grabbed from the mini fridge in the salon.

"I'm good. I'm fine," she says as she unscrews the cap and chugs down the entire bottle.

She dumps it in a trash bin when we emerge into the parking garage. But instead of heading to our car, she pauses at the curb and checks her phone again.

"Eonni, aren't we getting the car?"

"Huh?"

I start to ask the question again when the elevator doors open behind us and Minseok walks out with a cheeky grin on his annoying face. "Well, fancy running into you here."

I'm initially shocked that he's acting like we didn't get into a huge fight at the photo shoot. Then I remember that Minseok is the king of avoidance. A dozen sarcastic responses sit at the tip of my tongue. I could say one of them—only Hongjoo is here to witness it. But I don't want to upset her, so I hold back, even though it pains me.

"Well, we *are* going to the same place." I can wait until I'm in the safety of my own car to curse his existence.

A black van with dark tinted windows pulls up with Hanbin in the driver's seat. The automatic doors open and Minseok climbs in. But I'm surprised when Hongjoo jumps into the passenger seat.

"What are you doing? Aren't you getting in?" Minseok asks from the back, watching me expectantly.

"Wh-what?" I ask.

"Oh, we're just going to ride with Hanbin and Moonster-ssi, since we're going to the same place." Hongjoo's hands are shaking a bit as she buckles her belt, and I realize she must be too nervous to drive.

Sighing, I climb in.

Be cordial, I remind myself. *It'll be over soon.*

"Ready?" Hanbin asks, glancing in the rearview mirror as he presses the button to close the door.

I start to nod when Minseok says, "Aren't you going to buckle up?" In my confusion I forgot. Still, he doesn't need to be so rude about it.

Embarrassed, I yank too hard on the seat belt, and it refuses to budge.

I pull again, trying my best to be gentle this time, but it's practically stuck in place.

"Come on," I mutter. I can feel myself becoming more and more frustrated with each pull, but I can't help it. I can tell everyone is staring at me, waiting for me to finish so we can go.

"You're still horrible at pulling out a seat belt," Minseok says.

"I'm not horrible at it," I say through gritted teeth, still yanking. "They've gotten more sensitive."

"Aish." Minseok leans into me, his body practically covering mine.

I press back into the seat, letting out a surprised gasp. My mind flashes to that moment backstage, when he lay over me, cradling my head to protect it from the falling glass, and every inch of my skin seems to burn.

I notice how long his lashes are. They brush against his cheeks as he glances down at me.

"Wh-what?" I barely stutter out, trying to make sense of what's happening.

Then he gently opens my fist and takes the seat belt from me, pulling it around me with ease. He leans back to click it into place. Without his body blocking mine, the air-conditioning vent blasts on me, a welcome reprieve, as I feel so warm, I worry I'm sweating.

Maybe I'm coming down with something, I think as I press my palm to my forehead.

Hongjoo notices the movement and eyes me in the rearview mirror. "Hyeri, is something wrong?"

"I'm fine," I squeak out, then grimace at the sound of my voice.

I think I notice Minseok's shoulders shaking with silent laughter. I turn toward the window so my back is to him for the rest of the ride.

When we arrive at the venue, we're ushered out of the van in an underground garage. An entourage descends on us the moment we're hurried out of the elevators. Stylists rush forward to make sure we didn't wrinkle anything on the way here. Someone from my makeup team pulls out a compact, and I obediently lift my chin so they can touch up my foundation.

We're stationed at the entrance to the press room. I hear the chatter of reporters behind the doors, and I turn to Hongjoo.

"Eonni," I mutter anxiously under my breath so Minseok can't hear. He looks relaxed, unaffected as he lets his makeup team touch him up.

"Just remember your answers," Hongjoo says. "You know how to do this. You'll be fine. And if you need help, Minseok-ssi will be there."

I resist the urge to roll my eyes. Minseok is too much of a wild card. He's just as likely to make me the butt of a joke for his own amusement as he is to actually help me out in front of the reporters. I'll just depend on myself—I've gotten better at press conferences, even if the constantly flashing cameras are so disorienting.

"Okay, they're going to announce you both," someone says. I think I recognize them as an assistant PD from HBS, but he's gone before I can confirm. Hongjoo and Hanbin are ushering the teams away, probably to take their place in the back of the room to monitor the press conference. And then it's just Minseok and me waiting behind closed doors to be called in.

"Stop that or you'll walk in with bloody fingers," Minseok says, pulling my hands apart.

I didn't realize I'd been picking nervously at my cuticles. Already my left ring finger looks a mess.

"Shoot," I mutter, sticking the manicured nail into my mouth to try to smooth out the jagged skin.

"Just take deep breaths. You've done press conferences before," Minseok says. He looks annoyed and it presses deep on my nerves.

"I know. I'm fine. I'll be fine," I insist, clasping my hands together to stop myself from picking at them more.

Why is it taking so long for them to call us in?

I just want to get this over with already.

It feels so hot even though the hallway is well ventilated. The air-conditioning is brisk enough that I feel the blow of it from the vents overhead. Still, I press my fingers to the pulse on my wrist to check. It's definitely speeding.

What if I'm coming down with something? What if I faint in the middle of the press conference?

"Ya, Hyeri." Minseok grabs my shoulders, and I realize he's been trying to say something to me.

"Sorry, I— Uh, what were you saying?"

"You still space out like that?" Minseok frowns down at me like I'm a small child with a bad habit.

"I'm just focused on the press conference." I glower at him as I pull out of his grip.

He tilts his head curiously at me. "Are you sure you're good?" Things must be bad for Minseok to actually sound concerned.

I'm about to give some brush-off answer, but for some reason I let out a heavy sigh that makes my shoulders droop with defeat.

"Why do you care? Don't you think I should deal with my own shit?"

He sighs. "Hyeri-yah, I'm sorry. That was a messed-up thing to say."

I want to hold my ground and not forgive him too easily, but he genuinely looks contrite. And I know starting a fight with him right before this press conference would be a mistake. So I nod. "Yeah, okay, let's just forget that conversation ever happened and focus on this press conference. I can't afford to mess this up." I press my hands against my cheeks. They're burning, and I can only guess how red I look right now with my rushing nerves.

"You won't." Minseok sounds so confident, but it just highlights my own intense doubts.

"But what if the public sees right through us? What if they hate me even more after this?"

"You still do that what-if thing, huh?"

"What?"

He smiles, and it's almost kind. "That thing you always used to do when we were younger. You'd ask the strangest what-if questions all the time. 'What if I lose my voice entirely in the middle of an evaluation?' 'What if I have an allergic reaction to a face mask?' 'What if I fall into a sewer hole and no one finds me for days?'"

"Sewer holes can be dangerous," I mutter.

"If you're a cartoon character." He laughs.

"It's a real concern."

"Okay, but what if it all works out way better than we thought?"

"It won't," I almost blurt out. Because things usually don't work out well for me. And when they do, it just means the other shoe is yet to fall.

The doors open then and that same assistant PD who first greeted us appears. He ushers us inside. Cameras start to flash immediately, and I resist the urge to check my cheeks again, but they actually don't feel flushed anymore.

I guess my annoyance at Minseok distracted me from my nerves. Right now, he's smiling and waving at the cameras as we pose in front of the large banner with the *Our Celebrity Marriage* logo. I have a set of poses I know work well from all angles. I am working through them methodically when Minseok steps closer, holding out his hand. I lean away, surprised by the unexpected closeness when I realize he's making half of a hand-heart. He gives me a raised brow, waiting for me to finish it. And I have no choice, it would be too awkward to leave him hanging. So, I finish the heart, sending a weak smile at the cameras.

A short table is set up with two mics for the question-and-answer portion. Minseok pulls out my chair for me with a smile. A show for the reporters. But I force myself to smile back at him and accept the seat.

This is just another performance, I remind myself. *You're good at that.*

The questions begin immediately.

"What made you agree to do this show with your packed schedules?" The first is an easy one given by a reporter known to be friendly to Bright Star.

I lean in to answer first. "I'm a huge fan of the show. I watched the entire last season, since one of our sunbaes was on it." A reference to a veteran actor represented by Bright Star, good cross-promotion for the company. "So, when the show fit into my schedule, I jumped at the chance."

"What about you, Moonster-ssi?"

"I figured I'd earn points with my mom if I finally settled down." He grins so naturally at the responding laughter, and I wonder if his answers also had to be pre-written or if he's making this up on the fly. I can't really imagine the staid marketing managers writing that kind of line.

"Moonster-ssi, will we be able to expect the other members of WDB to make an appearance on the show?"

"We haven't finished planning for the episodes, but I'm sure they'll come to the wedding if they can. If Jaehyung comes, we'll have to double the catering budget."

That gets a few more good-natured laughs. He's so good at this, it's making me feel even more stiff in comparison.

"What about you, Hyeri?" another reporter asks. "Will any members from Helloglow be attending the ceremony or housewarming?"

I lean in with the prepared answer, remembering to add a smile for the cameras. "I'd love for some of the girls to come. With our busy schedules we rarely have the chance to get together these days. But they're all definitely invited."

The response isn't as enthusiastic as Minseok got, but I see some nods at the acceptable answer. I feel like I'm somehow failing even as I perfectly recite the answers. If only Minseok wasn't here to make me feel so stiff and unskilled.

A reporter in a dark red windbreaker raises their hand. "What do you think of the video from backstage at the midsummer K-pop festival?"

I tense even though this is an expected question. Minseok leans forward to answer first; he'll smooth the way with the explanation and I will add my short apology at the end. I recite the words in my head to prepare: *I'm sorry for being lacking; I have reflected on my actions and will work harder in the future.*

"We're embarrassed about that accident and grateful that no one was hurt. We were so impressed by how the staff took quick action to make sure that the space was made safe so the show could move forward smoothly. We regret that any of our actions created any concern or worry among fans but appreciate that they continue to support us both."

I lean forward to add my part when red windbreaker interrupts. "How do you feel about the rumors that the fight was due to jealousy over Kim Ana?"

That wipes my carefully rehearsed answer out of my brain. It wasn't one of the questions we were anticipating. It's obviously a question for me, but I don't know how to answer it in a graceful way. If I say I'm not jealous they won't believe me. If I try to brush it off, it might come across as caustic. Still, everyone is waiting for an answer and it feels like the flashes of the cameras are getting faster.

"Well, um, I think . . ."

"Is there a rumor Hyeri's jealous of me and Kim Ana? That's impossible," Minseok says with a laugh. "Hyeri's seen me at my most awkward before I discovered CC cream."

Some of the reporters laugh along. Shock has me turning to stare at him, but Minseok doesn't even spare me a glance as he continues. "The accident was just that, an accident. But we do realize it could have been worse and we're sorry for being so lacking. Hyeri and I have both reflected on our actions and will work harder in the future. Next question?"

He so clearly and brusquely moves things along. And with nothing to say now, I lean back, nervously picking at my cuticles.

I try not to glance at red windbreaker, but I can't help it. He's slowly shaking his head, mouth in a tight disappointed line as he types something. Does he think I was being rude by not answering his question? Does he think I'm not taking responsibility? I want to ask Minseok what he was thinking, but, of course, I can't.

The next asks their question. "Have you met the other couples cast in this season?"

"Not yet," I answer, trying my best to remember the pre-written answer. "But when I saw who was cast, I was really starstruck. I've been a huge fan of those sunbaes since before I debuted."

The rest of the questions are among the predicted list. And Minseok and I take turns answering. We're nearing the end of the press conference, and I finally feel like I can let myself relax. The final questions are always throwaways. We did it, we survived.

Then red windbreaker lifts a hand. I wish there was a way to call on someone else, but ignoring him would be too obvious. He's staring at me with sharp, almost predatory eyes. And my stomach clenches in apprehension.

"Hyeri-ssi, what do you think of the rumors that Kim Ana was in talks to be cast in the show before you, but turned it down to take the role in *Idol Academy* that you were passed over for?" He directs the question at me this time. Like he learned his lesson with the last. It's blunt and rude, but the reporter shamelessly watches me for my reaction.

I can feel my hands go numb as I grip the edge of the table. I find Hongjoo in the back of the crowd, her eyes wide as she holds her hands in an X. She doesn't want me to answer. But not answering could be misconstrued as dismissive or petty. What should I do?

I didn't even know that Ana was under consideration for the show. Or is that a lie made up to get a rise from me?

I start to lean forward, clearing my throat. The sound is caught by the mic—it echoes like an awkward cough throughout the room.

"Hyeri-ssi? Do you need me to repeat the question?" Red windbreaker looks like he's smiling a bit, satisfied that he's caught me in this trap.

"Um, no, I just—"

Minseok grabs my hand, squeezing it hard.

He leans forward to answer. But that's not right. The question was for me this time. There's no reason he should be answering this one.

Minseok grins. "Hey, this isn't fair. Shouldn't you also be asking me how I feel about the rumors that Rowoon-sunbae was almost cast?" He lifts a challenging brow, and I'm surprised that he'd call out the unfair treatment so blatantly. Then he gives a charming grin. "And my answer would be that I'd love to be married to him."

Everyone laughs at the obvious joke. "But in all seriousness, I was thrilled when they told me Hyeri would be on the show with me. To be honest, I have no idea what I'm doing, but I've known Hyeri since we were kids dreaming of being where we are right now." He turns to smile at me, and I realize I've been staring at him. Stuck in place as I watch him effortlessly divert the trap question as easily as swatting away an annoying fly. He keeps my gaze in his as he continues. "I think it will be fun to catch up with an old friend. No matter what, it will be worth it to spend time with someone who's known me for so long."

"And Hyeri-ssi, what about you? How do you feel about your new future husband?" one of the other reporters asks, but I don't know who, as I'm still staring at Minseok. I can't pin down the mixed emotions spinning inside me like a cyclone.

He gives me an encouraging nod. A way to let me know that

everything is fine. Crisis averted. Because he saved me. I let out my breath to pull another in. It's a little shaky, but I'm able to replace my smile again.

There's an old familiarity in the way Minseok looks at me right now. It pulls me back to the way I felt when I was fifteen, in awe of the way he exudes confidence and kindness in equal measure. I'm still watching him even as I lean into the mic. I can't remember the pre-written answers. So, I just say whatever comes to mind. "Yes, I am really pleased with my new fake fiancé. I can't wait to live fake happily ever after as long as he always remembers to take out our fake trash."

The reporters all laugh along with the joke.

And Minseok's lips quirk up in that signature cocky grin of his as he pats my hand in approval.

K-Pop Newsfeed article: "WDB's Moonster and Shin Hyeri Show Off Childhood Friendship as Newest Couple on *Our Celebrity Marriage*"

WDB's Moonster and rookie actress Shin Hyeri joined HBS's *Our Celebrity Marriage*, season 4.

Moonster and Shin Hyeri became the newest and, to date, youngest couple on the show. HBS also announced that they will cater to the show's growing international viewership by doing their segments partially in English. It won't be a problem for either as Moonster was raised in both London and Shanghai. Shin Hyeri was born in Los Angeles before moving to Seoul to train as an idol. Many might recognize Shin Hyeri from her time in the mega-popular girl group Helloglow and this year's drama *Youthful Exchange*. Moonster is back from WDB's world tour, which wrapped up in Chicago this spring.

The casting announcement was met with surprise and excitement.

The press conference showcased Moonster's effortless variety skills and Hyeri's fresh brightness, as well as the chemistry between the two. Not a surprise, as the idol and rookie actress were trainees together as children.

A joint statement for both artists was released:

"Many know that Moonster and Shin Hyeri are friends from their trainee days. We hope that through *Our Celebrity Marriage* the fans will get a peek into the close relationship between both artists."

The first episode with Moonster and Shin Hyeri will air July 20.

THIRTEEN
HYERI

"Okay, this is a good start. The company sounds like they're happy with this." Hongjoo is pleased, I can tell by the way she taps the steering wheel in excitement.

I look at the article on my phone.

Like many of the others I've seen, this one doesn't use any of the carefully posed shots from the photo shoot, but a candid from the end of the conference. Minseok and I are looking at each other, soft smiles on our faces. If I didn't know the exact anxiety parade that was streaming through my brain at that moment, I'd think I was enamored with Minseok. And it doesn't help that both of his hands softly cradle mine. Something I hadn't realized at the time.

The photo looks sweet, like we really do get along.

So, I suppose this is all working out so far. If I can keep this up.

But that's a big *if*, as my stomach is already rolling like a monsoon as I sit in the van waiting to be called to set.

It's an outside shoot for the "first meeting." An important episode because it sets the tone for each couple, so they're often set in iconic romantic areas around the city. But ours will be a little different, since we already know each other.

We're at the playground outside our old trainee dorms, where Minseok and I both lived when we first came to Seoul. A strange flood of memories assaults me. This is where I lived when I still thought being an idol was all I ever wanted. When I couldn't see anything except for the desire to debut.

Looking back, I feel foolish for how I thought debuting would solve everything. How I thought it would fix my anxiety, my relationship with my mother. How I thought it would finally make me happy. I gave up everything to succeed. My old friends back home. Studying. Any chance at making new friends in Seoul.

But even though I succeeded in debuting, it all feels wrong. It would be easy to blame *Citizen Producer* and my scandals, but there's this gut-deep unsettling sensation that I started to get about three months before the show even started. Something that I was too scared to tell anyone about.

I was so certain that if I told my company I'd had doubts about going on the show, it would ruin my chances of ever debuting with them. And I'd have to find a completely new company and start over. At sixteen I hadn't been "old" yet, but I didn't want to risk any delays. I wanted every advantage I could get to ensure I debuted.

So, I buried it even deeper and pushed forward.

Seeing the playground with its bright plastic slides and orange metal railings, nostalgia fills me. Gray metal exercise equipment sits on the far side, mostly used by the older residents early in the mornings. I'd see them huffing on the mechanical elliptical or bar press when I left at dawn for the practice rooms.

There's a giant teddy bear in front of the main slide with a giant bow on it. I roll my eyes at the corniness of the gesture. But I know this is par for the course for variety shows.

David hurries up as I climb out of the car, Jeongho trailing behind. I say hi to him and he gives me a nervous nod. I wonder if his awkwardness is because he's seen the articles. I wonder if he thinks they're true.

But I tell myself he's probably just nervous because he's new. Plus, the company has a strict policy that staff cannot be fans of the artists. He could get fired if he fawned all over me.

David comes over and air-kisses me. I remind myself that at least I have him. He doesn't care about showing preferential treatment—the benefit of being so in demand in this industry.

"You didn't have to come," I tell him. "I know you're too busy to attend all of my schedules."

"I wanted to be here for your first shoot," he says. And even though he doesn't mention it, I know he's worried about me.

It both comforts me and makes me feel like a burden.

"Thank you." My voice cracks a bit, and I hate myself for letting my emotions get the best of me. I should be better at this by now.

But, for his part, David skillfully ignores it, letting me have my moment without any embarrassment. Instead, he pulls out a can of hairspray and spritzes it over my head in a light mist. "I'm glad we went with the simple pony. The humidity is deathly today." He smiles. "I saw the press conference. You did well."

I want to ask if he really means it. I'm still not sure it went that well. Despite the mostly positive articles, there are still a few saying that I hid behind Minseok when it came to the midsummer festival incident. Though there were far fewer than I thought there'd be.

"Don't worry. This is all going to blow over. Just keep being your sweet self," David says with an encouraging wink.

"Thanks." I try to hold on to the comfort his smile gives me. To not let it dissipate too quickly as I turn toward the set and the waiting crew.

The main PD walks over to greet me. He's short, only a few inches taller than me, with an avuncular face framed by big square glasses. "Hyeri-ssi, looking forward to working with you."

"It's an honor, Han-PD," I say with a bow, and I mean it. Han-PD is the most successful variety show producer on HBS.

As an assistant starts pinning my mic, Han-PD goes over the shoot. This is just the meet-and-greet scene. I listen intently even though I've read the pages for today over and over. Not having some kind of script makes me nervous, so I wanted to be as prepared as possible. I haven't gone on this kind of variety show since Helloglow broke up. The kind with vague missions that depend almost entirely on the participants' personalities to provide entertainment. I'm not sure if I'm enough all on my own to be interesting without some kind of script to follow.

Calm down, Hyeri, I tell myself. *This show would not have cast you if people weren't interested in seeing you on it.*

But what if Bright Star pressured the production to cast me? What if they dangled Minseok in front of them, and they wanted a member of WDB so badly they were willing to take me on as extra baggage? Isn't that the unofficial narrative of my whole career? I supposedly coasted into K-pop on my oppa's coattails. And now I'm doing it here with Minseok and this variety show. It's a path I'm stuck on no matter what I do to try to escape it.

"Hyeri-ssi?"

I look up to see Han-PD and the staff all staring at me. Obviously waiting for me to do something.

"Sorry, what did you say?" I glance at Hongjoo, who grimaces. Great, I'm already making mistakes.

"I asked if you're ready to start rolling," asks Han-PD.

"Sorry, yes, I am." I take my position, waiting intently for the signal.

"Can you do the clapper for the cameras?"

"Oh, yes." I almost curse myself out under my breath, but I'm careful not to, as I'm mic'd. I clap my hands, but it's weak and sloppy. And in my nervous state I clap again to make up for it.

"Ah, can you go again? Just one clap this time." Han-PD isn't unkind when he says it, but I think I see some snickers from the crew.

I clap again, this time succeeding in getting it in one go.

Embarrassed at messing up already, I hurry over to the bear. There's a giant envelope in its hands with a heart on it and I open it and read the message.

It's up and down.

Add the numbers of home.

Don't forget the strawberry milk.

It's a riddle, but clearly meant to send me on a mission to find Minseok. I didn't realize I'd have to solve puzzles. Without anyone to help me.

"Um, Hyeri-ssi? Can you do or say something?" Han-PD calls out, and I realize I've just been standing here rereading the riddle quietly to myself.

I mentally berate myself for messing up again so quickly.

"Sorry." I bow low in apology to the entire crew. I am not making a good first impression at all. "I'll start over."

"No, it's okay, just start at your current mark and read the message aloud. Let us know what you think about it. Just talk us through your process, okay?" Han-PD sounds like a teacher explaining a very simple activity and I'm so embarrassed.

The staff is all watching me like I'm a complete rookie. Which we all know isn't true. I should be better at this by now. They all probably think the rumors are true, that I'm a total flop who's been helped along this whole time.

I clear my throat and read the message.

"It's a riddle, right? To find Minseok-sunbae? Wait, am I supposed to say his name or should I pretend I don't know it's him?"

Han-PD sighs before he answers this time. Definitely annoyed with me. "You can know it's him. Your segment is different because you were already announced."

"Ah, okay. Sorry." I bow again and I can see Hongjoo out of the corner of my eye covering her face with her hands.

"Um, yeah, so it's a riddle. I'm not that great with riddles," I admit trying to keep my voice steady, hoping that this is usable material for the production team. I don't want to be fired before I even finish one episode. "So up and down." I look around and then walk over to the seesaw and examine it. I'm hoping for another clue, or maybe an arrow pointing me in the right direction. Nothing. "Okay, that's not right."

I walk to the swings. "These go up and down, right?" I say aloud for the cameras even though I feel like my commentary is less than useless. "Or is that more back and forth?" I want to just ask for a clue, but I know it's way too soon and I'm scared of annoying the production team more.

Finally, I see Hongjoo gesturing toward the apartment complex, then lifting and lowering her hand like a platform.

I squint in confusion. What is she trying to mime? She's mouthing something. *Sell a gator? Mel Vader?* No . . . "Elevator!" I practically shout, and see the sound technician wince as he lifts his headphones. I lower my voice and spin to face the building. "The elevator goes up and down."

I hurry to it and one of the mobile cameramen follows me. The doors are unlocked for us, and I push inside. I press the call button for the elevator, and it opens immediately, like it was waiting for us.

Inside is a small bag. I grab it and see two strawberry milk cartons inside.

"Okay. This is good." I turn to the buttons and realize I have no idea which floor to pick. "Um, do you know which one it is?" I ask the cameraman before I realize I probably shouldn't be talking to him.

He lifts a brow and looks pointedly at the message still gripped in my hand.

"Oh right, the clues. I told you I wasn't good at this." I look at the paper, now completely crinkled in my nervous fists. "I already have the up and down. And I have the strawberry milk. So, it must be 'adding the numbers of home.' Numbers of home?"

What's a home number? A phone number? No, I don't think I'm meant to expose my phone number on national television.

"Maybe a unit number?" I say aloud, and the cameraman lifts his brows again. A silent prompt. It must be right. Or maybe he's just reacting to my total stupidity. Well, I have nothing else to try, so I add the numbers of my apartment in my head. It gives me ten. I start to press that number when I hesitate. Wait, this doesn't feel right. Something is off here. I almost pull out my phone and just call Hongjoo to ask for her help. But I know I shouldn't give up so easily. I just have to be logical.

"This is about when we first met, right?" I ask the cameraman. And he doesn't say anything, but he does move his eyes up and down. Like miming a nod.

"So, when we first met, the apartment I lived in . . ." It was unit 1829. And those numbers all added up come to twenty. The roof.

I press the button for the top floor. It feels right. Either way, I can't just keep running around alone. I need Minseok. And I hate to admit that, but right now, I am desperate.

The doors open and I race through them, the bag of strawberry milk banging against my stomach as I practically sprint for the staircase leading to the roof. I hurry up the stairs, taking them two at a time, not caring about being ladylike or demure.

I burst out to a scene of flowers gathered in a veritable garden. Minseok stands in the middle of the roof with a bouquet in his arms.

I hurry to him, barely registering the setup of cameras around him or the secondary crew. I'm just glad I'm no longer alone. I fling my arms around him. "I did it! I found you."

He laughs and gives me a one-armed squeeze. "I've been waiting forever, Shin Hyeri. What have you been doing all alone? You trying to keep the camera time all for yourself?"

That gets a surprised laugh out of me as I say bluntly, "Don't worry, most of the footage is me failing miserably. I hate riddles."

"Well, the reward is worth it, right?"

He's giving me one of his cocky grins and I have to use all of my willpower not to roll my eyes. "Depends on what my reward is."

"Am I not reward enough?" I know he's play-acting, but my heart does jump a bit at the words. So arrogant but still designed to make me blush.

"I thought this was my reward." I hold up the bag of strawberry milk.

He laughs and says, "It's my apology."

Now I frown, too confused to hide my reaction. "What are you talking about?"

"You don't remember? The first time we met I spilled your strawberry milk on the playground. You cried."

"I did not!" I protest even as the memory returns. He's right. He did spill my strawberry milk.

I'd just had a horrible review where I was told I needed to start counting calories more. I was only thirteen and bitter about it. So, I'd purposefully taken the last strawberry milk in the trainee fridge even though it was all sugar. My private act of defiance. I'd set it on the ground next to the swings while I moped and Minseok was playing basketball with his friends. And when he missed a throw the ball slammed into my milk, spilling it everywhere. Pissed, I'd flown off those swings, yelling at him until angry tears fell down my cheeks.

"You did. I remember it and I always felt sorry for making you cry." He lifts his hand, runs a thumb down my dry cheek like he wants to wipe up the memory of those angry tears. "Sorry my apology is so late."

I can't speak. My skin is still tingling from where his thumb touched, a trail of sparks that spin wildly like starbursts in my brain.

"I don't know what I'm supposed to say," I whisper, unsure what's expected of me in this moment.

"How about officially forgiving me?"

I nod because it feels like the only thing to do now. And he grins, pulling me into his arms. "Great. Slate clean, right?"

I pull away from him. "You did way more to me than spill my strawberry milk. Are you going to make up for every little thing?"

He laughs as he holds out the flowers. "Let's start with the milk and these."

He plucks up one of the cartons, uses the disposable straw to stab it, and offers it to me. When I take it, he holds out his own for a toast. "To us."

I nod and tap our cartons together. "To no more spilled milk."

FOURTEEN
HYERI

W e're strolling down one of the side streets close to the apartment now, the strawberry milk left behind after a single sip. Still have to be careful of calories.

I can't figure out what to do with my hands. It's as if I've never walked beside another person before. I'm so aware of the cameras on us that I worry I look stiff and unnatural beside Minseok, so I end up stealing glances at him to see what he's doing.

Finally, he sighs. "Can we take a quick break?"

I'm surprised. It's not diva behavior necessarily, but I'd just never even consider asking for a break before the main PD calls for one.

"Oh, sure, Moonster-ssi," Han-PD says amicably. "Let's take five minutes."

The camera people all gratefully lower the heavy equipment. Assistants run forward with cool water bottles to help with the afternoon heat. Hongjoo hands me one herself, and I take a long gulp.

Minseok leans in and I'm startled enough to jump back, spilling some of the water on my sleeve.

"I just think we should talk."

"Talk?" I'm confused enough that I don't put up a fight as he grabs my wrist and pulls me to the side, into the shade of one of the buildings.

"You need to calm down," he says, voice lowered so only I can hear.

"What?" I wonder if he's messing with me, but for what purpose?

"You're overthinking everything and it's making you stiff and jittery. Like when you used to be all wired right before an assessment test."

I pale at the memory. I was always a mess before monthly assessments when I first came to Bright Star. It was bad enough sometimes that I'd freeze in the middle of a song or dance routine. For the first six months as a trainee, I was always convinced I was about to get kicked out. But now, I just scowl. "I'm not thirteen anymore. And I don't need your criticisms on my performance."

"It's not a criticism. I'm telling you that you're fine. Don't focus on being on the show."

I laugh. "Um, that's kind of hard, since there are literally cameras everywhere."

"Why are you here?" Minseok asks.

"Huh?" What nonsense is he spewing now?

"Why are you doing this show?"

"Because I have to."

"No, that's not what I'm asking. What are you trying to prove by coming on this show?"

I shake my head, about to laugh off his question. Then I stop and actually think about it. With a sigh, I admit, "I guess I want people to realize

I'm more than all that bullshit gossip the antis make up about me. I want them to give me a freaking chance to prove it."

He smiles with satisfaction. "Just remember that. Don't let the antis win. You're too talented to give in to them anymore." With that he walks back toward the PDs and cameras.

What the hell? Did he really mean that? Or is he just gassing me up so I stop acting so awkward?

I don't have time to wonder as Han-PD calls out for everyone to set up again to continue the shoot.

Immediately, Minseok points to a small hole-in-the-wall kookbap restaurant.

"You remember begging Miss Ha at that shop for an extra fried egg?"

"Huh?" I frown, still confused by Minseok's last words to me.

"Wow, you seriously don't remember Miss Ha?" He slaps me on the shoulder hard enough to sting. "She practically kept us fed five years ago and you don't remember?"

"Of course I remember her," I say indignantly, rubbing at my shoulder. "She always gave me a can of cider for free and told me to practice hard for debut. I wonder if she's still running it."

"She is," Minseok says. "I visit whenever I'm here."

"Really?" I stare up at him in genuine surprise. When does he have the time to do that?

"I would have starved some days without her soup."

At his words, I remember the early days. When Bright Star was a struggling agency. It didn't have the giant organic cafeteria it does now, famous for bringing in celebrity chefs to cook for its artists. Back then it could barely afford to give us food tickets to the restaurants close to the dorm. But Miss Ha always made us meals on credit even if we'd run out of tickets.

I suddenly need to see the woman who made me home-cooked food when my own mother never did.

"Let's go see her." I pull on Minseok's arm.

He laughs and lets me tug him toward the shop. It looks exactly the same. With only four scuffed tables all along one side of the room. The other side is taken up entirely by a cramped kitchen space separated from the dining area by an old metal counter. On it sits the same banged-up register where she'd carefully tuck away our meal vouchers from Bright Star. Two large fans work valiantly to cool the small cramped space.

A woman in her late sixties is stirring the contents of a giant metal vat, the steam filling the room with a familiar scent. And despite the heat and humidity, I immediately have an intense craving for the warm soup.

"Ajjuma," I call out, and she turns around. The moment she sees us, her smile spreads wide.

"Woori saekki-ya." Miss Ha comes over and pats us both on the hips. The universal Korean halmeoni gesture of affection and approval. "You've come back to let me feed you."

"Yes, please. I miss your kookbap so much." I wrap her in a hug. Has she always been so small? She barely comes to my shoulders now. When I first met her, I was a head shorter than her. But I've skyrocketed now to 170 centimeters.

She ushers us to a back table, the one I always sat at when I came here. Above it now sits framed photos of us. Minseok with his group, and Sohee and me in a shot at a concert with Helloglow. I remember the day she asked me to sign it. I'd cried and she'd hugged me gruffly before shoving a bowl of kookbap in front of me and telling me to eat.

Now, as Minseok and I sit, a wave of nostalgia hits me. This place was my comfort after hard practice days when I thought I'd never debut. Or moments after I'd had a fight with Mom. Or when Hyejun ignored me or left me behind again.

There's no telling how stained this old table is with my own tears and snot.

I remember suddenly that I came here after Minseok broke my heart when I was fifteen. I eye him, but he's happily looking around the space, lost in his own memories.

Minseok grins as he looks up at the walls with handwritten messages and doodles from the many patrons. He points at one. "I drew this my first month as a trainee."

I lean in to stare at it. Anything to stop thinking about all my awkward memories. It's a cartoon sketch that looks like a smushed llama with a date scribbled underneath. "What's this lump?"

Minseok's smile fades a bit. "It's Moonie."

Moonie is the cartoon werewolf that's his representative character in WDB. All the boys have one (personally my favorite is Robbie's little droid named Robi-bot). But this thing looks nothing like the cute chibi werewolf.

I angle my head closer. "I don't see it."

His smile drops fully now. "These are the ears and this is the snout."

He points to the lumpy face. I tilt my head, squinting in exaggeration at the drawing. "Maybe it could be a pancaked goat. A wombat at best."

"Wombat?!"

"The ears are curved," I point out.

"It's faded," he says defensively.

"They're round," I insist, holding back a smile at his distress.

He opens his mouth, clearly about to argue and then gives in. "You're right, they're round."

"It's cute, for a lumpy wombat," I say to console him.

He shakes his head in defeat. "Maybe I should talk to the marketing team about changing Moonie to a marsupial."

I laugh at the thought. "The fans might not like it."

"Well, if my wife wants it, I'd rather make her happy."

I freeze, remembering we're filming a show. I let myself become too relaxed in an old familiar setting. I can feel the tension returning to my shoulders as I work hard not to turn to the glaring lenses of the cameras. Thankfully, Miss Ha arrives with a tray of food, setting out the small plates of banchan before giving us each a steaming bowl of kookbap.

"Masitgeda!" I exclaim, leaning in to breathe in the salty broth.

"It's so good to see you kids again. I'm so proud of you two. You've worked so hard and you're both so talented."

I grin with pride. Miss Ha was always reliably around with bolstering compliments.

"What is this you're doing now?" Miss Ha asks, pointing directly at the cameras. I cover a laugh at how little she cares about show etiquette. The unspoken edict is to try to ignore the cameras as much as possible. Though some of the bolder, more charming celebrities ignore that rule. I've seen Minseok do it a time or two. Not that I'm monitoring his shows, it's just when scrolling the feed.

"We're on our first date," Minseok says plainly.

I give him a sharp stare. Why isn't he providing more context?

"Eh?" Miss Ha looks back and forth between us, then breaks into a wide grin. "I knew you two would get together eventually." She looks directly at Han-PD, clearly marking him as the one in charge, and addresses him now. "This girl had such a huge crush on this boy. Couldn't take her eyes off him whenever he was around."

"Ajjuma," I groan, trying my best not to make eye contact with Minseok or any of the crew. I drop my face into my hands to hide the bright flush that burns my cheeks. It's bad enough that I'm forced to pretend I like spending time with Minseok, but now the whole country is going to find out about my old silly crush on him.

"Aw, Hyeri-ya, you've been pining for me that long?"

I glower at him. "Seriously? Did you forget how you—"

Minseok plucks up a piece of pickled radish and shoves it in my mouth before I can finish my sentence. I am so shocked I almost spit it back out at him. Instead, I glare pointedly at him as I crunch the radish cube.

"What was that for?" I ask.

"Isn't it supposed to be romantic to feed each other?" he says with a cocky grin.

"Oh yeah? Should I feed you now?" I stab my chopsticks into the head of a grilled fish and pick the entire thing up.

Minseok laughs nervously. "Let's not get carried away."

"Yes, yes, eat before it gets cold," Miss Ha says, waving at the table of food.

"Ne, chal meokaesumnida," I say obediently, setting the fish back down and scooping up a big bite of kookbap. Even annoyance at Minseok can't stop me from enjoying this meal.

$$\star \; \text{☆} \; \star$$

I stuff myself, completely forgetting my diet in my enjoyment of the comforting food.

"Oof, I'm so full," I groan, leaning back and patting my stomach after everything has been completely devoured. Then I freeze, eyes sliding to the red light of the camera. I shouldn't have done that. It's not very ladylike. And I'm sure the netizens will say it means I'm rude or classless. But it's already captured and I just close my eyes to hide my embarrassment.

"Good. You know I like a girl who eats well."

I open my eyes to stare at him suspiciously, but Minseok just grins at me.

"Really?" I ask slowly. "I thought that was Jaehyung."

"Jaehyungie just eats fast. If we took our time, I could eat him under the table."

Despite myself, a laugh breaks free. "Remember when you ordered a pound of chicken by accident instead of just one serving? We ate the whole thing because we almost never got fried chicken when we were trainees. I thought I was going to explode."

Minseok laughs at the memory. "Yeah, and we had to eat it fast because we weren't supposed to have food in the practice rooms."

I see Han-PD smile and nod. He seems to like it when we talk about our friendship moments. And I want to please the production.

"If Jaehyung hadn't been there, we'd have been screwed," I muse. "What are the guys up to right now?"

"Who knows," Minseok says, pushing out of his seat. "Come on, I have another surprise for you."

I'm confused. Does Minseok not want to talk about his members?

He's already calling goodbye to Miss Ha, and I have to hurry to catch up with him.

He turns a sharp right down a narrow side street beside the restaurant. I remember cutting through this alley to get to the bus station.

In my hurry to keep up I almost stumble over an empty crate. I didn't notice Minseok turn back, but he's suddenly there, grabbing my hand to steady me. He doesn't let go, even when I right myself. Instead, he pulls me along after him.

I can feel my palm getting clammy in his. I'm worried Minseok will feel it too, but I also don't want to pull away either.

I'm so focused on overanalyzing the hand situation, that I don't look up until we're halfway down the next street. And then I see it.

"It's the old arcade!" I exclaim, excitement and nostalgia hitting me all at once. "The trainees went there almost every day, remember?"

Minseok grins. "I remember you got banned for a month because you practically wiped them out of dolls in the crane games one weekend."

I nod, pride lifting my shoulders. If claw games are ever added to esports, I'd change professions in a second. I'd sweep every competition.

When we were trainees, every time I got a bad review or a critique at the agency, I'd come here and work out my frustration in the arcade. I suppose I got a lot of criticism at the beginning, because now I'm unstoppable.

We hurry inside and I make a beeline for the first flashing crane game.

"Which one do you want?" Minseok asks.

"I can get my own." I'm already surveying the stuffed animals inside and choosing my optimal target. I feel like a seasoned athlete returning to the ring after years away. "You know how good I am at them."

"I want to get you one, though. We're on a date."

The statement still catches me off guard enough that I fumble with my response.

Get it together, Hyeri. You can't forget that you're on the clock right now.

"Why don't I get one for both of us?" I offer, trying to find a compromise.

"I'll just win you one," Minseok insists, his face set in stubborn lines. It reminds me of when we were younger and he was determined to learn a new dance in a day. Minseok often changed his mind about his performance review songs, switching within days of assessment. It always gave me proximity anxiety, but he always pulled it off.

"I'm not so sure if you can. You weren't really that good at crane games when we were kids." It's one of the only things the great Moon Minseok could never master. Proof that he really was human.

"Hyeri-ya, I *have* gotten better at things since I was sixteen." He rolls his eyes, but I can see his jaw clenching. He's annoyed. "Just let me win you one."

I purse my lips, somehow drawing perverse pleasure in knowing I can tease him over this and he has to let me. "I'm just saying I'm not sure if you've had time to hone your claw game skills; it takes a lot of practice and you've been too busy touring the world."

"Fine, if I get it within three tries, then you have to do something for me."

I shake my head, sure it won't come to that. "Okay, what is it?"

"If I get the doll, then you have to start calling me Oppa again." He grins as the smile finally falls off my face.

I promised myself a long time ago that I would never call him that again. I almost refuse the challenge. But I know that will give it more importance than I want to admit. Already he's watching me with a smug look. He knows that this bothers me. That's why he's doing it. So, I lift my chin.

"Fine, but you won't win."

"Just tell me which one you want."

I turn and consider picking a difficult one, but give in and choose the easy target I'd pinpointed before. It's a wily white rabbit that's the representative animal of an older idol.

"Leebit?" Minseok's brow furrows, and if I didn't know any better, I'd think he was jealous.

"Yeah, you know how much I love Sunbae's dancing." I can see that Minseok is giving me a little frown. I send him a sly side-eye. I tell myself I'm just playing up the teasing for the camera, but I'm secretly pleased at his reaction. It reminds me of when we were kids and we could act foolish without worrying who was watching.

"What? You can't get mad. They don't have a Moonie stuffie in there," I say, batting my eyes innocently at him.

"Fine." He shakes his head. "I hope Sunbae appreciates that I respect him so much."

He fails. Nine times.

It's almost sad as he shoves the tenth bill into the crane game. I want to tell him to stop wasting his money. He's already lost the bet.

"Look, I'll show you." I try to take the controls. By now we've moved targets after his fourth attempt buried Leebit more. (To be honest, I half suspect he might have done it on purpose.) Now we're aiming for a small stuffed bear with a tiny hanbok on.

"I've got it." He bats my hand away.

"You don't." I grab the joystick but he won't let go of it. "You have to calculate the best place to grab it. You can't rush it."

I move the claw, forcing Minseok's hand to obey my pressure. I can see the perfect angle and I'm practically pressed against the glass to spot it better. I know if I position it just right, I can hook the claw around the bear's arm and head.

"There," I mutter with a nod. It's as good as I'm going to get, I'm sure.

I start to press the button, but remember that this is Minseok's game. So, I take his hand and place it over the button. "Ready?" I ask.

Minseok doesn't reply, just stares at me so long I start to feel nervous. In this position, I'm holding both his hands, my side pressed tightly to his. It's as good as a half embrace. I tell myself it's not like that. But the way he's looking at me, I'm sure he's thinking the same thing. And then he smiles. It makes my brain tingle, like staticky prickles. I start to pull back when he turns his hand to grip mine. He uses our joined fists to press the button.

I turn at the whirl of the claw, my attention stolen by the metal pincers approaching our target. Should I have moved it a bit to the right? No, it's going to be okay. I wince as the claw does that annoying thing when it lowers a little too low, turns crooked, seems to miss its target.

But as it lifts, it hooks right onto the arm of the stuffed animal. And it rises, but it doesn't just have the hanbok bear, but another bear wearing a heart-patterned T-shirt.

I let out a little gasp as Minseok grips my hand. "We did it!"

"Wait," I say, not daring to celebrate yet. Still, I can feel his excitement vibrating through our joined hands, and it fuels my own as we wait for the two dolls to be deposited safely in the bin. The claw jerks before reaching its destination and I let out a squeak as the heart bear almost falls, but the claw stays hooked in its T-shirt.

And when both are successfully dropped, we let out twin shouts like we just won the World Cup instead of a crane game. We clap our hands together in a rapid pattycake of triumph. For a moment, I was really scared we'd lose it. Excitement at the win feels like firework spinners sparking inside of me. He wraps his arms around my waist and lifts me in the air in a little victory spin.

It's dizzying and thrilling at the same time. And I have to wrap my arms around his neck so I don't slip. When he finally sets me down, I'm a bit wobbly but still pumped up on the win. My arms are still around his neck, pulling his head slightly down toward me. He's smiling so wide that it creates creased dimples at the tops of his cheeks. His signature look that the fans go wild over. It sends those internal sparklers of mine spinning again.

It's too much. He's too close. I let go, pushing away hard enough to stumble back into the machine. It lets out a little clatter as I bump it.

"Whoa, you okay?" Minseok reaches for me again, but I skitter out of his reach.

"I'm fine. Just got overexcited." I force out a laugh to maintain the celebratory mood, but I know I've kind of ruined it.

Clearing his throat, he leans in. I sidestep, but he just pulls the two stuffed animals from the machine.

"Here, your prizes." He holds them out and I take them gingerly, making sure our hands don't touch. He shoves his into his pockets once they're empty. And for the first time today he doesn't have a self-assured grin or a cocky comment. It makes me feel guilty for ruining the mood. So, I hold out the heart bear to him, like a peace offering.

"This one is yours. We won them together. We should both get one."

"Really?" He looks genuinely delighted. "I'll give him a place of honor in the dorm."

"You better. And every time you look at him, remember who helped you win."

"I won't forget. You're officially my lucky charm." He presses the bear's little stuffed mouth to my cheek like a kiss.

I blink in surprise. I know that he's just doing this for the cameras. So, why is my heart racing? He's too good at this.

I force myself to smile. Force myself to play my part. "Happy to help."

I'm trying to calm down as we step out of the arcade. But the moment the doors open, screams surround us. Already skittish, I jump in alarm before I recognize them as fans. WDB fans. They're waving signs and the aforementioned Moonie plushie. Cameras and phones are lifted in the air to get a shot. Moonster gives a congenial smile and wave, completely unfazed. I can barely hear my own thoughts over the screams.

One of the assistant PDs comes over and yells close to my ear. "Someone must have leaked where we were. We'll have to wrap up."

They hurry us through the crowd toward the waiting vans. The date is prematurely over. But I can't help but think it's for the best. I was already starting to forget what was real and what was just pretend.

FIFTEEN
HYERI

did use to call Minseok Oppa.

In fact, it was something I secretly relished, the moment we were close enough that I could call him that. It made my heart flutter every time he'd turn in response. It meant he recognized our close relationship too.

Hyejun made fun of me sometimes. Miming the word and pretending like he was air-kissing someone. But I didn't care what he thought. My crush on Minseok-oppa was too strong to be swayed. And Hyejun wasn't in our company. So, he couldn't deter me from engineering moments for me to run into Minseok "coincidentally" in the halls (when really I'd waited, leaning against the wall outside his practice room until he took a break to go to the convenience store for a snack).

I'd ask to tag along. A tentative "Can I come too, Oppa?" and he'd send me that friendly smile that creased the tops of his cheeks and say, "Of course, Hyeri-ya. Oppa will buy you a drink." And my heart would take off in flutters as I hurried after him.

But a stronger memory blocks out any of the warmth from those naive moments.

Minseok's harsh voice telling me, "Stop calling me Oppa! You want someone to hear and misunderstand? I don't have time to deal with this right now. I have to focus on the group, not your immature crush."

The words were cruel. But I know now that they were necessary. Though they worked to shatter my sensitive heart at the time, I'm better for it.

It helped me along the path of learning the realities of what our lives were about to become. That no matter how we might want normal lives with normal crushes and relationships, as celebrities, we belong to our fans. Nothing we have is just ours anymore, not even our own hearts.

SIXTEEN

HYERI

The first episode airs and the company couldn't be happier.

Despite my certainty that we'll be the first ever couple on *OCM* to be fired, the viewers don't hate us.

Actually, it's hard to trust it yet, but they seem to *like* us.

I monitor the entire episode, making little mental notes for myself so I can do better in the future. As predicted, I was completely awkward during the initial riddle-solving segment. Though, the producers kindly edited my struggle to frame it as adorably fumbling with the clues.

But once Minseok is on the screen with me, things smooth out. Our bickering is presented as banter. The captions on-screen keep labeling us as old friends, probably at the request of Bright Star. And the commentary is definitely that our little jabs at each other have the undertones of young flirtation.

It's embarrassing, especially knowing Minseok is probably watching as well. He wouldn't actually think I was flirting with him, right? He has to know it's just the editing of the show.

The most surprising thing is that the crew somehow got Miss Ha to do a testimonial interview. When they got it, I have no clue. But she's standing in her kitchen talking about us as kids, coming in to eat together, thick as thieves.

To my dismay they do air the scene where she mentions my crush. But then it cuts back to the testimonial interview. "The thing is those kids don't know that Miss Ha sees everything. And I noticed him noticing her too. That's why I'm not surprised they're together now." She shakes her ladle at the camera like she's lecturing it. "It was just a matter of time, if you ask me."

I'm not sure how they got her to say that. It can't be true, but maybe the director thought it would add a bit of flavor to pretend my crush wasn't completely one-sided. After all, it feeds the romance angle of the show.

At least the producers seem to like how much better I am at the crane game than Minseok. Me teaching him how to win the doll is an entire segment at the end of the episode. Including our hug when we won.

After the episode airs, the narrative online quickly becomes focused on any moments from our debut and pre-debut time. Clips surface of small moments of us interacting.

The power and sleuthing skills of netizens has always scared me. But maybe that's because it's always been used against me. Now, there are screenshots from old vlogs. A fuzzy zoom-in of us at a music show when I was promoting with Helloglow and Minseok with WDB. We're on opposite sides of the stage, but netizens insist there's a moment where we make "meaningful eye contact." Amateur body language analysis claiming we were secretly waving or smiling at each other. They even find a still from CCTV footage of us at a convenience store pre-debut.

The netizens seem to love the idea that Minseok and I have had some secret friendship we were so good at hiding that it hasn't come out until now.

It all feels like another lie, though. Minseok and I are not friends. Acquaintances. Frenemies. A passing embarrassing childish crush. But friends? I don't know if I could claim that.

Yet this half-truth helps me.

Does letting it spread make me a hypocrite? When I've been the victim of nasty half-truths meant to drag me in the past? Or is this something I'm owed after surviving all that?

SEVENTEEN
HYERI

he restaurant we're filming in today is one of those fancy (read: expensive) places with private rooms in Gangnam. Places where exclusive business deals take place. But also, the place you go to meet your future in-laws when you're trying to impress them.

Of course, I'm not trying to impress the people who will show up as Minseok's stand-in family for the "family meeting" episode. But I am nervous nonetheless. It all seems both so real and so fake at the same time. It feels different than filming a drama. Because even though we're still telling a story, we're supposed to be ourselves—just a more entertaining, more palatable version. And it all just feels like more lying.

Get over it, Shin Hyeri, this is your job. Just do it and do it right.

"Okay, kids, we're going to start filming soon," Han-PD announces, pushing his square glasses up his nose. He's in a good mood today. Probably because of the positive reception of the first episode.

Minseok has already settled at the table and is laughing at something one of the assistant PDs said. He looks so casually handsome and I'm suddenly reminded of all the viewer comments saying that we make a good visual pair.

Just thinking about it makes me blush just as Han-PD tells us to take our places.

I'm supposed to sit next to Minseok, but I feel self-conscious all of a sudden and I keep a foot of space between us.

"Okay, Hyeri-ssi, can you do the clapper?" the PD asks.

"What? Oh yeah, sure." I hurry to clap my hands together, much smoother this time than last.

When I settle into my place again, Minseok pats my shoulder and I freeze. "Are you nervous?"

"Nervous?" I repeat, wondering if he's picking up on my awkwardness.

"To meet my family?" he clarifies with a laugh. "Guess you are."

My instinct is to lie. To pretend I'm fine. But I know the point of these shows is to give people a look at the "real" you. So, I nod. "Yeah, I guess a little. I want it to go well."

I don't add that it's not about meeting family but about doing it on camera. I wonder if they brought Minseok's actual parents over.

Instead, the door opens and two familiar faces walk in.

"Noona!" Robbie gives me a quick half-hug before I can fully react.

"Hyeri-noona." Jaehyung, who has always been far more reserved, sends me a friendly smile and bow.

I've known them since we were kids, trainees together at Bright Star. But it's been months since I've seen them. And I'm struck by how much they've grown since we were starting out.

Robbie used to be shorter and now he towers over me. It's weird to think that he's still in high school. He's been in the industry longer than I have, growing up in the public eye.

They settle on the other side of the table and I send them a relieved grin. I'm glad it's them. It should make it just a little easier to get through.

"How are you dealing with Hyeong so far?" Robbie asks with a teasing smile for Minseok.

"I'm not that bad," Minseok insists.

"Sunbae is fine," I say with a shrug.

"Sunbae?" Robbie looks between the two of us. "Oh."

It's just a single word, but it holds a ton of questions in it.

Minseok laughs. "She refuses to call me Oppa."

"There are other things. Oppa isn't the only option," I insist.

"Then why did you choose Sunbae?" Minseok asks.

I can't help it, my eyes slide to the cameras. I can't say the real reason. That his warning all those years ago still echoes in my head. That he rejected me. And calling him Oppa represents a time when I was too naive to realize his platonic kindness wasn't any more than that.

"What do you call Hyeri-noona?" Jaehyung asks.

"What I've always called her, Hyeri-ya."

"That's not very romantic either," Robbie points out.

"What would you call your girlfriend?" Minseok asks, and I almost gasp. Is he allowed to say that? Bright Star has never confirmed that Robbie is dating, and I'm sure they're doing it on purpose because of the Jongdae scandal.

Robbie just shrugs. "I call them Constellation. Obviously."

Jaehyung lets out a surprised laugh, and Minseok rolls his eyes.

They're so natural, letting these awkward moments slide off them so easily. Why can't I do that? This is why WDB is so widely beloved, because their rapport with each other is so natural and fun. Filled with inside jokes and sibling-like bickering. They grew up together and it's clear to anyone who watches that they're not just teammates, but family.

With the three of them here, my nerves are smoothed out, and I'm able to join in on the conversation a bit more naturally than when it was just Minseok and me.

We're served injeolmi, a rice cake dessert covered in roasted soybean powder called konggaru.

"We hope the newlywed couple will stick together like these injeolmi," the waitress says with a professional smile.

"You should feed one to your bride, Hyeong," Robbie says mischievously.

Minseok picks one up and to my horror, it looks like he's going to comply with Robbie's request.

"I'm okay!" I yelp, and quickly snatch it from his hand. Some of the konggaru falls onto the table.

I shouldn't have done that, but it's too late now. Embarrassed, I stuff the injeolmi in my mouth. Then immediately realize I've made another mistake as the chewy rice cake completely fills my mouth. I can barely bite down.

Minseok smirks at me. "You look like Jaemunk."

I'm confused until Jaehyung lets out a surprised laugh. Jaemunk is the cartoon chipmunk that represents Jaehyung, his cheeks always puffed out with food.

"Hey," I mumble through my mouthful.

Minseok laughs and leans forward. I want to pull away, but the rice-paper wall is right behind me. So, I'm trapped and he knows it, if his slow grin is any indication. He takes his time lifting his hand, then wipes the edge of my mouth with his thumb.

"You had some on your lip," he says so quietly I wonder if the mics even pick it up.

There's a thing Minseok has always done. He speaks to you like you're special. When I was younger, I couldn't wait for the times I could have that focus on me. To let it make me feel somehow important to him.

And I'm horrified to learn that it still gives me that glowy feeling, being the center of his attention.

He shouldn't be able to pull me in like this when I know all his tricks already. I should be immune. I've worked so hard the past four years to be. Except I've clearly failed.

I hear Robbie and Jaehyung's low "Oooh."

Minseok's gaze flickers toward them in annoyance, and finally I'm able to snap out of it and push him away. Not hard, but enough to get him to move back.

I'm sure I'm flushed, but for once I don't care what I look like on camera. Jaehyung and Robbie start teasing Minseok, who plays along. I know I should participate. I will, I just need to catch my breath first.

EIGHTEEN
HYERI

When the shoot ends, everyone is in good spirits. Han-PD comes over to give both Robbie and Jaehyung hearty handshakes, thanking them for being on the show. I know this will get good ratings. It's one of the only chances in months that the fans will get to see members of WDB officially interacting for a show.

Even Minseok looks like he's in a good mood, smiling as he chats with his group members. I start over to thank them too when there's a commotion in the hall. Hanbin walks in, carrying holders filled with coffee. Behind him comes Jongdae, holding a bag with pastries even as he leans on a crutch with the other arm. His leg is encased in a brace.

I hurry forward to help, taking the bag as people start to crowd around. "Jongdae-sunbae, shouldn't you be resting?" I ask.

He smiles and it makes his already handsome face even more stunning. "I wanted to come show my support for the couple."

"Thank you." I notice the pastries are from Minseok's favorite café chain and turn to show him the bag. But he's stepping out of the room. He hasn't even acknowledged Jongdae's presence.

I notice JD's eyes tracking Minseok, his smile slipping for a moment before he turns to Han-PD, who came over to greet him. I set the pastries on the table and step out of the room to look for Minseok, but he's nowhere to be seen.

An assistant PD hurries over, telling me she'll take me to a side room to shoot my testimonials. I do another scan of the hall but finally give up on Minseok and his mysterious mood change. The interview is pretty straight-forward. I just give my commentary on meeting Minseok's "family" and how I felt it went. Since I'm perfectly comfortable around Jaehyung and Robbie, it's not hard to talk about how much fun I have with them.

I wonder if I'm actually getting the hang of this.

After, I find Robbie leaning against the hood of one of the company cars typing on his phone.

"Robiya!" I call, and he turns to greet me with a grin.

"Noona, this was so fun." He catches me in a quick hug. I know I should be more careful about the easy affection in public. But I'm still in too good a mood to worry about who's watching or judging right now.

"It really was," I say, surprise lacing my voice. "Thanks for making the time to come."

Robbie shrugs. "It's not like my schedule is stacked these days."

He grins so good-naturedly, but I wonder if it bothers him more than he's letting on. The unplanned hiatus because of WDB's scandals must be stressful. I know it always bothers me when my scandals force me to lie low.

"How are you doing?" I ask cautiously.

"Good. Great actually," Robbie replies, and I'm surprised at his bright smile. It's the look of someone who's not worried at all.

It's not what I expected.

"Hey, we should hang out," Robbie says.

"Didn't we just do that?" I laugh.

"Nah, this is work. We should hang out for real. I've missed that. You always took good care of me when we were trainees."

I blush. Robbie was one of the few trainees younger than me when I joined. I never had a younger sibling, so I latched onto him as an honorary younger brother.

"I'm thinking of having a small birthday party," Robbie says. "You should come."

"Didn't your birthday already pass?" I ask, mentally calculating the days. Am I so out of it that I don't even remember what month it is anymore?

"Yeah, but I didn't get a chance to celebrate yet." Robbie scratches at his temple while giving a rueful smile. It makes his adorable dimples flash, reminding me of how he loved to use them to disarm the vocal and dance coaches when we were trainees. "So, you in?"

"Oh, well, maybe." I struggle to figure out how to answer. I'm not sure if it would be a good idea for me to go to a party. If the antis find out, they might accuse me of partying when I should still be apologetic for what happened at the midsummer festival.

"I'll text you the details," Robbie promises.

"Okay. Sure," I concede, figuring he'll either forget or I can just politely pass via text, where it's less awkward. "Hey, have you seen Jaehyung?"

Robbie glances around. "I think maybe he went back to one of the other private rooms with Minseok?"

"Okay, I'm going to thank him too before you guys leave." I give

Robbie a pat on the arm as a goodbye before stepping back inside. The other private dining rooms were set aside for the shoot to put equipment. A couple at the back are staging areas where Robbie and Jaehyung probably waited before filming. I hear a murmur of voices from the farthest one.

I recognize Minseok's voice and figure he must be in there talking to Jaehyung. But I stop when I hear the hard tone. "... why I told you not to come!"

"What's so wrong with coming to show my support, Seok-ah?" Jongdae's voice asks.

"Is that what this really was? Or were you checking up on me?"

"Are you kidding? You think I don't trust you or something?"

"I don't know, do you?" Minseok sounds angrier than I've ever heard him. I've rarely seen him lose his temper, let alone sound so vitriolic toward someone. And his best friend at that.

"What the hell is that supposed to mean?"

"Never mind."

"Hey, will you just talk to me?"

The door bursts open and I jump back, tripping over a set of stacked chairs. When I fall one of the chairs clatters against me. I cry out when the wooden leg hits my arm.

"What the hell, Hyeri? Were you listening to us? And now look at you, you've hurt yourself!" His anger feels severe as he looms over me.

I spot Jongdae just inside the open door and am that much more embarrassed at having an audience.

Minseok starts to reach down, but I push his hand away and scramble up on my own. I feel embarrassed at being yelled at, and in front of Jongdae. "I'm fine. And I wasn't listening in on purpose," I insist, rotating my wrist carefully. My arm throbs where the chair hit, but it doesn't seem that bad.

"Well, whatever you heard, forget it. And stop following me around."
He strides past me so fast that I almost stumble back again. I catch my
balance but stub my thumb in the process. The pain makes it hard for me
to hold back my frustration and I yell after him. "I wasn't looking for you!
The whole world doesn't revolve around Moon Minseok."

He pauses midstep. His back is tense, his fists clenching at his sides.

I think maybe he'll come back. And I'm ready for it. I didn't do anything wrong. He's the one who's acting like a raging a-hole right now.

But he continues down the hall, slamming out of the restaurant.

NINETEEN
HYERI

don't really go out that much.

After the first few times random people yelled at me on the street for being a bully to Ana, I'd slowly stopped going out unless absolutely necessary. Choosing instead to order most things online, even groceries. Plus, I had Sohee, who almost willfully refused to change her routines just because of her fame. She'd always go out on random errands or to grab us late-night snacks.

And, at first, I didn't mind staying in. I like being at home most of the time. But now, it's not the lack of going out that gets to me. It's the lack of options. I'd like the *choice* of going out, even if I ultimately decide to stay in.

So, I started going to the one place that I always know is safe. The company building.

It's actually a really nice place, with multiple dining options and cafés.

There's a gym and a screening room we can watch movies in. There's even a bowling alley and arcade in the basement. And it has a convenience store inside that only employees can access where I can use my company points.

I know I sound like a weird advertisement for the joys of the Bright Star Entertainment building, but if there's only one place I can go to every day, at least it's a place with a lot of things to do.

Plus, the two things I am always expected to do, even on break, are to keep up my practice and keep up my skincare. And Bright Star even has a skincare clinic in the building. (Insider hint: Celebrities will be in dozens of commercials for miracle products, but the real secret to our flawless skin is almost daily clinic visits.)

Today, I'm antsy, and Sohee is busy with the photo shoot for Kastor's album jacket. She texted me photos of her outfits this morning. They're going with a mermaid concept, a play on Kastor being part of the Gemini constellation, known for guiding sailors in the olden days. It's also why there are six members, because of the six stars in the Castor constellation. I used to love how deeply complicated the concepts were for idol groups. But now, I just get confused trying to memorize all the details for all the new hoobae groups.

Yet more proof that I was probably never truly cut out for being an idol. It's why I need to safeguard my new life as an actress with everything I have. Even if it means playing nice with Minseok for another couple of months.

"It's fine, the show is being well-received. You're doing well," I whisper to myself.

"Shin Hyeri." Someone shouts my name and I spin around in surprise.

Did they hear me talking to myself? I'm already mortified before I recognize who was calling me.

Kwak Dongha is standing by the curb wearing a protest sign about "artists ruining the image of Bright Star." And I know it's about me.

I take a step back, ready for anything. Food projectiles, spit, even a slap—which has happened to me once before.

He thrusts out a paper, and I skitter back, almost falling on my butt. But he shakes it at me until I finally take it.

It's a list of my perceived crimes (I'm not explicitly named, but I know it's about me). I try not to read it, but I spot Kim Ana's name and the words *stolen costume*. I sigh. Of course he believes the lie. Why wouldn't he?

I want to ask him to leave me alone, but I just know it will spur him on. So, I just walk away as fast as I can without breaking into a run.

An employee is already coming out of the lobby, having witnessed the situation, and I breathe out a sigh of relief as he ushers me inside.

"You shouldn't be so shameless!" Dongha shouts after me. "How dare you film a show when you should be reflecting on your bad behavior!"

I can't help the reflexive hunch of my shoulders as the Bright Star employee uses his bulky arm to shield me and the automatic doors slide shut behind us.

But I can still hear Kwak Dongha shouting outside, even if I can't hear the words he's saying.

"Don't worry, Hyeri-ssi. I've already alerted security."

I nod, grateful, but also worried that they won't be able to do much. He isn't breaking any laws. Technically. I might have to wait in the building all day before I can leave.

I'm also embarrassed. Other artists don't cause this kind of trouble to the company. I wonder if I'll ever be free from this kind of hate. And if not, when will the company finally reach their limit when it comes to me?

The front desk guard opens one of the glass security gates for me with a polite nod. I can barely return the greeting as I keep my head down. I hate that this keeps happening to me. I hate that they keep witnessing it. I wonder if they will talk about it after. They must. Who wouldn't? If I didn't know how much gossip can truly hurt, I'd do it too. It's human nature.

Luckily, there's no one else in the elevator bank and I snag one alone. Finally able to lean against the back bar and settle my nerves.

"You're going to be okay. You have things to do here. You can wait for him to leave. One anti doesn't matter." Except Kwak Dongha represents hundreds of faceless keyboard warriors who say so much worse behind their anonymity. He's just the one who's willing to show up and harass me in person.

The doors of the elevator open, and I start out before I realize it's not my floor. I step back to let the others on, smoothing out my shirt and putting a polite smile on my face. It drops when I see Minseok with two of the younger producers. Thankfully, they don't stop talking just because I'm here, and I slide to the corner, trying to make myself as small as I can.

Minseok doesn't even glance at me as he listens to one of the producers explain the jazz concept of the sample.

"It sounds like his thing, but I thought he was leaning more hip-hop and R&B?"

"Yeah, we know."

Minseok laughs and from my angle I can see the corners of his eyes crinkle. Dammit, why does he have to be so effortlessly attractive? I hate him for it even as I keep sneaking peeks.

"So, you already pitched it to him and he said no."

"We just thought you could at least get him to listen to it." The second producer holds out a flash drive.

Minseok sighs like it's the biggest burden, but he takes the drive. "Next night of drinks on you, not some pocha. A nice bar."

"Done!" the first producer says, patting Minseok on the shoulder. "You're the best, Minseok-ah."

"I know." Minseok shrugs, his grin widening, and I hate that it makes his eyes practically sparkle with charm.

The doors open on my floor, and I squeeze past the group, scurrying away to the safety of the empty hallway.

But after the elevator doors ding to signal closing, I hear someone call my name.

My throat clogs with fear as I hear an echo of Kwak Dongha saying my name outside. But when I turn, it's Minseok jogging toward me. "Hey! We should talk."

"Why?" I turn into the small kitchenette on this floor, the closest place I can think to escape him. I'm still on edge from the confrontation in front of the building, and I don't think I can handle Minseok's irritating brand of teasing right now.

Unfortunately, he doesn't get the hint and follows me. "It's for the show."

Dammit, why'd he have to bring that up? I feel like I'm required to listen now since it has to do with work. I didn't realize that agreeing to do this show would give him a tool to control me with.

"Fine," I say as I throw open the slim fridge, pretending this is the reason I came in here.

Minseok reaches past me for a Coke. It traps me between him and the fridge. Even though he already has his drink, he roots around, then plucks up a bottled iced Americano. He hands it to me. "This is your brand, right?"

It's what I probably would have picked, but I'm annoyed enough to put it back. "That's not what I want," I say, and pick out a Pocari Sweat instead. I don't really love the taste of it, but I hate that Minseok assumes he knows me. Even if he does.

He just shrugs and settles at one of the three small tables, opening his own soda. "So, I think we should decide what to call each other."

"What?" I frown. "Why?"

"Robbie and Jaehyung thought it was weird, and the fans seem to agree. We should decide what to call each other."

"Why can't I just call you Sunbae?"

"When have you ever called me that?" Minseok laughs.

I hate the idea that he's laughing at me. So, I reply defensively. "I call you that all the time." *On broadcast.*

"What about Ya! Neo!" He suggests the rude informal way of calling someone.

"Why not just Ee Nom," I say dryly. It's as close to cursing him out as I can get even without cameras around.

He laughs. "If that's how you want to address me, I support it. But then I get to call you Riri."

I roll my eyes. "Why not just yeobo or something?"

He winces. "That's what my parents call each other."

"Yeah, because they're married. Isn't that what we're pretending to do here?"

He shakes his head. "What about aein?" He wiggles his eyebrows as he suggests the Korean equivalent of calling me his lover.

I pretend to gag. "Why can't we just use what we always have?"

"Okay, fine, what about jagi?"

It's still cringey. I might as well call him babe. But it's the least offensive of the suggestions. "Fine."

"Try it." He leans in, grinning like he's relishing the discomfort clearly splashed across my face.

"I'll do it on the show." I'm too embarrassed to say it right now. It feels weirdly intimate when it's just the two of us.

"Come on, you should practice. You said you get nervous on the shoots. It'll help if you try it out now." Is there something strange in the way he says it? Like he's trying to pull something over on me? But as I narrow my eyes at him, I can't tell.

"Fine." I try to force the word out, but all I get is a stilted "Ja—"

"Come on, jagi-ya," he practically purrs, his smile widening. "Say it, jaaa-giii."

I can't stop my jaw from clenching as I grit out, "Ja . . . gi."

"Really? That's all you can do?"

"Jagi-ya!" I practically shout it, annoyance bursting out of me with the word. "You happy now?" Why does he have to insist on jabbing at me all the time? Can't he just cut me a break every now and then?

"I'm very happy." His smile just sparks my anger even more.

I grab my bag to leave. "I hate you."

"You know we'll have to reenact this conversation for the show!" he calls after me.

I hate that he's right and that he's throwing this in my face right now.

The producers will want us to reenact the pet-name debate for the camera; it's too good a piece of content not to have for the show. And I hate it. Because I already feel like a fraud, and I know that we'll create a much friendlier version for the cameras. Just another way of watering down the reality of my life so I'm palatable for the viewers.

"Screw you, *jagiya*." Now it's easy to say the word, as it's saturated in all the sarcasm and frustration I feel.

"See you on set," Minseok calls after me cheerfully as I let the door slam behind me.

TWENTY
MINSEOK

Minseok stares at the bottle of Pocari Sweat that Hyeri left behind, untouched, unopened. The condensation is dripping down the sides now.

He came to the studio to get some alone time. The dorm is a busy place these days since the other guys don't have a schedule.

Minseok had to get out of there. But he'd just stepped off the elevator when the two young producers pounced on him, begging him to listen to their tracks. They kept him in the hallway long enough for him to overhear the squawk over the comm device at the small security desk on that floor. And the name Shin Hyeri.

When the guard reported that someone was bothering Hyeri outside the building, Minseok jabbed the call button for the elevators. He wasn't sure what he was planning to do, but he never had to find out, as the elevator opened to reveal her inside. She looked okay, but he had to be sure, so he got on. Except, the two producers followed him, and he was forced to chase after her to get a moment alone.

He had no intentions of teasing her. But she's always so intent on acting cold and distant around him that it makes him want to needle her until he gets a reaction.

What is it about that girl that feels like a wasp's nest begging to be poked?

Minseok doesn't have to pretend to guess. He knows why he can't help himself when it comes to Hyeri.

Because she used to love him and now she doesn't.

And he knows it's his fault.

Maybe it was a mistake to do the show. It just seems to make her hate him more. But he wasn't given much of a choice.

After that unfortunate pitch meeting with the directors, Hanbin had cornered Minseok.

"Minseok-ah, this show is the best solution for everyone involved."

"And if I say no? Will you find a way to force me?"

Hanbin's face set in hard lines, the look he gets whenever he's about to put his foot down. "Let me be blunt, if you don't do this for her, then there's nothing that anyone here can do for her."

Minseok didn't like the way that sounded like a threat. "What are you saying?"

"Shin Hyeri's scandals have gained a life of their own. She lost out on a role because of this. If she cannot recover with this variety show, she might be out."

How could he not do the show? He couldn't be the one who was responsible for Hyeri losing everything. Not when he had the power to help. Though, she'd hate to hear that's how he saw it. So, he didn't tell her. Let her think he was just doing this solely for his own PR.

After filming the first few episodes, he thought he'd made a little headway. She seemed to have fun at the arcade and walking down memory lane. But maybe she really is just pretending for the show. And it kills him to think she hates spending time with him.

Because maybe he agreed for more than just PR or saving Hyeri's career. Maybe he agreed to do it because it gives him a chance to be close to her again. To show her how effortless it used to be with them.

And he's already messing it all up. Sighing, he pulls out his phone and dials Hanbin.

"Hyeong, I need a favor."

TWENTY-ONE
HYERI

That night, the doorbell rings and I'm surprised to see Hanbin on the other side.

"Did Hongjoo-eonni send you?"

"I'm just acting as a delivery boy." He holds out a gift bag.

"What is it?" I ask even as I take it.

"Minseok is going through a few things. Don't be too hard on him, okay?"

I'm surprised to hear the gift is from Minseok, but I just nod.

"Great, see you at the next shoot."

When Hanbin leaves, I bring the gift into my room, settling cross-legged on my bed before carefully pulling out the tissue paper. I tell myself that he can't just buy me something and I'll pretend that he wasn't a complete ass.

But when I uncover the gift, I let out an involuntary laugh. It's a jumbo bag of Honey Butter Chips. I hate that he knows me this well.

A text from Minseok dings on my phone.

It's a picture of the little stuffed bear from our first date. And he's holding a handwritten sign: *I'm a dumbass. Forgive your faux-fiancé?*

I hate that I'm charmed by it. It's so silly and unserious. But it's also kind of sweet.

Will forgiving him make me a pushover?

Or is it better to let this go? It would make my life easier on set if we weren't at each other's throats.

So, I type back: *I'm only forgiving you because I ran out of Honey Butter Chips.*

Minseok: *Thank you. 1004.*

It's a stupid code kids used a lot when we were younger. 1004. Pronounced *cheonsa* in Korean, which is also the word for "angel." And I roll my eyes, but my heart reacts with a quick flutter.

"Stop it," I say aloud. I don't have time to revisit old crushes right now.

TWENTY-TWO
HYERI

The next day, I walk out of my room and almost scream as I practically run into one of the new trainees. Minjung or Minyoung. There are three of them, and I haven't memorized all of their names yet. I'm pretty sure they're all like thirteen or fourteen, which makes me feel old.

"Oh, hi, Sunbae. Sorry. I was just coming to tell you there are packages for you."

"Thanks, Min. . . ." I trail off, feeling bad at not knowing what to call her. "Um, have you eaten yet?"

It's a generic question in Korea. Akin to asking someone if they're doing well. But her eyes widen in shock. "Oh, um, yeah, we got lunch already. Sorry, did you want to come? We can go out and get you something!"

"No." I wave my hand, feeling bad for upsetting her. Of course she'd go out with the others, they're all trainees together. And the same age. I'm just an ex-idol half a decade older than them with no friends and nowhere else to go.

"Thanks for telling me about the package." I give her a reassuring smile, and she scurries into the first room where the three trainees have all claimed beds, leaving the second room for me.

I realize that maybe it's time to finally let go of this place. My presence here is making the new trainees uncomfortable. I pull out my phone as I walk out to the living room. I text Hongjoo, asking her if there's another company apartment I can live in temporarily while I look for my own.

There are a few packages stacked on the table.

I look through the boxes; some of them are things I ordered myself. Skincare, a new pair of sneakers, and a replacement case for my phone.

But one box doesn't have a shipping label. Instead, it has a Post-it attached with Hongjoo's handwriting: *fan mail delivered to the company.*

I can't stop the grin. I know I don't get as much fan mail as other Bright Star artists. And I definitely don't get the level of gifts they do, often delivered during their appearances at events or shows. There was one disastrous fan event where I received nothing, and I had to sit at my empty table while the other girls were photographed with their piles of gifts. I wouldn't have minded receiving nothing if it hadn't been so embarrassingly public.

There's something so insidious about how public the love for idols is, creating an unspoken implication that you're a failure if your fans aren't as vocal. It's something that caused me such intense anxiety that my doctors considered starting me on medication before my mother vetoed the idea.

"Celebrities have to learn to deal with rejection gracefully, Hyeri-ya. What will people think if they hear you take drugs?"

Still, I do get a few notes sometimes. And it feels like a special event whenever Hongjoo delivers them. Usually in a single manila envelope, but

I don't care how few there are. It's a reminder that not everyone out there hates me.

I rip it open, the tape pulling some of the cardboard away with it in my rush.

The first few notes are in cute stationery, and I carefully open the envelopes, wanting to preserve them to place in a scrapbook. When I was in *Citizen Producer*, all the girls were gifted one at the end of the show, pre-filled with fan letters. The others filled the rest of their pages quickly, but I still had space in mine at the end of Helloglow promotions.

I don't put the new fan mail in there. I started a new album for them. A symbol of a fresh start. And slowly the envelopes have been getting fuller and fuller.

Now it's an actual box.

So many of them are decorated with little bears and I realize it's fans who've seen the first episode of *Our Celebrity Marriage*. There are small packages with stuffed bears just like the ones we won in the crane game. One fan even sent me a Leebit. I laugh and set it aside to show Minseok.

I can't believe *OCM* is actually helping. I hate to admit it, but it seems like joining the show was a good idea after all.

The next envelope is plain. It doesn't have any of the stickers or handwriting on the outside like the others. And it feels thin as I carefully open it. At first, I think it was mistakenly included. Then a small slip of paper flutters out, falling face-up on the ground by my feet.

Angry block letters are slashed across the ripped piece of printer paper: *POISON IS TOO GOOD FOR YOU BUT IT WILL HAVE TO DO.*

TWENTY-THREE
HYERI

know the hate mail is from the HyeriTopAnti account, the one I suspect Kwak Dongha runs.

But Hongjoo says I'm not to worry myself about figuring that out. She promises the company is taking care of it. That they're taking the threat very seriously. In the meantime, I'm not to accept any food deliveries for now and only eat what she drops off for me or what I get directly from the company cafeteria.

It's not an issue. I can barely eat anything, as my anxiety burns a hole in my stomach like an ulcer. And the worst thing about it is that in the past couple of days I've actually thought that this is better than any diet I could force myself on.

Sometimes I wonder if this is really the life I worked so hard for. Wasn't I supposed to feel excited or content when I achieved my dreams? Instead, I just feel tired all the time.

At least I don't have any other scheduled appearances outside of *OCM*.

So, I can hide away, telling myself that most threatening letters are fake. That I probably shouldn't worry about it. That giving it to Hongjoo and the company is enough.

And today I don't have time to worry about it.

Because today I'm getting married.

I am currently encased in the bulbous skirt of a bridal hanbok in bright reds and golds. The jeogori is tight around my shoulders so I can't fully lift my arms. It's the long-sleeve top of a traditional Korean dress, shorter than a crop top, knotted shut with a single loop called an otgoreum. I always feel self-conscious the jeogori will pop up and show the hanbok petticoat underneath (I think the woman helping me dress called it a sokchima). But with the bridal outfit, a long top coat, or wonsam, is worn. You can't even see the jeogori, which makes me wonder why the costume person forced me to put it on when it restricts all my movement.

The wonsam trails low in front of me, the bright green of the overcoat a huge contrast to the vivid red of the skirt. And the sleeves are like two feet longer than my arms, so I'm having trouble keeping them pushed up right now so I can play on my phone as I get my styling done.

"Are you sure I have to wear the full getup?" I ask as David carefully slicks back my hair. I pick up the long gold-plated binyeo that will be speared through the tight bun he's creating at the nape of my neck.

"Be grateful I'm not making you wear the bridal wig." He nods toward the monstrosity that looks like a braided re-creation of Darth Vader's helmet.

"Thank you for your generosity," I mutter. "Where's Jeongho?"

"He's at the salon, bothering another stylist."

I laugh. "You can't keep going through assistants," I say. "You're way too busy to do everything on your own."

"The pressures of being so in-demand for my skills." He gives an exaggerated sigh.

I sigh along in sympathy.

The door bursts open. "Eonni!" Sohee shouts. "David-oppa!" She gives him a quick air-kiss before turning to me with a wide grin.

"Sohee?" I get out through my confusion.

She squeals as she grabs my hands, jumping up and down. "Look at you! It's like you're in a sageuk drama! You look like my eomma in her old wedding photos!"

Sohee looks delighted, but I'm still confused. "What are you doing here?"

"I was invited as a guest." She's still looking me over. She runs her hands over the bright red folds of my skirt. They trace the gold embroidery at the edges. "I wish they'd told us it was a traditional wedding. I'd have asked to wear a hanbok too."

"But what about your schedules?" I ask. "Don't you have to be with your group?" Is the company really letting her appear in the show?

"We don't have anything today. And I really wanted to be here. What kind of best friend would I be if I missed your wedding?"

I want to remind her that it's fake. But I feel tears suddenly pricking at my eyes. I didn't realize I'd be so emotional to see her here. "Thanks for coming," I choke out.

She smiles and tries to hug me. It's more of an awkward lean and back pat through all the layers of material I'm wearing. "Don't wrinkle her," David warns as he stabs the binyeo through my tight bun; it makes me wince a bit.

"Today is going to be fun," Sohee declares.

I laugh. "I'm not sure about that. But it'll be a little easier with you here."

"Okay!" Hongjoo comes in. "Who's ready to get married?"

★☆★

The ceremony itself is quick. It's blazing hot outside, and I think Han-PD knows that I'm two seconds away from heatstroke under all my layers.

Minseok's traditional hanbok is much simpler. Made of the same material, but a quarter of the layers. Plus, he can use his hands. I have to be led around like a child, with two older women on either side of me, helping me bow and drink the ceremonial water. I feel like I'm delirious by the time we're brought inside for the "reception."

As I walk in, loud cheers erupt and I stumble backward, ramming into Minseok with a soft "Oof."

Jaehyung, Jun, and Robbie race forward, singing a congratulations song used for anything from a promotion to a new baby.

"Chuka-ham-*ni-da*! Chuka-ham-*ni-da*!" they crow as they dance around us, high-fiving Minseok.

I try to smile along, but all I can think is that I want to drink a gallon of water.

"Eonni, are you thirsty?" Sohee asks, coming over to me. I suppose she's my sole wedding guest.

I nod enthusiastically. But before Sohee can deliver, Minseok is there with a cup.

"Here," he says.

"I can do it," I start to say, but when I lift my hands, my long sleeves cover them.

"It'll be faster if you just let me help you." Minseok doesn't wait for a reply. He just cups my chin and lifts the water to my lips. His fingers are firm but gentle as they hold me in place. And our eyes meet over the metal rim of the cup.

I'm glad for the material covering my hands now as they involuntarily clench into fists.

"Hello, my daughter!"

I almost spit out the water as Hyejun escorts my mother in.

Her bright red cocktail dress sparkles as she sashays over to me.

I know I should say something. Or at least smile. But my brain feels like it's malfunctioning; what is she doing here?

Mom takes care of it for me. Stepping forward with a bright smile she wraps me in a hug that suffocates me with all the layers between us. When her smooth cheek brushes against mine, she whispers, "Close your mouth, you look like you're trying to catch flies."

I do as I'm told, but I'm still not fully processing this.

"I—I can't believe you're here," I stutter and hope to god that it reads as excitement to see my long-distance mother.

She must read my hesitancy because her smile drops before she pulls me into another forced hug. "I had to come. It's my daughter's wedding."

I let out a surprised laugh at hearing my mom say those words.

Mom scowls—clearly this was not the reaction she wanted from me.

To make up for it, I force a bright smile. "I just can't believe you came."

She laughs. "How could you doubt I'd be here on such an important day?"

I'm saved from forcing a fake answer as one of the attendants comes over to direct her to sit behind the table with Hyejun for the pyebaek.

The decorations in here include a large Korean folding screen painted with soft watercolors of trees and cranes. Mom and Hyejun settle behind a low table set in front. It's covered in a blue-and-red cloth. Wooden and brass stands hold towers of chestnuts and ginkgo nuts, dried meats, and dates. There are two giant dried fish laid across the table.

The cameras start rolling and the attendant explains the pyebaek for the audience.

This part of the ceremony is when the family throws dates and chestnuts at us to decide how many kids we'll have. I eye the stacks of at least three dozen of each sitting on the table. I really hope it's not meant to be a literal count.

My mom tosses a gentle handful, but Hyejun has a glint in his eyes as he loads up two giant handfuls and lobs them at us. I let out a small scream as I recoil from baby-blessing projectiles. Minseok catches me before I roll back like a turtle on its shell. But even when I'm steady again, his arm stays comfortably around my shoulders.

"Careful, Hyejun-ah, you might go bankrupt buying gifts for all these nieces and nephews," Minseok jokes.

I force myself to smile along. I can see that my mom is watching me, stony-faced. She's not happy about something. And I'm sure I'll hear about it later.

An attendant hands me a fresh date.

I'm about to eat it when the woman stops me. "It's not for eating. You have to hold it in your mouth and your husband will bite into the other side."

I almost choke at the word "husband."

"Um, what part of the ceremony is this?" I ask to cover my awkwardness.

"You two have to see who gets the seed. They will be the boss in the relationship," the attendant explains.

"Okay!" Minseok says brightly. "Like a competition? Nice."

He gestures for me to bite into the date.

I'm not sure if I like the idea of this. It feels like a game made to force a couple to kiss. But I have no choice, everyone is watching, waiting for us to begin. So, I put the very end of the date in my mouth, barely gripping the skin with my teeth. I don't care about getting the seed. I'm more worried about keeping our lips as far apart as possible. Shows love these forced-proximity games. Like when idols are made to do a Pepero kiss or pass thin pieces of paper with their mouths.

I just need to stay as still as possible. Of course, when that's your goal, suddenly your entire body starts to shake. I feel like I'll drop the date in a second if Minseok doesn't hurry up.

But the moment he gets too close, I can feel his breath on my mouth and I lean back.

"Hyeri, stop moving!" Hyejun commands from behind the table.

"I'm trying," I grit out through clenched teeth.

"Just keep still." Minseok moves in again, tilting his head to the side. It reminds me of the moment in dramas before a deep kiss.

"Don't!" I squeak, dropping the date in the process.

"Hyeri-ya!" Minseok whines with a laugh. But he's still close enough that I can see his pupils are quaking. And I realize he's nervous too.

"Sorry, sorry," I say, plucking up another date from the bowl. "I'll stay still this time."

I carefully hold the skin of the date with my teeth. And this time, when Minseok approaches, I do my best not to move. But as he leans in, my eyes start to cross trying to keep him in my sights. I want to close my eyes, but I worry it would be read as too brazen. Isn't that what someone does when they're expecting to get kissed?

Finally, I can't handle it anymore. I don't care how it looks, I can't watch him moving closer and closer. I squeeze my eyes shut. But without something to focus on, I become dizzy and start to sway

Minseok solves the issue by cupping my cheeks firmly. I grip his wrists, to further steady myself by holding on to something.

Then I feel the pressure of him biting down on the date.

"Steady," he murmurs, and the low timbre sends shivers down my spine. I hold my breath, trying not to drop the date. But as soon as I feel him tug I let go. I don't care about winning or getting the seed, I care about this being over so I can catch my breath.

"Minseok wins!" Robbie declares, and I finally open my eyes. He's still sitting way too close, almost the entire date in his mouth. I hold a measly centimeter of the skin in my teeth.

"Guess I'm the boss." Minseok winks at me.

"Keep telling yourself that," I mutter, and then glance at the production crew.

A few hide smiles and I know that was definitely caught on the mics. I can't help but look at my mother, who is shaking her head in disapproval.

★☆★

After the shoot ends, I'm whisked away to change into normal clothing. I'm grateful to be out of the heavy wedding hanbok, but I'm anxious the entire time I'm changing. I know my mom will want to talk. And this is the first time we've spoken since I told her I lost the *Idol Academy* role.

I leave the changing room, moving toward the back of the venue where the vans and cars are parked.

Beside them sits a coffee truck. The kind friends and family send to sets to cheer on the production. This one has my name and face on the banner: *Shin Hyeri Fighting! Cheering for my princess! From your abeoji.*

I've never had someone send me a coffee truck before.

The crew is already gathered around it, happily ordering coffee drinks. It will definitely buy me a lot of goodwill on set. I remember when I first got onto *CiPro*, my mom insisted I bring these expensive vitamin drinks for the crew. She claimed making good with the staff would go a long way. But we were forbidden from bringing outside drinks or food onto set. I wonder if they'd have made a difference. Would they have swayed the staff not to air my most embarrassing on-camera moments?

Hyejun slings an arm around my shoulder. "How much you wanna bet Eomma organized this for good family PR?"

I shrug nonchalantly, because I don't want Hyejun to pick up on my disappointment at the thought. For one brief second, I thought maybe my dad had really put in the effort. But Hyejun's right, it's much more likely Mom did this and slapped our dad's name on it.

"At least everyone's happy."

I stiffen when I hear the telltale click of Mom's high heels approaching. "Hyeri, I've been looking everywhere for you." She's talking in her clipped, no-nonsense voice. She's definitely still upset at me.

"Sorry, I was just noticing Dad's coffee truck. It's nice, isn't it?" I'm hoping the sight of the happy banners might change her mood.

They don't. "I'd like to talk in private, Hyeri."

"Eomma," Hyejun interjects. "Why don't we all get a drink together?"

But Mom ignores his offer. "Hyeri, come." She sweeps past the truck, expecting me to obey.

I sigh and pat Hyejun on the shoulder. At least he tried.

I follow her behind the building, close to where all the production vans are parked.

"Is everything okay?" I begin even though I know it's not.

She crosses her arms, her lips turned down in disapproval. "Is this how you've been behaving here? Throwing yourself at Minseok?"

That is not what I was expecting her to say. "Wait, what are you talking about?"

"You were acting too familiar with him on camera. You're not here to actually flirt with him, you're here to fix your reputation. Bimbos don't keep fans."

I feel like I've been slapped. Her words sting just as bad as an open palm. Worse. I blink quickly to stave off threatening tears. Crying never softens my mom. If anything, she'll yell at me for ruining my makeup.

"I-I'm sorry."

"Sorry isn't enough. How are you going to fix this?"

I'm racking my brain for an answer that she'll find acceptable when I hear the shuffle of footsteps behind us.

"Hey, what's going on?" Minseok calls out.

Mom's eyes widen in surprise.

I close mine in utter embarrassment. Minseok is all smiles as he walks over, but I can see his jaw is tense. He clearly heard part of our conversation.

"It's nothing," I say.

My mom's face has transformed back into her sweet congenial facade. "I'm just having a quick chat with my daughter. It's nothing serious, just catching up. You should go back to set. Get yourself a coffee from the truck Hyeri's father sent."

"I'm sure I must have misheard, but I'm hoping you're not being too critical of Hyeri when she's been working so hard." Minseok's tone is pleasant, but his expression is cold.

Surprise at his quiet defense of me wars with my continuing embarrassment. Why isn't he pretending he didn't hear anything like a normal person? Why does he always insist on making things even more difficult for me?

"Excuse me?" Mom says pleasantly, though her smile has dropped a degree.

Please let this go, I silently beg him with my eyes.

Of course, Minseok doesn't. "Your daughter is doing really well with these shoots considering the way the show was sprung on her."

Now Mom's smile is completely gone. "This show is the only thing saving her drowning career." Little lines are forming next to my mother's mouth, which is a sign that things are getting bad. Mom would rather die than let her frown lines show. "She needs to learn how to avoid bad publicity and endear audiences to her better. Once she has them on her side, the media will fall into line."

"Hyeri is talented. She was one of the hardest-working idols I know," Minseok says, and my mouth practically falls open in shock. I don't think I've ever heard him say that before.

"Well, she's not an idol anymore, is she?" my mother says bitterly.

"Yes, but surely you can't blame her for how that happened, right?" Minseok replies, and I feel a flush rising up my neck. Can't he just leave this alone? I can see my mom's lips pursing in a tight line. She's angry, but she would never lose her temper completely at Minseok. Not when he's such a huge star. She pinches my arm, adding an urgent twist, a signal that I need to step in and fix this *now*.

"Minseok-ssi, leave!" I grit out, trying not to let my voice squeak.

He gives me a startled look. Clearly, he thinks I should be groveling at his feet for the few kind words he's bestowed on me. But I never asked him to help me.

"This is between me and my mother," I tell him. My mom's pinching fingers loosen a bit and I breathe out a little sigh. "Can you please go?"

He looks upset. Like my words somehow hurt him. But then the expression is wiped away as he shakes his head.

"Sorry for interrupting." He bows to my mother in apology. "I can see I overstepped."

When he lifts his head again, I swear I see disappointment on his face. It feeds my annoyance, growing it into hot anger. He has no right to be disappointed in me.

As he strides away my mother leans closer to speak in a harsh whisper. "Don't embarrass me any further, Hyeri. I will not be happy with you if you mess things up more."

"Yes, Mother," I reply obediently as I watch Minseok turn the corner back to set. If my fake wedding is any indication of how my fake marriage will play out, this is going to be an excruciating summer.

HYEJUN PROFILE

STAGE NAME: Hyejun
NAME: Shin Hyejun (신혜준)
GROUP: AX1S (악시스)
GROUP POSITION: Subvocal, lead dancer
BIRTHDAY: December 20
SIGN: Sagittarius
HEIGHT: 180 cm (5'11")
BLOOD TYPE: B
MBTI: ESFJ
FAMILY: Mom, Dad, younger sister (Shin Hyeri, formerly of Helloglow)
BIRTHPLACE: Los Angeles, California, USA
HOBBIES: Video games, basketball
EDUCATION: Global Cyber University

HYEJUN FACTS:

• Debuted with the group AX1S.

• Was cast at a Korean festival in Los Angeles.

• Moved to Seoul from Los Angeles at the age of 13 to become a trainee with HQ Entertainment.

• Friends with WDB's Moonster, Astro's Sanha, The Boyz's Sunwoo and Eric, Stray Kids' Felix, AB6IX's Lee Daehwi.

TWENTY-FOUR
HYERI

ater in the week, I get a message from Hongjoo that she's found me a new apartment. It might be a temporary situation, but I don't mind. There are two new girls in the trainee dorm now, and I feel like a squatter at this point.

So, I'm currently lugging my giant roller bag to the new building. Hongjoo wasn't able to come get me today, but I told her I didn't want to wait until tomorrow. I figured I could just take a taxi. This building is actually closer to the company. I count it as a win, even if it's just temporary.

I'm still listening to my music on full volume in my earbuds. It's a technique I use in taxis so the driver doesn't try to make small talk with me. I'm horrible at it. I drag my luggage to the apartment door and I can't remember the code. So I fumble with my phone to find Hongjoo's text, trying not to drop any of my bags, when someone grabs me from behind.

I immediately have an image of an anti-fan following me inside to make good on their threats. "Let go!" I shout, swinging wide. But my wrist is captured in a strong hand before it makes contact.

"Hyeri, it's just me," Minseok says, giving me an annoyed glare.

I quickly pull my earbuds free, the music becoming a small, tinny sound before I click it off. "What are you doing just grabbing a person with no warning?"

"I called out to you," he claims, and I realize I didn't hear him over my music.

I narrow my eyes at him. "Are you following me?"

"What? No. I live here."

"Why?"

He frowns and I realize it's a silly question.

"What are *you* doing here?" He's eyeing my luggage.

"This is my apartment." I gesture at the gray door.

His brows go up. "I thought you lived in the trainee dorms."

"I wanted my own place." I didn't realize the WDB dorm was in this building. Probably because I make a great effort not to know anything about Minseok if I can help it.

"Guess we're going to be neighbors," he says, leaning against my luggage. I resist the urge to wheel it away.

"Temporarily," I say. I'm already wondering if I can ask Hongjoo to find me another place.

Minseok's face falls at my curt answer. "Well, welcome to the building," he says, turning to the door across the hall.

"Wait, *that's* your apartment?" I gape. Not just the same building but literally across the hall from each other. This has to be a joke. Or maybe Minseok is just messing with me—I wouldn't put it past him.

"Yup, let me know if you need to borrow a cup of sugar."

"Not likely," I mutter under my breath.

He starts punching his code into the keypad, but stops midway and turns back to me. "Are you mad at me?"

This is unexpected. Minseok almost never brings up a past fight. His strategy is always to ignore and move on. "Why would I be mad?" I say.

He lifts a brow. "You really want me to answer that?" When I refuse to reply, he makes good on the bluff. "Maybe it was you shouting at me in front of your mother at the last shoot."

Disbelief at his gall makes me lose my cool. "Are you seriously saying *I* was wrong? You had no right to butt into my family business."

Minseok lifts his hand as if in immediate surrender. "I don't know why you take everyone's bullshit all the time. You should push back sometimes."

I want to roll my eyes. "Yeah, 'cause that would go over so well. I definitely wouldn't get dragged by the netizens for acting out like that."

Minseok cuts me off with a derisive laugh. "You know, maybe the fans would like it if you'd let go of trying to keep a perfect image."

"No, you're not allowed to criticize that when you're the one who first taught me that lesson."

"What are you talking about?" Minseok looks confused now.

"You're the one who told me I had to be careful," I remind him. "You said we had reputations to protect now."

When he just stares at me blankly, I'm annoyed. Does he really not remember? It's such a core memory for me. The first time I ever got my heart broken. And he doesn't even remember?

Then his eyes widen with realization and he lets out a heavy sigh. "Shit. That was so long ago, Hyeri."

So he does remember. "Yeah, well, it's kind of hard to forget your first big crush telling you that you're acting like a child."

"Hyeri, I was just a kid myself too. I was an idiot."

"It's fine, whatever."

"So, you're still making me pay for something stupid I said four years ago?"

"That's not what I'm doing," I insist. He's making me sound so petty. But he's the one who goes out of his way to mess with me all the time. Not the other way around.

"I'm sorry, okay? I'd just debuted and I was so focused on that. I didn't want anything to screw it up. You just happened to be a convenient target to take my stress out on because you were always popping up like my shadow."

His shadow? I don't even have words to express the offense I feel in this moment. I want to tell him he's not forgiven. To tell him where he can shove his late, half-assed apology. But whatever response I was going to give is lost as the elevator dings and Jaehyung and Jun step out.

"Hey, Hyeong," Jaehyung calls out. "Do you want to order ssambap for lunch?" Then he notices me. "Oh, hey, Noona."

"Do you two have a shoot today?" Jun asks.

"I think she's moving in, Hyeong," Jaehyung says, taking in my luggage. "The company just bought the apartment across from ours."

I nod. Jaehyung has always been very perceptive. "Just here temporarily."

Minseok looks annoyed at the disruption to our conversation. But I'm grateful; I don't want to talk about the past anymore.

"Do you need help?" Jun asks.

"I'm good, just have one bag." I quickly type in my code before they can ask more questions. "See you around," I chirp, avoiding Minseok's eyes as I escape into the safety of my new apartment.

TWENTY-FIVE
FOUR YEARS AGO

ebut was everything they'd warned Minseok about and nothing like he'd hoped it would be, regardless of the overwhelming probabilities.

Minseok had been raised by two very logical parents. His father a businessman, his mother a former lawyer. He'd known the statistics for kids with dreams of debuting as idols. But he also knew none of those kids were Moon Minseok.

He'd known Bright Star was a brand-new company. That so far, they'd only represented a few established soloists, models, and actors. That WDB was their first idol group.

He'd known that they'd have fewer connections due to being such a new and unknown company with a new unknown group.

But still, naively, perhaps foolishly, Minseok had believed the group's talent and determination would shine through.

But it was hard to shine on no sleep and constant rejection.

Their debut showcase had been underwhelming. The venue practically empty. The boys had gone out on the streets to hand out free tickets and promote the group. They'd even filmed it as content to release on social. But the public reaction had been so dismissive and unenthusiastic that the company had decided to abandon that idea.

And even today, their first time on a music show was over a month after releasing their mini album. And, though the younger members were excited and optimistic, Minseok had heard Hanbin talking on the phone about how they'd been a last-minute replacement for a group that canceled due to a missed flight from their concert in China.

WDB hadn't been given a real dressing room like the more senior groups. Which, Minseok told himself, was normal for a rookie group. But they also hadn't even been given their own cubicle space in the large area divided by temporary privacy screens. They had to share their small section with an aging trot singer.

Minseok came back from buying drinks at the vending machine to see Robbie and Jaehyung standing outside the cubicle, hands folded, heads lowered.

As he approached, Minseok saw one of the trot singer's managers smack Jaehyung on the back of the head with a rolled-up paper.

That made Minseok see red. Jaehyung was the politest of all of them.

"Hey!" Minseok rushed forward. "What's going on?"

"Hyeong," Jaehyung sobbed—there were clearly tears in his eyes.

"Jaehyung-ah, what happened?"

"These two stole from us," the manager said, shaking the rolled-up paper at them.

"I'm sorry," Robbie muttered. "We didn't know it was just for you."

"It's not our fault that your no-name company can't afford to buy you food," the manager said, pointing at a half-eaten sandwich on the ground.

"We're sorry," Minseok said, also lowering his head. He knew he should take responsibility as the hyeong. "We will order a replacement."

The manager sneered. "Can your broke-ass company even afford it? If its own sorry excuses for singers are stealing food, that's pretty pathetic, no?"

"I said we'll replace it," Minseok said through gritted teeth.

The manager shook his head. "Just forget it. We don't want some shitty convenience-store sandwich." He sneered at Robbie and Jaehyung. "If this is the kind of trash your company thinks can pass for idols, then it'll go under in a month." He turned to leave, gesturing at the smushed sandwich. "And clean this up before we come back."

Minseok wanted to yell at him that this wasn't their job. He wanted to tell that guy he had nothing to be cocky about. His own singer was a has-been in this industry. But Minseok knew he couldn't because the has-been trot singer had still sold more records than WDB. And he was senior. Seniority wasn't something Minseok could ignore.

He turned back to Jaehyung and Robbie and saw the dark circles under their reddened eyes. "Why don't you two go wash your faces? I'll clean this up."

"Yeah, okay." Robbie looked and sounded pissed as he stalked away. Minseok would normally warn him to drop the attitude, but he didn't have the energy for an argument.

"Sorry, Hyeong," Jaehyung muttered before hurrying after Robbie.

Minseok turned back to the crushed sandwich. Mayonaise was smeared across the floor. He closed his eyes, letting his head fall forward in defeat and frustration. Then he picked up some paper towels, kneeling to clean the mess. He hoped he could erase any trace of the incident before Hanbin and the others came back. He really didn't want to explain this embarrassment to anyone.

At the sound of crumpling tissue paper, he froze before turning to see Shin Hyeri standing behind him, eyes wide. She gripped a bouquet of flowers tightly in her arms.

"Oppa," she said in a sad voice.

Minseok stood quickly. His hand clenched involuntarily, squeezing mayo from the smushed sandwich he held. It dripped out of the crumpled paper towel back onto the stained spot on the floor. "Hyeri-ya, what are you doing here?"

She didn't reply at first, nervously chewing her lip, her eyes looking pointedly anywhere but at the sandwich in his hand. "Oh, uh, I, uh, I wanted to surprise you." She held out the flowers with a small smile. "Congratulations on your music show debut, Oppa."

Minseok felt the fire of embarrassment race through him. It was becoming clear to him that WDB wasn't the huge hit he'd dreamed of as a trainee. But to be treated as trash the way they were had been a shock. And he didn't want anyone to witness that. Least of all Hyeri.

"You shouldn't be here," he said coldly, and her smile faltered a bit.

"Oh, well, I thought I could keep you company if you're done with rehearsal?"

It made Minseok sigh.

He wasn't obtuse; he'd known for a while that Hyeri had a little crush on him. He'd thought it sweet at first. She was smart and fun. And she had a great sense of humor, definitely a plus in Minseok's book.

If they were two normal teens, he might have even asked her out on a date. But they'd both been given the chance to reach for something so much bigger. And he couldn't put those dreams at risk, not right now.

He'd always thought that with time Hyeri would catch on to the reality of things. After all, she was a trainee too. She knew the rules. She understood what was at stake.

He realized now that perhaps the crush was a little bigger than he'd given it credit for. He really should have taken care of this sooner.

"You should go back to your dorm," Minseok said. "You probably have training today, right? Did you even get permission to leave this early?"

"No one knows I left. And my vocal lessons are in the afternoon today." She held out the flowers again with a smile. "It's sweet of you to worry about me, Oppa."

She wasn't getting it. Maybe he was being too subtle. Or maybe she was being too stubborn.

"Hyeri-ya," he said. "You should stop having a crush on me now."

Her face fell, panic filling her eyes before she lowered them. She heaved a sigh. "How long have you known?"

"It doesn't matter," he said. "But I think you should stop now. There's no space in our lives for something like that."

"I promise I won't bother you with it."

She sounded so sad as she begged for permission to keep liking him. It made Minseok feel a hot, uncomfortable twinge of guilt. But he steeled himself against the urge to comfort her. It was better to cut off her feelings completely in one fell swoop than to drag it out unnecessarily.

"Just stop, okay? I'm trying to start my career. It's an important time and I can't have anything distracting me or getting in the way of that."

A flash of defiance ran across Hyeri's face, surprising him a bit. "I'm not a kid or a random fan. I know what's at stake here."

Minseok forced his lips into a derisive sneer. "You're not acting like it."

"But, Oppa—"

"Stop calling me Oppa!" Minseok snapped. He was starting to feel actual annoyance. Why couldn't she get the hint and let this go? Why was she forcing him to play the role of the bad guy? He felt like he was always putting out one fire after the next and he was exhausted. "You want someone to hear and misunderstand? Don't you see how difficult things are for us? I don't have time to deal with this right now. I have to focus on the group, not your immature crush."

"It's not immature," Hyeri whispered.

Minseok sighed. "Nothing we do is private anymore, Hyeri. All of our actions are watched and dissected. And the smallest thing could make or break a rookie's career. You should learn that now before you debut."

"Why is everything just about debuting? There are more things than that!"

Minseok's face hardened. "Maybe to you, but it's the only reason I'm here and the reason your parents sent you halfway across the world. You should have more respect for them and stop messing around. Stop being so selfish and leave. Now, before someone sees you."

He turned back to the mess on the ground just as something smacked into the wall beside him. Crushed flowers rained at his feet and he turned to see Hyeri storming away.

Minseok told himself he did what he had to do. This was for the best for both of them. She'd hate him for a few days, but then she'd get over it.

"He keeps sticking his nose in my business! I went *so long* without seeing him and now he's everywhere. I wouldn't be surprised if he was hiding in the closet." I jab my finger at the storage closet beside the salon wash basin.

"So you've said." Sohee is sitting in the styling chair, foils covering her head. The music video shoot is tomorrow and they're updating her hairstyle for it. A bright seafoam teal. I can already tell it's going to be a lot of early mornings for her with this style. But she doesn't seem daunted by it.

"And he's such a hypocrite. He acts like I'm so annoying whenever I have one bad moment, but god forbid anyone catches him in a bad mood. He'll bite your head off."

"Hopefully not literally. That'd be some weird praying mantis stuff."

I laugh despite myself. Sohee's always able to make me do that. "I think it's the females that do the head biting."

"As it should be." Sohee nods in satisfaction, and I can't help but laugh again.

"Anyway, it's fine, I'll just work harder at steering clear of him when he's in a bad mood."

"That's a good strategy," Sohee agrees. "But how will you do that if you're traveling with him?"

"Ugh, don't remind me." I sigh. "I can't believe I have to go on this ridiculous couple's vacation with him."

"Do you think you're going abroad?" Sohee hums, and I can practically see the dreamy smile on her face.

"Doubt it; I don't think we're bringing our passports." Though that's usually something Hongjoo takes care of. "I swear if I have to hear Minseok brag about himself in another language, I'll throw myself into the ocean."

"The show seems to be going well, though," Sohee points out, gently patting her foils.

"Don't touch," I chide her, and she drops her hands obediently. "The show is fine, I guess. Not as bad as I thought it would be, even though Minseok does everything he can to annoy me."

"You really think he's *trying* to be annoying? Or is he being charming and it annoys you?" She eyes me in the mirror.

"Let's talk about something else. Are you excited about the shoot tomorrow?"

She grins and pushes against the counter to spin her chair toward me, leaning forward eagerly like she's about to tell a secret. "I know it's going to sound silly. I've done all this before with Helloglow. But I'm so nervous. It's just that Kastor feels more like *my* group. Does that make sense?"

I smile because it does. We all knew there was an expiration date to

Helloglow. One that came much sooner than we all expected. Though, by that time, I'd been low-key relieved. But I know it hit Sohee hard. She loves performing, and now she can again.

"Kastor is going to be amazing. I love your lead single." It's a funk and alternative pop song about being true to yourself. It's much more intense than the bubblegum-pop cuteness that Helloglow portrayed. "How are the other girls doing? Any of them freaking out yet?"

"All of them are dealing with it in their own way. They're mostly excited, though there's a meltdown almost every other night. Minji still sometimes calls me Sunbae, but it's kind of cute. She's like a little puppy." I can hear the easy affection in her voice. Minji is the maknae of the group. She's fourteen, practically a baby still. But I remind myself Sohee was that age when she debuted. For some reason that feels like so long ago, though. Maybe because I've worked so hard to move past that time.

"I want to hear all about how it goes when I get back," I tell her.

"And I want to hear about your romantic getaway." Sohee wiggles her brows at me.

I groan. "Please stop calling it that. I'll be lucky if I don't strangle Minseok on camera. He's so nosy. You know he tried to lecture my mom about me?"

"Yeah, you told me that already," Sohee says.

"Oh, I did?"

"Eonni, have you ever heard of mention syndrome?"

"Huh? Is that like Munchausen syndrome?" I ask.

Sohee laughs. "No, it's this phenomenon that's really serious."

My heart drops. Is Sohee trying to tell me she's sick? "What is it?"

"It's when you start to mention one person more and more. And you don't even realize you're doing it. But it's kind of your brain's way of alerting you that you're probably into them."

"What?" I laugh, realizing it's nothing serious after all. "Why are you telling me this?"

"Because you're talking about Minseok-sunbae a lot these days."

"What?" An electric shock flies through me. "No, you're misinterpreting it. It's just that I have to deal with him and this show all the time. It's natural to talk about what's going on in your life."

"Yeah, but it's not like you're complaining about the show. Or the producers or writers. You only ever talk about Minseok-sunbae." She grins mischievously at me. "Be honest, Eonni. Do you still like him?"

"Definitely not," I spit out. Of all people, I know how fruitless it is to like Minseok.

TWENTY-SEVEN
HYERI

My family didn't really spend lots of quality time together. Even before Oppa and I came to Korea as trainees.

My dad is what people used to call a workaholic. And my mom overcompensated by spending all the money he earned to show off a flashy, luxury lifestyle to all our neighbors and friends. I suppose that's why she was so excited when Oppa and I were scouted. It was another thing to brag about.

Since I came to Korea, I don't think I remember a full day I spent with my whole family.

But I do have one perfect family memory. It was a Saturday when I was in second grade. My dad decided to pack us all into the car and drive to the beach for the day. My mom had grumbled about it, but even at eight I could tell she was in a good mood.

We played games in the ocean and ate sandwiches. And just goofed around all day, getting sand everywhere. I was so exhausted by the end that I fell asleep in the car. I woke up at one point and saw my parents holding hands as my dad drove us home. It was the perfect day.

Every time I saw the ocean after, I'd remember that day. But at some point, it stopped being a happy reminder. And instead became proof that perfect days didn't exist for us anymore.

So, of course, *OCM* decided that the ideal shooting location for our faux-honeymoon episodes was the beach.

Now here I am, walking on the sand with Minseok. We ate at a well-known seafood restaurant, the kind with dozens of photos of other celebrities or shows that have graced it before. We took a picture with the owner and provided our autographs to add to the wall.

Minseok was his usual charismatic self the entire time. You'd never know that he and I had a fight. I guess I should be grateful. But it just makes me uneasy. Is he really not mad at me? Or is he pretending for the show?

After, Minseok suggests we get ice cream and walk along the beach.

I agree, because it's part of the schedule for the shoot and the brand of ice-cream cone we eat is part of a product-placement agreement. Even so, I don't love the idea of walking along the beach in my outfit. They have me in a dress that hits just below my knees. It's gossamer light in a sweet peach color. But it's windy by the water today, an issue when your dress is designed to be worn in cute city cafés and not beach excursions.

My fears are proven right as I have to juggle between holding my ice cream and holding down my skirt.

Minseok, oblivious to my struggle, veers toward the water, dipping his feet into the ocean.

I stay put up the beach. My dress is so thin that if it gets wet, it'll become completely see-through.

My mom's voice echoes in my head reminding me that *Bimbos don't keep fans.*

Minseok glances back and rolls his eyes at me. "Come on, what's the point of coming to the beach if you don't put your feet in the water?"

"I'm still eating my ice cream," I say, holding up the cone as proof. Though, I've barely even licked it. With my diet, it's more like a prop at this point. Such a waste.

He jogs back. His feet are caked in sand now and all I can think is that it's going to track everywhere.

When he grabs my hand, I reluctantly let him lead me to the very edge of the water. It would be too hard to resist him and keep hold of my ice cream at the same time. The tide is just coming in and it splashes against my calves. I let out an involuntary yelp of distress and yank my arm free to skitter back.

"Oh, come on, jagi-yah." Minseok laughs and I'm glad for the wind blowing my hair in my face. It hides the fact that I'm still so flustered whenever he calls me that. He's waded back into the water, almost knee deep. Though he's rolled up his pants, they're still getting soaked.

"I can't go any deeper. I can't swim," I say.

He looks skeptical. "That can't be true. What kid from Southern California can't swim?"

"This one," I insist. And it's true. My mom enrolled me in classes, but after I freaked out during the first lesson, she never brought me back. And I just never learned how.

Minseok gets a gleam in his eyes, one that tells me nothing good can come from what he's about to do. I start to back away, but it's too slow.

He races forward, swooping his hands through the water to splash it on me. I let out an unladylike scream and temporarily forget I'm holding an ice-cream cone as I lift my hands to shield. The top scoop of vanilla plops right into my chest.

"Oops." There's laughter in Minseok's voice. I see it in his eyes, and he folds his lips together to hide a smile. "You okay?"

I close my eyes and take a deep, calming breath. It wouldn't do to lose my composure. I've learned by now that Minseok doesn't care when I'm shouting mad. My revenge will have to take a different form.

"Hyeri?" Minseok says my name hesitantly.

I open my eyes and force a nonchalant smile even as I feel cold ice cream drip into my bra. "I'm okay."

Minseok narrows his eyes in suspicion. "Really?"

I let out a light laugh even as I calculate my retribution. "Yes, I said it's fine." I'm proud of how smooth and low my voice is. Guess I really have gotten better at acting.

I calmly lift my left hand to wipe at the ice cream. I'm still gripping the cone in the right.

He inches closer and I force myself to keep still, like a black widow spider waiting for the perfect moment to strike.

"Do you need a towel?" Now he does walk the rest of the way to me.

"I don't know, is it bad?" I ask innocently.

He leans closer to study my dress and that's when I strike. I smash what's left of my ice-cream cone into his face. He lets out a gasp of surprise before lurching back a step. With timing even I couldn't have calculated, the tide comes in and takes him out. He falls backward with a satisfying splash.

I let out a laugh that turns into a crow of victory, pumping my arms in the air like a triumphant Olympic athlete. Minseok is half soaked as he sprawls out on the sand, ice cream dripping from his shocked face.

"Wow, I wish I had my phone. This is something I want to remember forever." I glance at the cameraman closest to me and notice him trying to hide a smile. "Do you think I can get a copy of the raw footage?"

Now he does grin, saying, "I'll see what I can do."

I shoot him a thumbs-up.

"Hyeri," Minseok says, his voice low and dangerous.

Suddenly, I realize that there is the very real chance Minseok will want to retaliate.

I back up, the cameraman following along with me. I turn to him and whisper, "Be ready to run."

He nods with a conspiratorial smile.

"Listen, jagi-ya," I say in my most charming version of aegyo. "You got me first. This was just a small bit of revenge. We can end it here, right?"

I'm still backing up, the sand too loose around my feet. I know that I won't be able to escape if he comes for me.

"Nope, this is not on the same level," Minseok says, scooping up water to wash the ice cream from his face before angrily flicking it from his fingers.

"Oh n—" My words turn into a scream as Minseok lunges at me.

I barely dodge him, trying to scramble up the beach. He gives chase, pivoting so lightly on his feet that you'd think he was on grass instead of sand.

"I'm sorry! I didn't mean it!" I scream, like that will deter him.

"Yeah, sure," he retorts as he almost gets a hold of my arm.

I try to race down the beach. But as predicted I'm awkward and slow on the terrain. I feel that lightheaded fear of being caught, but I also have the strange urge to let out a loud screaming laugh. Like the thrilled noises children make during a game of tag. I make the foolish mistake of pausing to look back.

Just as I do, he takes me down with a tackle.

My scream is cut short as I land with a hard *Oomph*. But at some point in our drop, Minseok managed to spin us, so I fall on top of him.

I try to push off to escape, but he rolls us to trap me under him. As his body presses mine into the sand, some of it seeps into my collar.

"Okay, okay, you win!" I admit.

"Do I?" he asks, poking at my ribs where I'm the most ticklish, an unfortunate fact he learned when we were younger.

"Yes, yes, you win!" I'm laughing so hard my eyes are watering. I'm so breathless from it I probably look red as a tomato. And I'm so desperate to escape that I'm squirming like a worm to get free. Sand gets into places I don't even want to think about. I'm certain I've destroyed both my hairdo and the dress. Not the calm, professional image I try to maintain on-camera. But I also haven't had this much fun in a long time.

"Do you give up?" Minseok demands with another tickle.

"Yes!" I grab his hand to stop him.

The sheen of laughter tears in my eyes turns the rays of sun into a hazy halo behind his head as he hovers over me.

I blink hard to clear my vision, but it just brings his face into focus.

His lips are open on the end of a breathless laugh of his own. His warm brown eyes are glowing with triumph at winning our arbitrary wrestling game. This close, I catch the scent of him, sea and sugar and just a bit of his aftershave. The same kind he used when we were trainees.

It makes me viscerally remember being fifteen again, anxious to prove myself and desperate for him to aim one of his smiles in my direction.

The barrage of sense memories must be why my body is tingling everywhere. Why my heart is racing like it used to every time he'd send me a wayward smile in the company hallway.

There's a bit of ice cream still at the edge of his cheek and in his sideburn. I reach up with my free hand and wipe it away.

I feel him tense when I touch him. Does he not like this? I start to snatch my hand back, but he catches it in his and glances down at the drip of ice cream I wiped off.

"Thanks," he murmurs, and now it's my turn to tense as strange shivers slide down my spine.

"Hey, ease up a bit, I need to catch my breath." I push at him and he sits back, letting the sea breeze sneak between us. It replaces the smell of him with that of the ocean. I'm both disappointed and relieved.

"So, what's my prize?" he asks.

"Prize?"

"Yeah." He stands up and the sun he previously blocked shines into my eyes. I squint, lifting my hand against the glare, and he grabs it to haul me up too. "I should get a prize for winning," he says with a grin that plays havoc with my already confused brain.

"What prize do you want?" I focus on wiping sand off my arms and hands instead of on that brief, indefinable moment that passed between us.

"I'll think about it," Minseok says. "Tell you during dinner."

He reaches toward me, and I pull back before I realize I'm acting like a scared animal and stop myself. Minseok gently wipes at the sand stuck on my cheek, then neck. I focus everything on standing still as he does it.

"Okay, yeah, at dinner," I agree quickly.

"Okay, cut!" Han-PD calls out. Immediately, I stumble back in retreat, pretending it's because of the uneven sand and not my need to create distance between us.

Hongjoo hurries over, brushing at the sand on my back with a towel.

"Thanks, Eonni. I can do that." I take it from her, wiping at my arms and legs.

"Okay! That was good," Han-PD says, walking over, trailed by two assistant PDs.

"Really?" I ask. "You don't think we were too . . . much?" I glance at Minseok, but he's busy taking the makeup wipes his manager offers to clean off the ice-cream residue and sand.

"No, it was exactly what we wanted for you two. The chemistry is great."

"Oh yeah? Good." I breathe out, not sure how to take the compliment. Is this really chemistry? Does chemistry make your mouth super dry?

"Eonni, can I have some water?" I croak.

"Sure." Hongjoo runs off to fetch a bottle.

"I'll let you get some rest before the dinner shoot." Han-PD slaps Minseok on the back lightly. "Great job." He pats me on the shoulder, and I can't stop the goofy smile that spreads.

"How's your new mattress, Kang-PD?" Minseok asks one of the assistants who came over. She's usually the one fetching us to set. She's young and energetic, and idolizes Han-PD.

"Oh, it's great! You were right, I like this new brand."

"I'm an expert on comfortable places to sleep," Minseok says with a grin.

"Oh, and thanks for the perfume suggestion, Hyeri-ssi. You were right, my sister loved it," Kang-PD says.

"Oh, I'm glad," I murmur, still feeling awkward around Minseok. I wonder where Hongjoo is with that water.

"We really do love the vibe between you two," says Kang-PD.

"Thanks," I say weakly, stealing a peek at Minseok.

"So, we were talking about what we think your prize should be," Go-PD says. She's older than Kang-PD, and has been at HBS for five years. She told me last week that her mom liked my drama. It's so odd, but, for the first time, I think I'm becoming friendly with the crew. I've never gotten close to people on set before. But Minseok has this habit of chatting with people between takes. And he always ends up involving me. I've somehow become closer to the staff as a byproduct.

"What prize?" I ask.

"Moonster's prize," Kang-PD explains.

"We think it should be Hyeri calling Moonster Oppa again," Go-PD says.

"What?" I blurt out.

"Really?" Minseok replies. "Why?"

"Well, it goes back to your first date when you made the bet on the crane machines. It'll be really satisfying for the full-circle moment," Go-PD explains. "What do you think, Hyeri-ssi?"

I bite my lip, hesitating. I'm not sure how I feel about being forced to call him that again. But as both PDs watches me, I realize that I don't think I can say no. I feel like I owe this show for helping me avoid fallout from the midsummer scandal. And what's the big deal if I call him that again? It's just for the show, it won't mean anything. I start to nod when Minseok replies.

"Nah," he says shaking his head. "I don't want it to be because of a bet or a wish anymore."

"Wait, really?" I ask.

"Are you sure? It would be a good moment for the show." Go-PD is frowning now, and I'm worried she'll be angry with us.

"If they want me to say it . . ." I start to say, but Minseok shakes his head emphatically now.

"No, it's fine. I'll come up with something else."

He starts to walk away, back to the hotel we're staying in tonight.

I jog after him, a little wobbly still on the sand as I catch up. "Why'd you do that? I can just say it if it's for the show."

"No, I'm not going to make you say it," he says.

"It's really okay," I assure him. "I'm a professional; I can do it for the show. It won't mean anything."

For some reason he looks angry. "No, Hyeri. I said I'll come up with something else."

Minseok turns to go, and I grab his arm to stop him. "Are you mad at me?"

He sighs and shakes his head. "No. I'm fine. I just don't want it to be like this."

I laugh, confused. "For what to be like this?"

He's staring at me now, his face too blank for me to read, and my smile drops a bit. Why does he look like he wants to devour me?

Despite the sun still blazing overhead, goose bumps rise along my arms.

When Minseok replies, he sounds more serious than the conversation should warrant. "If you're going to call me Oppa again, I want you to mean it."

He continues toward the hotel, but I stay where I am, because for some reason my legs feel too weak to walk right now.

TWENTY-EIGHT
HYERI

He wants me to mean it? Is he saying he thinks of me like a younger sister?

The thought makes me cringe.

Maybe I should stop being so pathetic and just ask him. But I can't bring myself to do it. He'll know I'm overthinking it. He'll assume I'm reading into it. Thinking he means something he doesn't, or worse, that I like him again.

Which would just seal my complete and utter embarrassment in front of him.

No, I'll just let it go. It probably didn't even mean anything.

"Dammit," I mutter, running my hands through my hair in frustration. It gets stuck in the tangle left by salt and dried seawater. "Ouch."

"Need help?" David asks, walking across the sand toward me. He's already tanning from the sun.

"What are you doing here?" I ask as he hugs me.

"Are you kidding, who would pass up a free trip to the beach?"

Jeongho trails behind David, sweating and huffing as he lugs the stylist's bag.

"Can we go inside?" he whines. "My shoes are filled with sand."

He looks like he's literally melting from the heat. Sweat makes his hair stick to his forehead and the bag slung over his shoulder must weigh a ton. It's safe to assume he's one person who might reject a free beach vacation.

"Should you be carrying all of that?" I ask, worried he might just pass out at our feet.

"Are you saying I can't do my job?" He glowers at me.

"No, I didn't mean it that way," I say urgently at the misunderstanding.

David pats Jeongho on the back. "Go to the hotel and check into our room."

Jeongho looks relieved, lowering in a bow before taking off.

I stare after the assistant. "Do you think I upset him?"

"Jeongho is just a nervous guy. Don't worry about him," David says, looping his arm through mine. "Come, I shall fix this tangle on your head."

I let David bring me inside to the hotel suite the production reserved for me. Hongjoo is already in there, hanging outfit options for tonight's dinner shoot.

We have a two-hour break, but I can't let myself rest. It's a quick shower to get the last of the sand and salt off and then right into hair and makeup. Even though we're going for a low-key style, it's kind of laughable how much effort it takes to do a no-effort look.

By the time I'm pulling on my dress, the sun is starting to set. I'm in a V-neck A-line chiffon dress in sky blue. The skirt is pleated, but light enough to flow around me with every step I take. It reminds me of my mother's skirts I used to try on as a little girl and spin and spin so they flowed around me.

The restaurant sits along the beach with an open deck covered in twinkle lights.

Minseok is already there when I arrive. He's standing at the railing, watching the water move in and out with the tide.

With the warm glow of the setting sun washing over him it could be a setup for a romantic photoshoot.

His hair looks expertly tousled, pushed back from his brow. I've always liked him with his hair styled like this. And those damn goose bumps rise on my bare arms again.

It's fine, I reassure myself. *He's objectively attractive; you'd have to be completely dense not to see that.*

Then he turns, the sun at his back, and a slow smile curves his lips as he takes me in.

My heart does a little somersault in response.

This is not good. It feels too much like how I reacted to him when I was fifteen and harboring a massive crush.

"Jagi-ya, you look amazing." He takes my hands, and I force a smile onto my face, though it feels like my lips are trembling just a bit.

"Thanks, you look nice too," I reply.

Please, just calm down, I beg my heart.

"Let's eat." He pulls out my chair, and I'm grateful I get to sit for the shoot. It feels like my legs are as steady as boiled spaghetti right now.

Food is immediately brought to us. A preset menu chosen for us. My mouth waters at the sight of the juicy steak. I can already tell it's cooked to perfection.

Minseok starts cutting his meat into small bites. "Did you rest well?"

"Mm-hmm," I reply, though I didn't. I was too caught up in wondering what Minseok meant on the beach.

I reach for my knife when Minseok trades our plates, giving me the steak he just cut. I want to laugh at the clichéd loving-boyfriend move. Wait, no, loving *husband*.

"Did you get all the sand out of your hair?" Minseok asks, grinning devilishly at me as he cuts his own steak and takes a bite.

"Oh, uh, yes, though my stylist is annoyed at you for tangling it," I try to joke, hoping my smile doesn't look manic or strained.

"I had to take an hour nap after that battle."

"Yeah," I say, rubbing at my sore neck. "I could have used a massage, or at least some aspirin."

I wait for some witty reply, like a suggestion we get couples massages or something. But instead, Minseok frowns slightly and sets down his fork. Then he reaches forward and takes my hand in his.

"I didn't push you too far on the beach, did I?" he asks.

"What? Where is this coming from?"

"I just don't like the idea that I might have messed up"—he frowns, like he's realizing mid-sentence that he might be making a mistake— "your dress."

"My dress?" I ask.

He shrugs. "Yeah, it seemed nice. I'd hate to think it's ruined." His smile is light, but there's something in his voice. An undertone that tells me he's not just talking about my dress.

"It's all right," I say slowly, wondering what this conversation is actually about. "I have other dresses."

Minseok's smile fades and his hand pulls away, and I think I've done something wrong. But he has to know what's expected of me. That I can't reveal my anxieties or fears, because they'll be twisted to be used against me.

"Yeah, I suppose you can get another dress. But if that's the one you chose to wear when you were with me, then I should've been more gentle with it."

I force another light laugh, but it comes out as a slightly too high trill of nerves. "You don't need to feel so bad about a dress." It's not even mine; my stylist sent it for the shoot.

"I just need you to know I always appreciate your . . . dresses."

"Oookay," I say slowly, still completely lost.

He picks up his glass, a charming smile replacing his pensive expression. "Let's have a cheers. To us."

I play along, figuring it best to move past my confusion. I'm sure what just happened will be cut from the episode. I should focus on creating more interesting content for the rolling cameras. "To our future."

"And our past." Minseok grins as he taps our glasses together.

I laugh. "I'd rather forget our past."

Minseok takes a slow sip of his soda. "Why would you say that?"

I'm still smiling, sure he'll agree. "Well, come on, we were so awkward. And I had that crush on you, right?" I've decided to own that narrative for the show. The fans actually received it well after episode one. "You said it yourself, I was so annoying."

"I never called you annoying," Minseok says firmly, setting his glass back down with a hard click.

"Well, you didn't have to say it, we both know it, right?" I laugh again, taking another sip of my cider.

Minseok is frowning at me now and I'm wondering why he's not going along with the lighthearted tone I'm trying to set. I'm trying my best to be casual and careless like him. He loves needling me about our past. Why isn't he doing it now when I'm giving him an easy opening?

Instead, he sighs. "Sometimes I worry that I never told you how much you meant to me back then."

His tone is far too serious. And the combination of candlelight below and fairy lights above makes his eyes seem depthless.

"Come on, it's okay if you say I was annoying. I was your friend's little sister," I reply, trying valiantly to return us to a lighter tone.

But Minseok refuses. He reaches out and takes my hand, letting our fingers link. "Maybe it was my mistake for never telling you. But you made everything so fun when you were around. I needed that, to be reminded we were just kids sometimes." I think I hear him murmur, "That we probably still are."

I want to yank my hand away, but I know I can't. Instead, I mutter, "I thought I was just your little shadow."

I see his slight wince, but he recovers expertly. "A shadow is important," he says, still gripping my hand tightly. Squeezing just a little too hard. "If someone has no shadow, doesn't it mean they're just in the dark?"

I want to laugh. I want to ask which writer scripted this. But I can't, because, damn him, his words make my heart lodge in my throat.

I hear the sigh of at least one of the assistant PDs. And I know that his charm is on full offensive. It's chipping at the shields I've built for four years.

This is so unfair. I wasn't prepared for this kind of emotional battle tonight.

"So, are you asking me to only be around during the day?" I try for a joke.

"I'm saying I should've been less careless with you in the past." His thumb moves over my knuckles, a soft caress. Static electricity runs over my arms, like lightning setting my senses on fire.

"I told you. Those things don't matter anymore." My voice barely makes it past my tightened throat.

"They matter to me," Minseok says.

It's just for the show, I remind myself.

But even if it is, saying something like this on camera, broadcasting it to the entire country—the entire world—is a declaration that he is willing to say such soft words to me. That I'm worth saying them to.

My neck feels hot and I'm sure it's red from embarrassment and something else. Something that's making my hand tingle under his.

Despite knowing that everything we're doing here is to entertain, I want to ask him if this is real.

A part of me needs to know as I feel my heart start to dip, as I feel myself start to fall back into the old familiar tingling rush of a crush. It's heady and exciting. And terrifying, because I know better now how impossible this is.

But I force a smile. "I guess our past is why we work, huh?"

Thankfully, he finally lets go of my hand now. Finally lets his serious expression melt into a playful grin. "Yup, and maybe it's why you'll let me steal part of your dessert?"

I laugh in relief at the more familiar mood and nod. "Sure."

As dessert is served, I keep my light and friendly smile in place. But under the table, my fingernails are digging painful divots into my palms.

It's all I can do to keep my entire body from shaking. I really screwed up. I've fallen for Moon Minseok all over again.

TWENTY-NINE

HYERI

When the dinner shoot ends, I escape.

I duck into the elevator before anyone can call out to me.

I can't believe I'm so weak. How could I like Minseok again? Or maybe I never stopped liking him. Maybe I just got really good at being in denial about my feelings because he hurt my pride so badly four years ago.

"No, it was just the moment," I say aloud to myself as I push into my room. "It'll fade now."

"What will fade?" Hongjoo asks from the desk.

I stumble back into the closing door, clutching at my heart as it almost falls out of my chest. "Eonni, you scared me."

"Why would you be scared to see me?" She eyes me suspiciously.

"I just didn't think you were in here," I admit. I wonder if I can escape into my room and avoid more questions.

"You look pale, are you okay?" She starts to stand, like she intends to inspect me closer.

I search for a plausible excuse to stop any probing. "You know what, I forgot my phone downstairs."

I race back out before any more questions can be lobbed at me.

On the elevator, I stare at the floors, wondering where to go now. Finally, I press the third floor, where the gym and indoor pool are.

The gym is way more crowded than I thought it would be. And the moment I walk inside I see Hanbin. I spin around, ducking my head to avoid him when I hear Minseok call out. "Hyeong, did you bring water?"

My whole being tenses at the sound of his voice. I hurry across the floor, ducking through the door to the indoor pool.

A big sign is pasted there, saying the pool is closed for cleaning today. Good, then no one will come in and bother me.

I just need a moment to myself. I've had eyes or cameras on me all day.

I walk to the pool, glancing down at my own watery reflection. The girl looking back at me looks frazzled. She needs a true break. But, since I don't have that luxury right now, I'll take an hour alone instead. I sit at the edge of the pool, taking off my sandals to let my feet dip into the water. It's colder than I thought. I suppose they turn off the heat if it's closed for cleaning.

I press my hand against my heart. It feels like I ran a mile instead of across the short gym floor. Is this really how I'm going to start reacting from just hearing Minseok's voice? What if this doesn't go away? I'll be screwed. There's still over a month left of *OCM*. And I'm pretty sure the company won't let me cancel the contract due to "an inconvenient resurgence of my old crush."

I kick at the water and it splashes high, falling at the hem of my skirt.

"Oh no!" I scramble up in fear of ruining another dress. And my hand accidentally swipes my sandal into the pool. "Why?" My shout echoes back at me, filled with all my frustration.

I lean over the edge of the pool, reaching desperately for the sandal. I almost get it, but I feel my balance tipping and I pull back with a small scream. Unfortunately, the move pushes the shoe so it floats even farther out.

"Come on, please, don't do this," I beg, though I'm sure if the shoe could reply it would probably tell me to screw myself. That's the luck I'm having right now.

I try to get it again, using the other sandal to lengthen my reach. I'm straining, holding on to the edge of the pool for balance as I just brush against the sandal.

I almost have it, I'm sure of it, when I go tumbling into the pool.

THIRTY
HYERI

t's like being submerged in ice water. The pool lights spin around me in distorted waves. The light material of my skirt, which swayed gently earlier this evening, is now wrapped around my legs so tightly that I can barely kick.

Terror has a scream trying to let loose. The chemical taste of chlorinated water fills my mouth.

Desperation takes hold of me. I can't swim. I can't breathe.

I see Minseok's face.

Is this that moment when your life flashes before your eyes? But he's not smiling the way he always is in my memories. His eyes are wide with anxious fear. And he reaches for me.

It takes me another beat before I realize he's really here. I grab him, let him pull me to the surface.

My first attempt to breathe causes me to cough up the water still lodged in my throat. Minseok hauls me onto the pool deck and I collapse like a rag doll.

The tile is cold against my cheek, but I don't care. I can't find the strength to sit up.

"Hyeri," Minseok says by my ear as I'm gathered into a towel. "Hyeri, answer me."

I try, but it just comes out a sobbing gasp.

"Okay, just breathe," he says.

I obey, leaning my head into his shoulder. And I don't even know when I went from gasping to crying, my tears joining the chlorine and pool water soaking his shirt.

"It's okay, you're okay now."

I burrow deeper into him, his body heat the only thing that I care about as I shiver so hard that my teeth chatter.

Once my crying has slowed to little hiccupping gasps, I feel his hand rubbing small circles on my back. My arms are still looped around his neck, holding him close.

"Minseok?" I'm finally able to croak out.

He leans back a bit, and I whimper in protest from the lost heat.

He immediately runs his hands up and down my arms to warm them. "What happened, Hyeri?"

I try to remember. I must have slipped, except it felt like I was some-how pushed. And, for a moment, when I was submerged, I thought I saw a shadow running away.

No, I must still be out of it. I was alone, I'd have heard someone else coming in. "I was reaching for the sandal," I say, "and I think I slipped."

"Okay, well, wait here and I'll get Hongjoo-noona."

When he makes to stand, I grab desperately onto him to hold him in place. "No, please, can we . . ." I trail off, embarrassed, but honestly, I don't care about decorum. "Can you just stay here with me?" I shudder at just the thought of being left alone right now.

"Yeah, of course," he says, holding me closer. "You scared the shit out of me, Hyeri."

"I scared the shit out of myself," I admit.

"You must be freezing." He wraps one of his hands around both of mine. "Your fingers are like ice."

"Yeah, the water was cold." My teeth chatter as if to prove it. He starts rubbing his palms over my frozen fingers, leaning in to blow his warm breath against them.

I blow onto them as well, hoping to warm them faster. His eyes lift, meeting mine over our joined hands. His expression moves slowly from concern, to confusion, to something that makes me shudder again. This time not from the cold.

He slowly lowers our hands until there is no longer anything between us. He swallows, a motion that makes his Adam's apple bob.

There's a part of me that knows this is ridiculous. I almost drowned just now. I should not be feeling the urge to press my face into his neck, right beside that Adam's apple.

I should back away. I should say something. I should at least let go of his hands. But I don't do any of those things.

Because there's still a small bit of the fifteen-year-old Hyeri who has always wondered what it would be like to be kissed by Moon Minseok.

He leans in. I let my eyes close. It's an invitation. *I'm not watching, so do whatever you'd like.*

I can almost feel the warmth of his lips on mine. I stay as still as I can.

Waiting for him. If he doesn't lean in, should I? Do I have the guts to do it?

Just as I'm about to take the risk, the door to the pool slams open, the sound a loud echo. "Moon Minseok! Where have you been?" Hanbin stands at the top of the stairs.

We break apart as Hanbin storms down to the deck. Then his eyes widen as he finally takes us in. "What happened? Hyeri? You're all wet!"

"She fell into the pool," Minseok explains as he helps me stand.

Hanbin grips my shoulder, looking me over. "Come on, I'll take you back to your room. Hongjoo has been going crazy looking for you."

I wince with embarrassment. When Hanbin glances at his own charge, Minseok says, "I'm fine, Hyeong. Take Hyeri. I can get back to my room myself."

"Come on." Hanbin's voice and arms are gentle as he steers me toward the exit.

I'm left with no choice but to let Hanbin lead me away from Minseok.

THIRTY-ONE
HYERI

ack in Seoul, I'm determined not to focus on what happened during the trip.

I heard the hotel ended up comping our rooms, an apology for not having better safety precautions. I feel bad; I saw the sign and went into the pool area anyway.

But it's not the accident that weighs on me as much as those moments with Minseok by the pool afterward. When I felt like maybe, finally, he was going to kiss me.

I tell myself I was probably just delirious from oxygen deprivation, adrenaline, and my residual confusion after the overly romantic dinner shoot.

From now on, it's probably best to treat everything involving Minseok with detached professionalism. This is a job. It's no different from being asked to do romance scenes in a drama. He is just really good at acting like he likes someone. Except, who would he have been acting for at the pool?

Every time I think about what happened, questions like that trip me up. So, instead, I'm in full avoidance mode. The last two days since returning home, I've holed up and focused solely on organizing my new apartment.

It's a three-bedroom that's clearly meant for a group instead of someone living alone. But Hongjoo did say it was temporary. Which is good. I don't think I can handle living across the hall from Minseok for long.

Sighing, I fall onto my couch even though I have a handful of towels in my arms that need to be folded. Why can't I stop thinking about him?

"Because we almost kissed," I reply to myself. "And I have to know if he's thinking about it as much as I am."

I stand up with purpose, letting the towels drop back into the laundry basket. "I'll just ask him. I'm not a kid anymore. I can just have a mature conversation."

Then I fall back on the couch, the nerves making my whole being squirm as I cover my face in a towel and let out a muffled scream.

"No, I can do this." I stand up again, and before I can overthink it again, I march across the hallway.

After I ring the bell, I have immediate regrets. This is a bad idea. What if the other members are home? I should wait for later.

But before I can dash back into my apartment, the door opens, letting out a blast of music.

I retreat a step as Robbie grins at me. "Noona, you actually came."

"Huh?"

"Come in." Robbie grabs my arm and pulls me inside before I can protest. I barely have time to toe off my shoes before I'm yanked into their living room. The lights are low, with what looks like a strobe light going in the corner. The TV is playing lyrics to a song. An old rock anthem from before Robbie was even born. And Jaehyung is singing on a Bluetooth karaoke microphone. Despite being younger than me, Jaehyung has always had such an old soul. I'm a little shocked to see Jisung, the maknae of Hyejun's group, belting it out alongside him.

He looms over Jaehyung as the tallest person in the room. But he's also the youngest. He's like a golden retriever, always so happy-go-lucky.

"What is this?" I ask Robbie, lifting my voice above the booming music.

"Didn't you get my text?" he asks.

I shake my head, not wanting to hurt my throat from shouting more.

"It's my birthday party," Robbie explains. "I invited you."

Oh yeah, I did see a text from him about this, but I'd been so caught up with everything that I'd only skimmed it and forgot to reply. Which was going to be a polite brush-off, but now I guess it's too late.

"Come on, sit down," Robbie says. "The party just started."

I do a cursory sweep of the room and don't see Minseok. Disappointment and relief war inside me.

Jun offers me a bottle of water. I take it with a grateful smile. At least now I have something to do with my hands.

"You're lucky." He has to lean down to whisper-shout in my ear over the music. "We actually cleaned for this."

I laugh, looking at the bags of chips and snacks strewn across the coffee table. Bottles of water litter both the table and the floor. What suspiciously looks like laundry is piled in the far corner. And three laptops are set up on the kitchen table, making it clear that space is used more for gaming than eating. I wonder how messy it normally is if this is clean.

There's a girl who looks vaguely familiar sitting on the couch, nursing a can of Chilsung Cider. Robbie has made a beeline for her, nestling in next to her and throwing his arm over her shoulder.

She settles comfortably into his side, like they've done this a hundred times. It's a shocking sight, but no one else seem surprised by it.

"Too bad we couldn't go to a real noraebang," she says.

"I like this more. I can do this here." Robbie nuzzles his nose into her neck like a puppy dog and she giggles as she tries to push him away.

"Don't be gross." She laughs.

"Too late," says a boy perched on the adjacent couch. He's tall and cute but a stranger to me. I wonder what agency he's with.

The girl sticks her tongue out at the boy, and I finally place her. Robbie's childhood friend that the gossip sites keep saying he's in a relationship with. And it seems that this time they're right.

Robbie smiles as he lets his head settle on top of hers lightly. They look so content. Like they're not in the middle of a noisy party but in their own private space. I feel a twinge of envy at the sight. It's not something I ever thought was possible for people like us.

The girl looks up and catches my eyes. Hers widen. "It's you!"

She jumps to her feet and I instinctively step back, ready for the attack or accusation. But she lets out a joyful giggle before covering her mouth. "I'm sorry, I just— I'm a huge fan."

Robbie laughs. "That's a huge compliment, Noona. It's hard to get Lani to admit she's a fan of someone."

"That is not true." The girl smacks Robbie on the shoulder. Then turns back to me with a grin. "He's just bitter because I refused to admit I was a fan of his when we first reconnected."

"Oh, I see," I say. "Well, nice to meet you . . . Lani?"

"Elena," she says with a belated bow of greeting. "Sorry, I'm so rude. I just really loved you in *Youthful Exchange*. I watched the whole drama with my como."

"Oh my god, yes! You were the mean girl!" The cute boy stands up and walks over, looking me up and down.

"Uh, yes." I take a step back.

"Can you throw water in someone's face?" he asks with a grin that makes me wonder if he's actually joking.

"Stop being embarrassing, Ethan." Elena pulls on the boy's arm and smacks him upside the back of the head. "I apologize for my twin; he never learned how to be a real human being."

I see the family resemblance now, even though Ethan is a good six or seven inches taller than Elena.

"He didn't mean anything by it, right, Ethan?" Robbie steps forward and slings an arm over the other boy's shoulder.

"Exactly, I was just trying to break the ice and be friendly." Ethan returns the gesture until the boys are half hugging each other.

Elena rolls her eyes. She leans toward me and mock whispers, "They've somehow bonded this summer and now they gang up on me like this all the time. It's infuriating."

I blink awkwardly at the overly friendly nature of the interaction. I'm not used to new people warming up to me like this. Including me in inside jokes or gossip so easily.

"Oh, um, well, Robbie has always liked . . . being liked. . . ." I trail off, not sure if that was the right thing to say.

But Elena lets out a laugh. "Robbie was right, you're really funny."

"What?" I laugh out the question because I'm sure I must have misheard. No one ever calls me funny.

"Come on, let's pick a song," Elena says, sitting on the couch again and scooting over to make space for me.

I sit down just as Jisung comes over to plop down on the other side of me.

"Hyeri-ssi, I can't believe you're actually here." He grins.

"I can barely believe it either," I admit.

Robbie lets out a laugh. "I guilted her into coming."

"Great job." Jisung lifts his hand for a high five. I want to be annoyed, but it's almost impossible to get mad at Jisung. He's like the embodiment of sunshine. "Is Hyejun-hyeong on his way?"

"You're asking me? You live with him."

Jisung's grin turns sheepish. "Well, he wasn't home when I left. I thought maybe he texted you."

I wonder if that's bad. So often I'm reminded that I have no idea what's going on with my own older brother.

A new song starts up, and Robbie joins Jaehyung to sing a vigorous version of hit trot single "Love Battery." Jaehyung sounds amazing. I've always loved his voice. So smooth and sweet but still fits into the EDM and dance tracks WDB debuted with.

The door bursts open. Minseok and Hyejun enter the room, holding on to each other and laughing at some previously shared joke.

Their entry energizes the entire room. Jaehyung and Robbie let out loud whoops. Jisung jumps off the couch to greet them.

I'm sitting stiffly, unnaturally straight-backed, gripping the water bottle I'm still holding.

Minseok greets Elena with a one-armed hug and lifts a hand to high-five Ethan. And then his eyes finally find me.

His brow lifts. "You're here."

"I-I was invited," I stammer, squeezing my water bottle so hard it spills over onto my lap. I jump up in surprise.

"Here, let's get you a towel," Jun says, pulling me into the kitchen.

I turn back to see Minseok throwing an arm around Robbie's shoulders. "Let's rock, woori maknae!" He takes the mic from Jaehyung and joins the song. Hyejun grabs a tambourine, jumping around and banging it into his head.

I was invited? Why did I say that? It makes it sound like I have to justify being in his apartment. Like I'm invading his space. But I don't have to explain myself. I'm not here to see him. Except, aren't I?

I return to the couch, using the kitchen towel Jun fetched me to wipe the damp cushion before sitting again.

The song has become less trot and more metal as the boys scream the end together. The song finishes and the screen announces that they somehow, impossibly, got a score of 92 despite the out-of-tune screaming.

Minseok lifts his fist in triumph. "Professional idols right here!"

"Fourth-gen kings!" Hyejun declares.

Robbie is rolling his eyes, but he's smiling.

"That was our gift to you, birthday boy," Minseok says into the microphone.

"*That's* your gift?" Elena asks. My eyes whip to her, but despite her shocked tone she's smiling. I realize suddenly that she's spent time with this group. She seems to already understand and enjoy the dynamic of them.

Robbie Choi really has a girlfriend. I can't stop myself from laughing at the idea of it.

"What's funny?" Elena turns to me.

"Oh, nothing. I mean, it's not funny so much as nice," I admit. I feel some of my jaded shields come down a little to just enjoy that idea. "I'm really happy for you and Robbie."

Elena blinks at me in surprise. "Wait, what?"

"Aren't you dating?" I wonder if I read it wrong.

But when Elena blushes, lowering her head to hide a smile, I know I'm right.

"Yeah, we are, but we've never officially confirmed it. Everyone still assumes, though, but Robbie says it's about making the choice ourselves about what we share."

"It can be a lot," I say, and see her smile drop a little. I feel bad for being the one to cause it.

"Yeah, I'm definitely not used to complete strangers having opinions about me and my life. But when it's just me and Robbie, we can ignore it." Her smile brightens again as she looks over at him.

Now Minseok has Robbie in a headlock as he demands a duet together. Robbie is laughing like a loon. Not even trying to free himself. Jun and Jaehyung have joined in, grabbing both boys in half-hug, half-wrestle moves. I'm not even sure if they're trying to separate the two or help one of them win. And if it's the latter, I'm not sure which side they're on.

"I'm glad Robbie found someone who likes him enough to deal with all the extra that comes with our lives." And I really mean it. I've often felt like it's virtually impossible to make true relationships outside of our bubbles. And even among ourselves, it's hard to know what the other person actually wants from you. I resist the urge to steal a glance at Minseok.

The music swells and the boys are really butchering an overly dramatic version of "Candy in my Ears" by Baek Jiyong-sunbae and Taecyeon-sunbae.

Minseok and Hyejun try to do the sexy dance with each other, which makes me cringe and avert my eyes. I do not need to see my older brother's hips shaking like that. Of course, they overdo it and they fall over each other. I barely catch Minseok before he bangs his head on the coffee table.

His weight is sprawled across my lap. This close, I can smell soju on him and see how red his cheeks are. He must have been drinking with my brother before coming here.

"Well," he says, lifting a hand to cup my cheek. "Haven't we been here before?"

I roll my eyes and release him. He drops to the ground with a grunt and a thud. He bumps into the coffee table and drink bottles scatter across the floor.

Just then, the door opens and Jongdae steps in. Behind him is Sooyeon, holding a cake box.

I start to stand. Sooyeon-sunbae is one of my favorite artists. I didn't know she'd be here tonight. I check my shirt and hair to make sure it doesn't look messy from the collision with Minseok.

But before anyone can greet them, Jongdae snaps out, "What the hell is going on here?"

The room quiets down.

"What do you mean?" Minseok asks lazily, not bothering to get up. Instead, he lounges across the floor like he's in a sexy photoshoot. "It's a party, we're partying."

"Are you drunk?"

Minseok scoffs, pushing himself up, brushing off invisible dust from his pants. "We just got a couple drinks before coming."

The way Jongdae is staring Minseok down, I'm worried he's about to explode.

"How could you do this with everything going on?" Jongdae demands. He takes a jerky step forward, leaning heavily on his crutch.

"Hyeong, it's fine," Robbie says.

"Don't get involved," Jongdae growls, clearly getting angrier by the second.

"Don't talk to him like that," Minseok says, his eyes hardening despite the drunk flush still on his cheeks. "And I don't really think you have a leg to stand on here." He lifts a brow and gestures at the crutch. "Literally and figuratively."

Jongdae leans toward Minseok and lowers his voice, but I can still hear him.

"This isn't the time to have this conversation."

"I thought you've been wanting to talk," Minseok says tauntingly.

An angry vein appears in Jongdae's temple. "You know we're trying to keep a low profile these days."

Minseok's jaw tenses, the first sign that he's not as unaffected as he's pretending. "No, *you* are keeping a low profile while I smooth things over so people forget your mistakes."

The room is now too quiet. I shift awkwardly in my seat, and I can hear the sound of the cushions squishing beneath me.

Sooyeon clears her throat. "I think maybe we all need to cool off. We're here to celebrate Robbie."

"Yeah, let's order food," Jaehyung suggests, pulling his phone out.

Robbie looks a little annoyed, but he just nods. "Yeah, who's next to sing? Jongdae-hyeong? You want a turn?"

JD still looks pissed until Sooyeon pats his shoulder gently. Her touch seems to relax him. He finally relaxes a fraction. "Yeah, let's look at the song list."

He moves to the couch with Sooeyon's help.

Everyone's shifting to make room for him, naturally catering to JD due to his injury.

But I'm still watching Minseok, so I see when he walks to the foyer and steps into his shoes. Should I stop him? Ask if he's okay? While I'm worrying over it, he slips out of the apartment.

THIRTY-TWO
HYERI

s he going to be okay?" Elena murmurs beside me. I guess she noticed Minseok leave too.

"I don't think he's in the mood to talk right now."

Even when we were young, Minseok rarely ever got angry. When he did, he usually needed time to cool off before he would listen to anyone.

"You should go talk to him," Elena says.

"Me?" I blink at her. "Why?"

"I think he'd listen to you."

I shake my head. It doesn't make any sense. Minseok would be much more likely to listen to one of the guys. But I get up anyway. Everyone is still too focused on Jongdae right now. And whenever I'm upset and storm out of a room, there's always a part of me hoping someone cares enough to come after me. Maybe Minseok feels that way too.

He's standing in front of the elevator but has yet to press the call button.

"Where are you going?" I ask.

"Nowhere," he mutters, letting his head fall against the wall with a depressing thud.

"Come on." I pull his arm, expecting resistance. But he follows me back like an obedient puppy.

Instead of going into his apartment, I open my own door.

He doesn't protest as I pull him inside and deposit him on the couch. Now that I see him in real light, I can tell that the drunken flush on his cheeks is deeper than I thought. He must have had more than a few drinks. I go to the kitchen and fill a cup of water.

"Hydrate," I tell him.

He obeys again.

I sit and wait for him to finish gulping it down.

"Are you done being mad?" I ask.

"No." He pouts like a little kid.

"Fine, but are you really going to stay away when it's Robbie's birthday party?"

He falters at that. His frown melting away as he puts the empty cup on the coffee table. "No."

"Let's go then." I start to stand, but he grabs my wrist.

"Not yet, okay? I'm still not completely cooled off. And if I see Jongdae right now, I might start swinging."

I'm surprised enough by the claim that I let him pull me back onto the couch. His hand lingering on my wrist. We sit there a minute awkwardly.

Finally, I can't take the silence. "Do you want to talk about it?"

"Not particularly."

"Fine." I pick up the remote, planning to at least turn on the TV.

But he blurts out, "He just won't admit that things are shit between us right now. He's acting like he's not the reason we're in this mess."

He jumps up to pace toward the kitchen before spinning around to pace back again.

It's weird to see him so jittery. I can tell he's hurting, but I suddenly realize I've never been the one to comfort Minseok. When we were younger, he was always the one pulling me out of a bad mood with a joke or a sweet gesture. He was always too go-with-the-flow to stress about anything, or at least that's how it always seemed.

"Maybe he's scared that acknowledging it will make it worse," I try.

"No, that's bull." Minseok shakes his head. "He's treating me like I can't be trusted. I have *always* had his back since we were trainees. I've always kept his secrets. And he couldn't trust me enough to tell me about Sooyeon."

He falls back onto the couch, perching his elbows on his knees to bury his face in his hands.

I am the last person to give advice on how to keep the peace in a group. I was obviously horrible at it in Helloglow. But I have to say something. "Have you tried telling him all of this?"

"No." He sighs. "First, I was too pissed and now there's never a good time. He's not really at the dorm these days; he's staying at his parents' house to recover from his accident."

"But he's here tonight," I point out.

"I can't have the talk now." He pushes his hair out of his face in frustration.

"I'm sorry." He looks so lonely. It's unsettling. A lonely Minseok feels wrong to me. "You'll figure this out. That's what family does."

He lets out a heavy sigh. Then, to my surprise, he turns to me. Leaning his face into my shoulder.

My arms hover in the air around him. Like they're not sure if they should embrace or push away. But he lets out another sigh, and I hesitantly pat him on the back.

His arms come around me tightly, like he's been waiting for me to do just this. And I give in to the moment. It can't hurt, right? I'm just a friend comforting another friend. I rub his back in small circles. "You're going to figure this out. You're closer than brothers."

"Yeah, maybe." He mutters it into my shoulder.

I pull back to look him in the eye and say sternly, "Stop over-thinking it."

He pinches my chin playfully. "You're one to talk. You're the queen of overthinking."

I'm about to rebut; instead I shrug with a rueful smile. "Yeah, you're right."

We're both laughing at ourselves when it strikes me that we're holding on to each other, sitting awfully close together. I have a flash of that moment by the pool, when we sat just this close. How I wanted so badly for him to kiss me. I push away from him defensively.

Jumping off the couch in a rush, I say, "We should get back to the party, right?"

"Hyeri," Minseok says, grabbing my hand so I can't escape.

"Yeah? What's up?" I try my best to pretend like I am not internally freaking out.

"Will you sit?"

I do, but my leg won't stop shaking. I press my hand against it to hold it still, but it continues to vibrate.

"I don't want things to be awkward between us," Minseok says.

"Awkward? What's awkward?" I want to die inside as it's very clear I am the awkward.

He gives me a pointed look, and I finally give up the attempt to ignore the topic.

"What do you think about erasing the last three days?" I suggest hopefully.

Minseok looks even more unhappy at that. "You think we can just ignore it?"

"Why not?" I'm confused. Minseok is the king of avoiding bad feelings. Didn't he just admit that he's evading a needed conversation with Jongdae?

"I think the show is just confusing us," I hedge. "It's no one's fault, right? When you have to pretend to like each other, it blurs the lines of reality."

"Is that what you really think is going on here?" A crease digs in between his brows, a small and perfect line.

This is annoying. What does he want from me? I have the urge to shake him. But an equal urge to lean forward and just kiss him so he can't say anything else that will confuse me.

"Hyeri?"

Great, I zoned out again instead of answering. "I'm just worried," I admit. "That I can't tell the difference between what's for the show and what's real." I wince on the last word. I might as well be confessing my resurrected crush. And desperation makes me quickly add, "I don't know, I'm probably just being stupid."

"Maybe you're right," Minseok murmurs.

"What?" I scowl, not expecting him to agree.

"I mean, no, you're not stupid. Yes, you're right. Shows can feel real sometimes."

"Right!" I cling to his agreement. These feelings are just because of the show.

"I don't think I've ever met someone so happy to hear that things *aren't* real." Minseok laughs. The good-natured kind that makes me grin too.

I shrug. "I guess I'm just special."

"Yes, sure," he says in a sarcastic voice.

"Ya!" I punch his shoulder and he falls back, grabbing his arm like I stabbed him.

"Stop it," I command. "You're such a drama queen."

He doesn't stop wincing. "I'm not joking, I pulled my arm working out earlier."

"Wait, really?" Did I actually hurt him? I scoot closer to see, and that's when his expression changes from pained to mischievous.

"No, not really."

He leans forward, poking at my ribs.

"Stop!" I squeal, but I can't escape him. I get an arm free and grab his knee, where I know he's extra sensitive.

"Ya!" he yelps, and falls over, rolling off the couch.

My triumph is short-lived as he pulls me down with him. But he immediately meets the consequences of his actions as I land heavily on his chest and he lets out a grunt of pain.

"Low blow going for the knee," Minseok complains with a wheeze.

"That's what you get for starting a fight," I say, unrepentant.

He shakes his head, laughing along with me.

A lot has changed about Minseok since he debuted. Polished and shined to create the perfect image of a celebrity. But this close, looking at his laughing face, I see the old Minseok, who joked around with me. Who learned my favorite drink and picked it out of the cooler before I could. Who always invited me along even when my own brother didn't.

He really is so handsome. It makes my heart do little pirouettes. This is dangerous, letting myself feel close to him again. Letting myself *like* him again. I need to do something to fix this, but it's like a speeding train that's picked up too much momentum at this point. I have to just hold on or I'll fall.

He finally notices I'm no longer laughing. "You okay?" he asks, a smile still lingering.

"So, we agree." My voice is too shaky but I can't do anything to calm it. "This is all just pretend, right?"

He looks confused. "You mean the show?"

"I mean, everything between us."

"Everything?"

I feel like my heart is going to burst free and flop across the floor. I grip his shirt desperately. "Just tell me it's pretend."

"Yeah, sure, Hyeri." He nods reassuringly. "It's just pretend."

I let out a relieved sigh, letting my grip relax just a fraction. "Good. Then this doesn't count."

I lean forward and kiss him.

THIRTY-THREE
HYERI

How do I explain the feeling?

It's like dreaming of having something that's just out of your reach. But also scared of it at the same time. Still, you can't stop yourself from imagining how it might feel. Creating hundreds, thousands, of different scenarios that might let you experience it. But when you finally do, it's nothing like you ever imagined. It's infinitely better.

That's what finally kissing Minseok is like.

His lips are slack with surprise at first.

A brief moment of anxiety slices through me, worrying that I misread the signs. That he'll pull away.

And then his mouth moves against mine. His hands cup the back of my neck. He doesn't pull me down so much as he nudges against me, suggesting I come closer.

And I comply. I can't help but do it.

He turns his head just a few degrees. Somehow the move parts our lips and his tongue dips past.

The shock of it has my eyes flying open. He's watching me with half-lidded gaze. And then I close mine again, an invitation for him to keep going.

Minseok rolls us to press me into the floor. We bump the coffee table, and I reach out to shove it aside. One of his hands pillows my head. The other grips right above my hip, shifting me into place so our bodies align perfectly.

It's like I've been waiting to be here for years. From the moment I laid eyes on him.

My heart is still thudding. But now I can feel the response of his own as his body presses into mine.

I feel like I'm vibrating.

Wait, no, that's not me. I push to sit up, moving Minseok back. My head spins, dizzy from him.

I pull my phone out and see that it's a call from Robbie.

"Yeah?" I answer. Is my voice too breathless? Will he know what we were just doing? Minseok leans against the couch. I scoot up as well, but we don't move apart. Our legs still pressed against each other's. "Uh-huh, yeah, Minseok is with me. No, he's fine. Yeah, we're coming back."

"Is Robbie about to send out search parties?"

"Sounds like it," I confirm as I hang up.

Minseok stands, and disappointment slashes through me.

He offers his hand and I take it, letting him pull me up. Our bodies bump into each other, but I don't immediately step back.

"Let's revisit this?" he says.

I nod silently because I can't trust my voice. I just made out with Moon Minseok.

And I'm pretty sure he just told me he wants to do it again.

THIRTY-FOUR

HYERI

have no idea what the vibe is going to be between Minseok and me the next time I see him.

The entire ride to the next shoot, I'm on edge. I barely drink the iced Americano that Hongjoo brought me, but I'm still wired.

I can't stop my leg from shaking as I wonder how he will act. How should I act? Should I pretend nothing happened?

I don't think that's possible as I blush every time I even think about him. I'll probably light up like red Christmas lights when I actually see his face. His gorgeous, perfect face.

Oh no, I'm screwed.

When Hongjoo parks, I don't move to unbuckle myself. I'm somehow more nervous than the first day of filming.

Hongjoo opens the door with a bright smile and says, "Everyone, out, last stop."

I frown at her chipper attitude. "What's gotten into you?"

"Nothing, I'm just happy that you've gotten so good at variety shows."

"That's a stretch," I mutter as I climb out.

Hongjoo wraps her arm around my shoulder. "You're doing really well, Hyeri. People love you in this show."

"Really?" The look of pride I see on Hongjoo's face triggers a need for approval that I never like to acknowledge. I'm a little horrified when unwanted tears spring to my eyes. "You really think it's going well?"

"Oh, sweetie." Hongjoo laughs as she pulls me into a full hug. She's shorter, yet her hug feels like it completely envelops me. "You're doing great, and I'm so proud of you."

She pulls back and looks around with a conspiratorial smile. Then she leans in. "Don't tell anyone I told you this. But there's interest in casting you in a really popular show in the US."

"What?" Those are not words I'd have ever thought I'd hear from my manager, definitely not while talking about me. "Wait, how? I mean when? I mean, what does that mean?"

Would that mean I'd have to go to the States?

"You're not supposed to know because it's just in beginning talks, but the higher-ups at the company are really pleased." She grins at me, and I force a smile. She's so happy for me, but all I can think is that the US is so far away from Seoul. And Seoul is where Minseok is.

Speaking of, Minseok's car pulls up behind ours.

He jumps out the moment it parks and starts to wave. Then he stops, eyes widening at the sight of my face, still red from crying. He runs to my side, grabbing my hands. "Hyeri, what happened? Did someone try to do something? Was it another anti?"

He's turning me from side to side as if checking for injuries.

"Calm down, we were just having a heart-to-heart," Hongjoo says, though she's watching him curiously now.

"Really?" He doesn't look convinced, and he's still holding on to me.

"Really," I say, pulling away gently so he'll let go. There's crew around and we don't want to start rumors. "I should get to makeup and fix my face."

"Oh, yeah, sure," he says, still watching me with concern.

As I walk to the prep area, I try to avoid Hongjoo's laser stare.

"Is something happening I should know about?" she asks.

"No," I huff out with a strained laugh. Great, some actress I am.

"Hyeri," Hongjoo says, voice firm. "You have to tell me if there's something I should be aware of."

"I swear, Eonni. There's nothing," I say, then call out to Jeongho, who passes in front of us. I jog to catch up with him, ignoring the questioning look on my manager's face.

✶ ☆ ✶

Today, the date includes wandering the quaint streets of Hannam, an area with steep inclines and narrow alleys with hidden gems. Some buildings decorated with artistic graffiti. Others built in a sleek industrial style.

It's an area I would enjoy exploring on any other day. But all I can focus on is Minseok. How he keeps standing dangerously close to me. How it makes me go internally haywire.

I actually giggle. Twice. It would be horrifying if I didn't see the approving nod of Han-PD.

Minseok keeps finding reasons to touch me. Tucking my hair back when the wind blows it in my face. Fixing the collar of my dress. Claiming a leaf fell on my shoulder that he had to brush away.

Is he doing it on purpose? He seems so unnaturally calm, when my whole body is tighter than a coiled spring.

I'm grateful when we break for lunch. We only have a shooting permit for a couple more hours. So, I opt to eat quickly in my car so I can be ready to return to the shoot as soon as they're set up again.

Just as I'm opening the sliding van door, Minseok calls my name, jogging between the cars.

"Minseok, what—" I'm cut off as he cages me in against the side of the van.

"I've been waiting all day to get you alone," he murmurs, his eyes moving to my lips like an archer zeroing in on a target.

"Wait," I blurt out, pressing a hand against his chest before he can close the distance.

"What?" He pouts but moves back. "What's wrong?"

I look around, making sure no one is watching before I pull him inside the van.

With the door closed behind us, I turn to him. "Do you think we should talk?"

He looks amused. "Is that really what you want to do with me right now? Talk?"

My pulse goes double-time at his words. Wow, he's really good at this. But I won't let him distract me. "I definitely want to do more than talk," I admit.

"Good." He grins as he starts to lean in again.

I press my palm against his mouth before he can make contact, and he rolls his eyes at me over my hand.

"But we *should* talk. Is doing this too risky?"

He peels my hand from his mouth, interlacing our fingers. "You're worried that someone might see us together and start rumors?"

I nod, grateful that he understands. "What if we're making a mistake?"

His smile falls. "Hyeri, do you not want to—"

"It's not that," I blurt out hurriedly. I'm suddenly desperate to take back my words. I'm scared of being caught, but I also don't want to lose this thing that I've wanted for so long.

"Well, maybe we should just tell everyone we're dati—"

"No," I say, cutting him off. "That's too serious. We can't know how they'll twist it to use against us."

His jaw tenses before he nods. "Fine, we won't tell anyone. But that doesn't mean we can't have fun together. Don't you want to have fun with me, Hyeri?"

"Yeah," I say slowly, wondering if I'm making a mistake here. "But we need to be careful. The whole point of this show was to fix our images."

"Well," he says, leaning in and pressing his lips lightly to my temple. I shiver involuntarily. "I suppose we could find a good meeting place." He lets his cheek rest against mine, his lips brushing my ear. "Somewhere we can definitely be alone." He starts to nibble at the lobe of my ear, and it sends electric shocks through my entire body.

I've kind of forgotten what I wanted to talk about. I turn my head toward his, ready to give in.

But he stops just before our lips touch. "What about your place?"

"Huh?" I murmur, my brain a fog.

"It's private, close to mine. And we can do . . ." He gives me the lightest kiss on the lips. Nowhere close to being satisfying. "Whatever we want."

Another shiver races down my spine. "Yes, my place. Perfect. Let's go."

He laughs as he leans away, and I feel a slight pang of disappointment. My arms itch to pull him back.

"I'll come by tonight," he says, then lifts our joined hands to his lips, pressing a kiss to my knuckles before climbing out of the car.

As he saunters away, I lean against the headrest, letting out a shuddering breath.

I don't think anything could have prepared me for the full powerful focus of Moon Minseok.

THIRTY-FIVE

HYERI

The day after our honeymoon episode airs my mother calls.

"Hello?" I answer cautiously, unsure how this will go.

"Did you see that Liza Kang posted about your honeymoon on her stories?"

"What?" I'm confused by the abrupt topic without even a hello.

"Liza Kang, don't you know her? Oh, Hyeri, you should be better at keeping up with Korean American celebrities. She's so hot after the first season of *Musical Dreams* aired on Disney."

"No, I know who Liza Kang is." She's slated to be the next big thing. Some people even think she'll take over the mantle from Olivia Rodrigo. And since she's Korean, everyone in the community is very excited.

"Well, she's obsessed with your show! Specifically, you and Moonster. This is such good news."

"That's great, Mom," I say weakly. It's like whiplash with my mom sometimes. Her disinterest is like a never-ending Westeros winter, but the moment she's happy with me she is like a bulldozer planning out the next ten years of my career.

"So, I read some of the viewer comments and it seems people love it when you and Minseok show skinship, so I think you should focus on that."

I roll my eyes to the ceiling and hold back my heavy sigh. It wouldn't be worth reminding her that she called me a bimbo after we barely touched at the wedding shoot. And now she's telling me to snuggle up to him more on camera?

At least she's showing a positive interest in you, Hyeri. Don't take this moment for granted.

"Okay, Eomma," I say, forcing brightness into my voice. "I'm glad you're enjoying it."

"Do you think we can get the show to have Hyejun-ie on it again? It would be nice to have some crossover promotion between you two."

"I think he's in Japan right now with AX1S," I remind her.

"Oh yes, I forgot. World tour!"

Asian Tour. But I don't correct her.

"All right, well, I can't believe both of my kids are doing so well! I just came from drinks with the girls. They're all so jealous of my talented children."

That must be the source of her energy right now. "I'm glad, Eomma. Maybe we can have a call this weekend if Appa's also home?"

"I have to go, I'm at the spa. Kisses!"

"Love you," I try to get out, but the call cuts off.

Well, at least she's happy, I tell myself. *That means I'm doing well.*

K-Pop Fan Attic forum:
Our Celebrity Marriage, ep.143

YeoBokki: Eomo, my heart is pounding at this scene! What's going on? Do I actually kind of like the scandal princess now?

    linosothercat: @YeoBokki Right? I'm totally into her right now!

        MoonstersWyfe4Real: @linosothercat She's still super awkward to me. It's all Minseok-Oppa!

            SunnyPaige6: @MoonstersWyfe4Real No way, Hyeri is super cute. They match vibes so well!

Weird_wurm: It's gotta be fake. She's a totally different person now. Probably got training from her agency. She IS an actress after all!

    3llsB3lls: @Weird_wurm She wasn't always so awkward! If you go back to look at the early videos from her trainee years or the first episodes of *CiPro* she was super friendly and sweet.

        SunnyPaige6: @3llsB3lls I agree! She just probably got stressed out by all the hate comments!

        AniAniAniAniAni: @SunnyPaige6 Still, she had to know that is something that happens. Maybe she just shouldn't be a celebrity. I don't mean any hate. I'm just saying if she can't handle it, she should do something else.

        Weird_wurm: @SunnyPaige6 It's what they sign up for! Don't become an idol if you can't handle the comments

            Daisy.4.9: @Weird_wurm What an asshole thing to say! No one deserves to be talked about like people do to Shin Hyeri.

Fangworl4783: @Weird_wurm So you're admitting she's a good actress then

    Weird_wurm: @Fangworl4783 Being a good actress just means she's a better liar!

        Fangworl4783: @Weird_wurm Whatever, keep being bitter!

M@rryMeJ@ehyung: So proud of our girl, showing everyone how lovable she is! Hyeri Fighting!

THIRTY-SIX
HYERI

The next few weeks are surreal.

Most of my time is taken up by *OCM*. They've doubled our air time because our segments are the most watched (and rewatched online).

It has strangely become a way for me to see the city. Even when I was a trainee, I didn't explore as much as I wanted, since I was always so busy with training.

Then being in Helloglow took up all my time. And after, I was too scared to leave my safe spaces.

But now, with *OCM*, Minseok and I have had dates at all the most popular spots in Seoul. The Coex Aquarium. Dressing in hanbok at the Queen's Palace. The Starfield Library. My favorite was actually after we finished at Namsan Tower, leaving a love lock like hundreds of other couples have. We walked down one of the winding roads instead of taking the car and found a small rooftop bar overlooking the mountainside. We just sat there, holding hands and watching the sunset together.

Too often, when we're recording, I forget that it's just for a show. But now, I don't worry about blurring that line anymore. In fact, I fully embrace the illusion; the show's dates have become like a way to live out my relationship bucket list with Minseok.

He's so good at creating a bubble around us. Like nothing outside of the two of us can touch what we have. It's such a skill, seeing as our relationship was literally created to entertain millions.

But Minseok doesn't seem to care about any of that. When he talks about us, he talks in the indefinite. He's always cracking jokes, sometimes shocking full snort laughs out of me. I can only imagine what my mom thinks as she monitors episodes. But it's too hard to try to hold back when I'm with him. I'm the most relaxed I've ever been on camera. Somehow, along the way, I gave up stressing about maintaining a specific image, which is good, since half the time Minseok and I end up bickering over something or another.

But somehow the fans still seem to think we have good chemistry. That even our fights are cute.

For the first time, people online describe me with words like "relatable" and "witty" instead of "stiff" and "rude."

There are still antis circling, commenting on articles about the show, but they're drowned out by the new fans. And when one anonymous post claims I was a school bully in LA, it's quickly shut down by other netizens picking apart the commenter for mixing up my middle school with my elementary school. I've never been so quickly defended online before like that.

I know I owe it all to Minseok. He makes me relax on camera.

And maybe sometimes I do have moments of worry about what will happen when I no longer have him beside me. But I tell myself that's a problem for future Hyeri. For now, I do have him. Not just on set, but after as well.

When we get back from shoots, we go to our respective apartments. And later, he comes to my place. At first, he'd text beforehand. But soon, it just became our routine. We haven't defined anything. It's like an unspoken agreement that as long as we don't say what it is, we don't have to worry about any consequences.

"Double scoops of ice cream," I say.

"Oh, that's a good one," Minseok hums.

We're sitting on my couch. Well, I'm sitting, Minseok is sprawling next to me—which I've found is his favorite position. His head is lying in my lap and he's playing with my hand, which is resting on his chest.

"I think the thing I miss the most since debuting is going to the movies."

"You don't go to the movies?" I ask, but then I try to remember the last time I went and come up empty.

"Well, we go to screenings sometimes when we're invited. But I miss just casually going to watch a movie. And also, the snacks." He twines his fingers through mine and presses my knuckles to his lips as he thinks—another habit he's picked up.

"Oh yeah, I love the movie snacks here. When I first moved from LA, sometimes I'd just go to the theater to buy snacks to bring home. I wouldn't even see a movie."

Minseok grins against the back of my hand. "Yeah, I remember you once came back to the trainee dorm with two bags of movie theater popcorn."

"It lasted me a week." I smile at the memory. Then, as if also remembering, my stomach rumbles.

Minseok laughs, glancing at his phone screen. "Wow, it's already almost dinnertime. We should order something to eat."

"You're not eating with the guys?" I ask.

He shrugs, already scrolling through a delivery app. "They'll survive without me."

I bite my lip, holding back my concern. I know that JD has moved back into WDB's dorm. I saw him with his suitcase in the hallway this past weekend. Minseok hasn't mentioned it at all, but he has been coming over to my place every day this week. "You're over here more than you're at your own place."

"You try living with four other guys and see how often you want to be home. They're all messy slobs," Minseok mutters, snuggling closer.

"I'm sorry, but I don't think you're any better." I eye the socks he took off and left on the floor.

"What are you talking about? Haven't you heard that the fans call me the mom of WDB? I'm always taking care of those boys."

"Yeah, right. You're just good at playing it up for cameras. I know that Jun does all the cooking."

Minseok sits up and gives me an offended stare. "Shin Hyeri, that is some archaic patriarchal BS to think the mom always has to do the cooking."

I laugh and smack his shoulder before he settles his head into my lap again.

"Fine, maybe you're right," I admit. "But aren't you worried one of the guys is going to get suspicious? What if they figure out you're coming over here?"

"If it's Jun or Jaehyung they won't tell anyone. If it's Robbie, I'll just bully him into keeping his mouth shut."

I notice he doesn't mention JD, but I wisely don't ask. Still, it does feed my worry that he still hasn't made up with Jongdae. Maybe I *should* say something. Isn't that what a good friend would do? Or whatever I am to Minseok.

What do you call someone who has finally successfully started a situationship with their longtime crush, but it's mostly secret kissing and heavy flirting?

Don't overthink this, Hyeri. Not this time. Just enjoy it while it lasts.

"Hyeri?" Minseok says, pulling me back to the present. "Where'd you go?"

"Nowhere," I say, pretending that I wasn't just spacing out with anxiety over our non-relationship. "What were you saying?"

He reaches up to ruffle my hair affectionately. "I kind of love how spacey you are, I ever tell you that?"

Love. My heart jumps before I purposefully squash the feeling.

"I was asking you if you were down for sushi?'

"Sure." I force a light grin, leaning in to peruse the menu with him.

Things are good for now, I tell myself. *That's all I can ask for.*

THIRTY-SEVEN
MINSEOK

Minseok steps back into his apartment and plops onto one of the kitchen stools. He's never been one to stress over a relationship, but he really thought Hyeri would be open to defining things by now.

He meant it when he told Hyeri they could start out casual. But he never said he had any intention of staying that way.

Maybe he needs to be more proactive in convincing Hyeri that they can have both their careers and each other. It will be hard, because he isn't certain he's fully convinced himself. But still, he has to try. Moon Minseok is someone who thinks it's worth trying even if the goal feels impossible. That's how he's already come so far in his young life.

"Hey, Hyeong." Jaehyung emerges from his room, carrying an empty bag of chips.

"Was that your dinner?" Minseok frowns, wondering if Hyeri's right.

Maybe he should spend more time here, if only to ensure his members eat more than salty snacks for meals.

"More like an appetizer." Jaehyung opens the fridge and stares at the contents.

"Any Spam? We could make bokkeumbap."

"Didn't you eat at Hyeri-noona's?"

"Yea but—" Minseok cuts off, turning to eye Jaehyung, who is considering a container of mystery pasta.

"Why do you think I was at Hyeri's?" he asks carefully.

"Because you've been there every day this week," Jaehyung says, clearly deciding the pasta is safe to eat as he pops the lid and digs in without even heating it.

Minseok sighs. He should have known. Jaehyung is always underestimated due to his resting confused face. It's what endears him to fans. He seems so innocent. But he's the most observant of the group. And he's clearly picked up on what's going on between Minseok and Hyeri.

"You haven't told the others, have you?"

Jaehyung shrugs, shoving another spoonful of pasta into his mouth. "If you wanted us to know, you'd tell us."

Minseok smiles, reminding himself that while astute, Jaehyung also likes to mind his own business. An introvert through and through, he doesn't like gossip because it means he has to say more than a sentence at a time.

"Does it bother you?" Minseok grabs a mug and fills it with water. He slides it down the counter where Jaehyung catches it and takes a long gulp.

"Do you want my honest opinion?" Jaehyung asks.

"Yes."

Jaehyung hums thoughtfully, taking another bite of pasta. He is not one to speak thoughtlessly, so he always takes the extra time if he needs it. He figures, if the other person wants a real answer, they should be willing to wait for it.

Finally, he takes a sip of water to clear his throat and says, "I think I was actually surprised nothing ever happened between you two before. But when it didn't, I also thought you'd both moved on."

"Well, we clearly haven't." Minseok grabs a mug for himself to fill with water, suddenly parched. He feels slightly uncomfortable talking about this. The relationship with Hyeri still feels too delicate. He's worried that overanalyzing it will show the cracks. "I think I've liked her since before we even debuted. But it just wasn't a good time to start something."

Jaehyung looks surprised, then he gives one of his slow smiles. The kind that takes a minute to spread, but that any Jaehyung bias can tell you is worth the wait.

"Then I'm happy for you. I like you and Hyeri together."

"Wow, really?" Jongdae steps into the kitchen. The look of anger on his face unmistakable. He no longer needs the assistance of a crutch, but the boot he wears makes his gait uneven. "You seriously gave me so much shit about not telling you that I was dating Sooyeon and you're in a secret relationship?"

"It's not a secret and it's not a full relationship," Minseok says.

Derision flashes across Jongdae's handsome features.

Jaehyung gives a careful cough, as if to remind them he's still there. "Hyeong, if it's still new, maybe Minseok-hyeong just needed time—"

"That's not the point. You acted all high-and-mighty at the beginning of the summer about how I screwed things up." He jabs a finger into Minseok's chest.

"Back off," he says through gritted teeth. It takes everything Minseok has not to grab that finger and give JD another broken limb.

"No, you've been calling me selfish all summer for wanting a relationship outside of this group." Jongdae shoves his sneering face into Minseok's. "Guess you're no better than me, huh?"

"I said back off." Minseok pushes Jongdae away. Not hard, but with his boot, JD can't catch his balance, and he stumbles into the couch.

"Hyeong!" Jaehyung races to Jongdae's side. "He's still hurt."

"Then he should be more careful." Minseok scowls. "You have no right to get into my personal business. Not when you worked so hard to keep me out of yours."

Jongdae shakes his head. "Yeah, well at least I'm not a hypocrite."

"What is that supposed to mean?" Minseok growls.

"You act like you're doing everything you can to save WDB. At least Sooyeon didn't have a reputation that could hurt us. Can you say the same about Hyeri?"

"You should stop talking," Minseok warns through teeth clenched as tight as his fists. He'd like nothing more than to hit that smug look off Jongdae's face, but he knows he has to hold back. He always has to hold back.

Jongdae doesn't listen. "Have you ever thought about how her reputation could blow back on us? Can she even survive another scandal if this gets out?"

That pushes Minseok over the precarious edge he's standing on. He can take all the jabs and criticisms for himself, but hearing Jongdae talk about Hyeri makes him lose his control. He grabs his friend's collar so forcefully that he hears the material rip. "Don't fucking talk about her like that."

Jongdae's fist is like lightning, a brick-hard blow to Minseok's jaw.

The surprise of the attack and the anger behind the hit makes stars explode behind his eyes.

"Hyeong! Stop it!" Jaehyung's shouting now, something that rarely ever happens.

It's enough to bring Jun and Robbie into the living room.

"What's going on?" Jun asks.

"Hyeong? You okay?" Robbie goes to Jongdae's side.

"Minseok-ah?" Jun asks, worry creasing his brow.

"It's nothing. It's over," Minseok says, wiping at his lip; it comes away with a smear of blood. "Just keep him the hell away from me."

As he escapes into the hallway, he stares at Hyeri's door. He wants to go to her. To hide away with her. But Jongdae's angry accusation echoes, too fresh in his mind.

Can she even survive another scandal if this gets out?

Instead, he turns to the elevators. He needs fresh air and time to think.

THIRTY-EIGHT
HYERI

haven't seen Minseok the last four days. The first day he didn't come over, he texted me that he had a headache. The next he said he needed to help Robbie with recording. And the third he didn't even give an excuse. Just said he was busy.

I tell myself that it's fine. This doesn't mean he's growing bored with me. This isn't the beginning of him ghosting me. He's an idol; idols have busy schedules. I know that better than anyone.

Still, I wanted to see him before our schedule today. Because we were invited to be guest hosts on HBS's *Music Showdown*, which means my return to a weekly music show for the first time since Helloglow disbanded.

I was already freaking out about the show and then I got the schedule last night, and Pink Petal and Kim Ana are both promoting new music. So, we'll all be in the same place for the first time since the midsummer festival.

My phone buzzes as I walk back from the restroom. I've already had to pee twice this morning, probably because I nervously gulped down two Americanos.

I pluck the phone out of my pocket, but the message isn't from Minseok like I'd hoped.

Sohee: *Eonni! I can't believe you're the guest host for our debut week! Make sure you take care of us!*

I can practically hear her squeals through the text and it eases my nerves a bit.

Maybe I can just focus on that. Kastor's album came out last Friday, which means they're doing the circuit of all the weekly music shows.

I type back: *Fighting! See you out there!*

She sends five muscle emojis and I can't help laughing at her enthusiasm.

I'm still smiling at how cute Sohee is when I look up and see Minseok walking toward me. I almost don't recognize him at first. He's wearing a cap low over his eyes and a face mask. But I'd know his gait anywhere.

"Minseok-ah," I call, and he pauses but doesn't look up. For a second, I think he's going to walk right past and ignore me.

My anxiety flares. Is he mad at me?

Finally, he looks up. "Hyeri-yah, you're here already?"

I try a smile. "Yeah, I was nervous, thought I'd get reacclimated to the space." Then I hesitantly add, "How are you?"

"Fine, good." The answer lacks any of the familiarity we've built up recently.

I wanted to convince myself his strange shift in attitude toward me was just in my head, but it's definitely not. He steps into his dressing room; it's right across the hall from mine.

The old me would have let him go. The old me wouldn't have wanted to push too hard for fear of making a bad impression. But this isn't right.

I walk into the room after him. The staff isn't in there, so it's just us. Good, we'll need privacy for whatever this is going to be.

"Are you mad at me?" I start to ask as he pulls off his hat and mask.

"What?" He spins around, clearly surprised. And that's when I see the bloom of a bruise on his chin.

"Oh my god, what happened?" I rush up to him.

He grabs my wrist before I can brush my fingers over the mark.

"It's nothing," he says, grabbing his mask again.

But I stop him from putting it on and lean in to examine his chin. It's already an angry purple, which means it's at least a few days old.

"Is this why you've been avoiding me?"

He shrugs.

"What happened? Ran into a really tall door?"

"Ran into Jongdae's fist," he finally says, dropping onto the couch.

"JD hit you?" I sit next to him.

"He's not really happy about this." He darts a finger back and forth between us.

"He punched you because of us?"

"He punched me because he's being an asshole right now."

I can't believe my relationship with Minseok is getting him into physical fights with his best friend. "Should I talk to him?" I wonder aloud, though I'm not sure if that'll help or make things worse.

"Leave Jongdae to me. We have bigger things to figure out between us." He scoots closer to lean his head on my shoulder. "I'm sorry. I didn't realize staying away would make you think I was mad."

"I might have been projecting," I admit. "Plus I've been spiraling about today. Kim Ana is promoting."

"Oh crap." He shoots upright, turning to run his hands down my arms. "I didn't even read the lineup, I'm sorry."

I smile at his sweet concern, already feeling better. "It's fine. You're here and so is Sohee. I'll be okay."

"You'll be great. And I'll be right next to you." He pushes my hair behind my ear gently, then leans in to kiss my cheek.

I sigh as I turn my head for a real kiss. I know it's risky, but it's been days since we've been together and I need this right now. In the quiet before the storm, when it's just the two of us. It grounds me. But when I hear the jiggle of the doorknob, I lurch away from Minseok, pushing him a bit too hard in my hurry to avoid getting caught.

He drops off the couch with a grunt just as Hongjoo and Hanbin walk in.

"Ah, there you are," Hongjoo says. "Did you get confused? Your dressing room is across the hall."

"Yes, sorry." I jump to my feet as Minseok pulls himself back onto the couch.

"Minseok-ah, you good?" Hanbin frowns at his own charge.

"Yup, just a bit off. Probably need some caffeine."

"I'll grab you an Americano." Hanbin scoots back out.

I hurry to join Hongjoo, shooting an apologetic glance back to Minseok as I slip out the door.

★☆★

Never in my year as a member of Helloglow would I ever have used the word *fun* to describe a broadcast experience. But honestly, I'm having fun.

It helps that I have a script again. Something to anchor me when I have a blank moment. But for the first time ever, I go rogue a few times. Making small jokes to play off something Minseok does or says. And every time he gives me an approving grin or wink it emboldens me. Maybe I do have decent broadcasting instincts. I just needed to get out of my own head. Or maybe I just needed the right partner to bring it out in me.

I'm the interviewer for the debut segment with Kastor. It's a bit nerve-racking being up there alone.

But the interview spaces on these shows are as small as a cubicle, with only one cameraman to film. So, it helps make me feel enclosed and safe.

Plus, the girls are absolutely adorable. It's strange and fun to see how they defer to Sohee as their leader. And watching them give her a hard time as one of the oldest in the group makes me laugh. The tables have truly turned from when Sohee was the beloved maknae of Helloglow.

"Sunbae," Bomi says. She smiles so big that her gums show, something I'd have been self-conscious about, but she doesn't seem to care. It endears her to me. I can tell she's just having fun and it's a refreshing change.

"Yes, Bomi-yah."

She giggles at the familiar address I use. "Can we convince you to do the dance challenge to our song?"

"Oh?" I glance toward the PDs; this wasn't in the script. But they don't seem upset about the tangent. "Um, it's been a while since I've danced."

"Oh, come on, Eonni," Sohee says, clinging to my arm. "It's been, like, a year. You can do it!"

I sigh and agree. Bomi and Sohee rush forward, teaching me the moves. I feel awkward at first, but I realize it's not as complicated as I feared. And soon, I'm so determined to do well, I don't care how stilted I probably look trying out the moves.

"Okay, I think I got it. Music, cue!" The chorus plays, and I actually keep up with the other six girls. We end on an agreed-upon pose where I'm in the center of a circle of jazz hands framing me as I cup my own chin.

I'm the first to break the pose with a self-conscious laugh.

"You were amazing!" Sohee insists.

"Yeah," Bomi agrees with her big gummy smile. "We should make you our seventh member."

"Kastor only has six stars," I remind her. "I will just cheer you on from here on Earth."

The girls laugh at my bad joke and the PD signals us to wrap up. I say the closing lines before introducing the next performance. And when the red light turns off, I am enveloped in a hug from Sohee.

"Oh my god, you are a natural at hosting! Were you hiding this the whole time we were in Helloglow?" She gives me a suspicious glare.

"I swear, I am barely holding it together." I laugh, but I feel good. I know the segment was fun. I know I did a good job. And I didn't even need Minseok to fill in the gaps this time.

"Sohee is right, you're such a natural. I hope you do more of these, Sunbae," Bomi says with a sweet smile. The other girls gather to agree emphatically. And I make a mental note to take the whole group out to dinner. It's what sunbaes are supposed to do. And I am suddenly really fond of them all.

"Good job," Minseok says, coming over as Kastor is ushered off by their manager to prepare for their performance.

"When did you get here?" I ask with a self-conscious flush.

"I snuck in at the end. You've still got good moves." He bumps my shoulder with his.

"I almost passed out with anxiety. But it was kind of fun," I admit with a grin.

"Look at you, growing some confidence on broadcasts. Soon you'll abandon me for bigger and brighter things."

I laugh, punching him playfully on the shoulder. But my stomach does a little uncomfortable flip at the mention of working without him. Does he mean he's looking forward to OCM being over?

Stop it, you're overthinking things again, Hyeri.

"Hey, you good?" Minseok asks, brushing a wayward strand of hair from my shoulder before letting his hand trail lightly down my back.

"Yup," I lie, trying to hide my worries.

"We have a little bit of time before the next segment. Do you want to get a snack? When's the last time you had a famous HBS commissary cookie?"

I know I shouldn't. Technically, I'm still watching what I eat. But it's been almost a year since I've had an HBS cookie. And they really are amazing.

"I can tell you want one," Minseok says in my ear. It makes me shiver. But I guess that's what thinking about cookies will do to a girl.

"Just one," I promise myself.

"Yes, just one." Minseok laughs as he grabs my hand and pulls me into the elevator.

"Ya, no holding hands in public." I pull away.

"We're the only ones in here."

"Really?" I nod up at the security camera in the corner.

"Fine, have it your way." He sighs in a heavy and dramatic fashion. "But it's your loss, I'm a really phenomenal hand-holder."

I laugh as the doors open. "Says who? Your mom?"

"And Junie. Jun loves holding hands."

"He does not." I roll my eyes as I follow him out of the elevator.

He lifts his phone to his ear. "Yes? Junie? What a coincidence, I was just telling Hyeri about our sweet nights of hand-holding I always look forward to."

"Stop being weird," I tell him, but he just grins at me as he ducks into the commissary.

I laugh as I chase after, so caught up in him that I don't see the person stepping into my path until I'm about to collide with them.

"Sorry," I murmur, starting to bow when I realize I'm face-to-face with Kim Ana.

THIRTY-NINE

HYERI

'm so thrown off that I don't take in the girls next to Ana at first.

It's Pink Petal. They're all staring at me with a mix of shock and judgment, and I immediately start to sink into myself.

"Shouldn't you apologize?" Yunseo sneers.

"Huh?" I blink at her, still trying to pull myself together. I haven't talked to Ana since Helloglow disbanded.

"She just did, didn't you hear?" Minseok replies, stepping up beside me.

Yunseo blinks up at him in clear shock before plastering a bright smile on her face. "Sunbaenim, I didn't see you. I was so excited when you were announced as guest host. I can't wait for WDB's comeback."

It's like whiplash to see her attitude change the moment she's talking to Minseok.

"I should go," Ana murmurs even though she's clearly waiting in line to pay. She looks down at the seltzer and salad in her hands. Then pushes them into Yunseo's arms. The other girl takes them obediently.

"Bye." She bows to Minseok, then turns and hesitantly lowers her head toward me before hurrying out.

She can't even be in the same room as me? Does she really hate me that much?

"Do you want us to bring these to you?" Yunseo calls, but Ana has already disappeared into the elevators.

Yunseo turns to me with an accusatory glare. I'm scrambling to think of an excuse or an apology.

But Minseok's arm comes around me, squeezing just slightly. "Come on, Hyeri. We have to go back for that new segment." He guides me out of the commissary.

I'm disoriented, trying to parse out my thoughts. So, I let him lead me without paying attention to where we're going. It's not until the door of the stairwell closes behind us that I snap out of it.

"She couldn't even be in the same room as me," I murmur.

"You don't know that," Minseok says.

"She didn't even look at me." *She acts like I'm really a bully.* I start to get heated. I've never done anything to her and she acts like she's scared of me. "*This* is why people think I bullied her. She acts like an injured deer when I'm around."

My anger flares brighter. It's surprising and shocking. I've never allowed myself to feel like this before. But I'm suddenly so overwhelmed with the injustice of it all. "You know, when the first bullying rumor came out, I actually apologized to her. I was worried that it would give her anxiety to be written about on the gossip sites. But she hasn't *once* asked me if I'm okay, not even when we were in Helloglow together."

"Wow, you're really pissed," Minseok says softly, and it pulls me slightly from the current of my feelings. It makes me self-conscious and defensive.

"What? Are you going to tell me that I should calm down? Or that I should be the bigger person? Or that no one will believe I'm worth investing in if I'm too messy and emotional?" I'm listing all the criticisms my mom always says to me.

Minseok lets out a laugh that echoes against the stark concrete walls of the stairwell. "No, I'm just really surprised you're actually letting this all out. I never thought you'd be able to." He grins as he pinches my cheek. "I'm glad."

"Glad?" I blink up at him in shock. "You're glad that I'm angry?"

"I'm glad that you know you're not responsible for the bullshit narrative the media made up about you and Ana."

"Really?" My voice is tight. I have to push it out from my constricting chest. "You don't think I'm making it worse by showing too much emotion?"

He shakes his head. "Any normal person would get pissed at a situation like this. Whether she's playing it up or not. You can't change that. But I'm glad you're not letting them convince you you're in the wrong here."

I laugh and it's like a release. As if someone opened the lid of a boiling kettle that lives in my chest. Maybe, this whole time, I was just waiting for someone to take my side, no questions asked. I grip his hand, squeezing it. "You're really surprising."

He grins and twines our fingers. "That's a good thing, right?"

I lift onto my toes to give him a quick peck. "I guess you could say that. At least I'm never bored with you."

"Oh good; a life of boredom is worse than death." He shudders dramatically.

"I'm not sure people would agree with you."

He shrugs, tugging me after him. "That's because most people are wrong."

I start to laugh, but it cuts off as I realize we're climbing the stairs. "Wait, we're not taking the elevator."

"You said I can't hold your hand in the elevator," he reminds me, lifting our joined hands to show me.

I laugh again. "You always seem to find a way to get what you want, don't you?"

He presses his lips to my knuckles, his smiling eyes bright over our joined hands. "Usually."

t can't be real, right?

It's a lucid dream or something.

But the message from Hongjoo is still there when I close and reopen my Kakao: *Congratulations, Hyeri! You're nominated for two Hallyu Wave Awards!*

Entertainment Couple of the Year and Entertainment Newcomer Award.

The Hallyu Wave Awards started only a few years ago, but they're slowly growing in influence. And like any of the awards in this industry it's all about who you know and who knows you.

Fine, Entertainment Couple of the Year makes sense. We probably got nominated because of Minseok.

I try not to dwell on the idea that people think Minseok and I make a good couple. Not when it takes all my self-control not to kiss him every time I see him these days.

But Newcomer Award, that must be a mistake, right?

Stop it, I tell myself. *You worked hard for this.*

But knowing I worked hard has never been the problem. It's the idea that anyone noticed or cares enough to acknowledge it.

When I hear the door beep open, I hurry toward it just as Minseok steps in.

He grins when he sees me and lifts me into a hug before he even has his shoes off.

"Congratulations, Newcomer Award nominee!" he says, leaning down to kiss me.

I press my hand against his lips to stop him, even though I'd love nothing more than to lose myself in him and ignore the swirling complicated mass of emotions tornadoing inside me.

"What if it's a mistake? What if they announce that I'm really not nominated?"

Minseok laughs but stops when he sees I'm serious. "Come on, Hyeri. How many times do people have to tell you that you're talented and you deserve to be here before you'll believe us?"

I shake my head and turn away from him. "I'm just not the type of person who gets nominated for these kinds of things."

"That's nonsense; you got nominated for so many rookie and newbie awards as an idol."

"No, *Helloglow* got nominated," I remind him.

He nods. WDB is such a powerhouse brand, so of anyone he has to get it, right? What it's like to get sucked into a group and lose your individual identity.

He steps over to cup my cheeks and hold me still. "But this time it's just you. And you should celebrate it."

"I don't feel like I can, just in case . . ." I stop myself and sigh, closing my eyes. I can hear myself becoming paranoid. "No, you're right. This is great. I'm happy."

He laughs. "Maybe practice saying that a few more times and you'll sound convincing."

"I'm happy," I repeat, forcing cheerfulness into my voice. "I'm happy!"

"That's more like it. Plus, we're nominated for couple of the year." He wiggles his brows at me.

"Stop being such a perv," I say, punching his arm.

"I just meant we worked hard as costars. What are *you* thinking?" He gives me a stern look.

I laugh at his teasing, relaxing the way only Minseok can get me to do. A part of me worries that this is bad. I'm coming to rely on him too much. I'm getting too used to him. But it's not something I want to worry about right now. I deserve this moment.

"Really? So, you just came over to say congratulations and that's all? That's fine, I'll just walk you to the door." I start for the foyer when he spins me back into his arms.

"Well, maybe I did think that as the Couple of the Year nominee, we should practice being a couple. To increase our chances of winning."

I smile and wrap my arms around his neck. "You're so smart, Oppa."

Minseok's smile falls. He goes completely still.

I frown with worry. "What is it?"

"You said it."

"Said what?"

Instead of answering, he picks me up again, jumping around so I have to cling to his neck because I'm afraid of him dropping me.

"What is going on?" My voice is bouncing as he continues to whirl me around.

"You called me Oppa."

I laugh now. "I guess it just slipped out."

He finally sets me down. "But you mean it, right?"

I pretend to think about it and he pinches my cheek in retaliation. "Yes, I meant it, Oppa."

He leans in, turning his ear toward me. "What? I don't think I heard."

"Oppa," I say with a laugh. "Oppa, Oppa, Oppa."

He grins so wide, his dimples crease. "Yup, that's what I thought I heard."

When he kisses me, I feel his giddiness transfer to me.

I keep waiting to get used to the sensation of kissing Minseok. But just the feel of his palms against my cheeks makes me light up. It's thrilling and comforting all at the same time.

I'm so engrossed in Minseok. That must be why I don't hear the door lock beep. I don't hear the click of it open. But I do hear the thud of something dropping.

Minseok and I jump apart to see Hongjoo standing over a crushed cake box, frosting splattered at her feet as she gapes at us.

FORTY-ONE
HYERI

'm sitting on the couch, hands folded, head lowered.

Before we could come up with a convincing lie, Hongjoo calmly asked Minseok if he could leave.

Now, I feel a little abandoned. He could have tried to stay and explain things with me. But, then again, as I watch Hongjoo pace angrily across the living room floor, I don't blame him. My manager can be fierce when she's truly pissed. And she definitely is now.

"So, you lied to me. No, you *hid* this from me. How am I supposed to help you, to *protect* you, when you hide things this huge from me?" I know she's not expecting a response. She's been pacing and muttering like this for five minutes.

But I finally can't handle the guilt or tension anymore. "I didn't mean to make things hard for you."

She finally stops pacing and turns slowly to glare at me. I immediately regret saying anything.

Then she lifts her eyes to the ceiling and sighs. "I just don't even know where to begin with this, Shin Hyeri. This is *not* something I have the bandwidth to deal with right now."

"Then maybe let's pretend you didn't see anything?"

"Yeah, sure." Hongjoo barks out a laugh. "And who do you think the company will blame first when your little secret comes out?"

"It won't," I insist. "We're being careful."

Hongjoo lifts a disbelieving brow. "Hyeri, this is too risky for both of you right now. The company won't be happy."

"Please don't tell them, Eonni." I lift my folded hands. I'm ready to get down on my knees if I have to. I can't give up Minseok, not yet.

She shakes her head sadly as she comes over to sit next to me. "You have to stop this, whatever it is."

"No!" I'd been expecting the demand, but still my stomach drops hearing the words. "It's not going to affect the show, I swear."

"It's not just about the show."

Her voice scares me. "Eonni, what's going on? Is something wrong?"

Hongjoo picks up the bouquet of flowers she brought along with the crushed cake. She stares at them in a daze. "I was coming over here to celebrate."

I feel the squeeze of guilt. I hate that I've put that worried look on her face. The person who's always been by my side through everything good or bad has been Hongjoo. "You mean the nominations?"

"Yeah, and to tell you that you got the offer. *Musical Dreams* wants you to be a recurring guest star next season."

"Wh-what?" I stutter out. That's not what I was expecting to hear. "How? I mean, when? I mean . . . how?"

"I know, it's huge. They want you in LA in two weeks for a table read."

"Two weeks?" I am shocked. "But what about *OCM*? The Hallyu Wave Awards?" *What about Minseok?*

"You'd fly out right after the awards. You'll come back to finish up your commitment to *OCM*. But the producers are already aware and even though they're disappointed, your contract with the show is over in a few weeks."

I nod. I knew that. But I've heard rumblings of extending our run on the show. I thought that maybe, hopefully, we could keep going. Because a part of me connected the longevity of my time with Minseok to our time on the show. But now, this opportunity feels like one I can't give up.

"If you say yes to the show, you'll have to move to LA. It's good timing since Bright Star is opening an LA branch this fall. They say you could be based out of there."

"They want me to leave?"

Leave Seoul? Leave Minseok and everything that I've been building here?

Hongjoo takes my hand in hers. "They think it would be a fresh start. You've done well to fix things here. But there are still antis who could be a threat to your safety. We haven't figured out who leaked the midsummer backstage video, yet. And we're continuing to investigate the death threat and the most heinous online comments. It might be bad enough that we'll have to take legal action. LA might be a safer place for you right now."

"I need time to think about it," I whisper.

"They want an answer this week," Hongjoo says gently, almost apologetically. "You worked so hard for this, Hyeri. It means that people are recognizing your talent."

"Yeah," I agree, but why doesn't hearing this make me happy? Isn't this what I've always wanted? "It's just a lot to take in."

"I know it's scary. But you need to figure out what your priorities are right now. And if you choose this, you have to commit."

She doesn't say it out loud, but I know what she's implying. If I choose this opportunity, I can't have Minseok too.

FORTY-TWO
HYERI

don't answer any of the calls I get. Not from my mom. Not from Minseok.

I know what my mom will say. That I have to take this role. That it's going to be a breakout opportunity.

And I know that if I talk to Minseok, I'll have to tell him about the show in LA. But I'm scared. What if he asks me not to go? Will I be strong enough to say no? Do I even want to say no?

The next day, I'm in the kitchen when I hear the soft knock on the door. I know it's Minseok. He has the code to my door, but he waits for me to answer.

"Are you hungry?" He lifts a pastry bag from a bakery that makes my favorite cream-filled buns.

"Yeah," I say, for once not thinking about my diet.

He sits on the couch and holds the pastry bag out to me. I take it with a wobbly smile, sitting next to him.

"What happened with Hongjoo-noona?" he finally asks.

"What?" I squeak out. Does he know about *Musical Dreams*?

And then I realize he's asking about her catching us together. I sigh, putting the pastry bag on the coffee table. My stomach is tied in too many knots to keep anything down. "She says it's too risky to sneak around like this."

"She's right."

My heart drops at how quickly he gives up.

"But we knew from the beginning it was risky," he says, eyes sharp and challenging. "Nothing has changed for me. Has it changed for you?"

I'm not sure how to answer. It feels like I care about him more than I thought possible, but I'm not a naive thirteen-year-old anymore. I know the price of this now. "I don't know. There are things I have to take into consideration."

"Like what?" Minseok frowns. "Did something else happen?"

This is the moment. I need to tell him about LA and the TV show. If he wants to walk away after hearing, there's nothing I can do about it. I should just rip the Band-Aid off.

"It's just that . . ." I can't force out the rest of the words.

Minseok nods and takes my hand in his. "I know."

Wait, *does* he know about the offer? Did someone at the company tell him?

"Hongjoo probably told you that you have to think about the fans. That we're still building trust with them again. And she's not wrong, but she's not completely right. We don't owe everything we are to the fans. We're allowed to keep some of it for ourselves." He lifts my knuckles to his lips. "And we don't have to figure everything out now."

"You really think so?" I ask.

He nods. "Why don't we sit down with Hongjoo and Hanbin after the Awards show and figure out a plan that works for us? That is, if you still want this."

Sparks race up and down my limbs. Minseok always seems to say the perfect thing to make me ignore my doubts.

"I want this," I say. I don't have to give this up yet, I still have time.

Minseok's smile blooms, slow but wide, and it chases away the worst of my anxieties.

"Oh thank god." He pulls my arm so suddenly that I'm not ready for it and I tumble into his lap. "For a second there, I was worried you didn't feel the same way."

"Don't forget I'm the one who liked you first."

"Eh, debatable," Minseok says with a grin. "This thing between us isn't for some show or for other people."

"I know."

He cups my cheeks, leaning in to rest his forehead against mine. "This isn't pretend anymore, Hyeri."

I nod in agreement a moment before he kisses me. Hard and possessive. But it's fine, because I feel just as needy at the moment. I'll tell him about LA and the show after the Hallyu Wave Awards. Not just yet. If we only have a few weeks left, then let it be just for us.

FORTY-THREE
MINSEOK

Minseok knows there are things to worry about. But he's just usually not the type to do it.

He knows Hyeri is, though. He can tell she's worrying a lot these days by the way she spaces out in the middle of conversations, getting lost in her own anxious thoughts.

Every time he prods her back into the moment, she smiles and insists she's fine. But Minseok knows there's something bothering her. And it's probably the fear that they won't be able to keep their relationship from the press.

There are many other idols and celebrities who do it. Some for years. But the media seems to have an obsession with catching Hyeri in another scandal.

Maybe the solution is to figure out how to make the press forget about her. But aside from Hyeri retiring from the industry, he can't figure out a way to do it.

He slips out of the apartment. It's early enough that none of the guys are awake. But he knows Hyeri will be. She's an early riser. So, he's also taken up the habit so he can sneak out and spend the mornings with her.

The door opens, but instead of Hyeri it's Hongjoo that emerges.

Minseok stops in his tracks. "Noona, good morning."

Hongjoo glances down at Minseok's slippered feet. He didn't even bother to put on outside shoes for the quick trip across the hall. He knows he's caught, but he hopes perhaps Hongjoo takes pity and pretends they're not blatantly disregarding her.

It's no use as she sighs and crosses her arms. "Minseok-ssi, this is not smart."

"We're being careful."

Hongjoo laughs. "That's the same excuse Hyeri gave me. Did you study the same script?"

Minseok tries one of his charming grins. "Noona, come on. We're not children. We can have a relationship if it's not hurting anyone."

"It will hurt your fans."

"They'll get over it," Minseok wants to say, but he knows it's the obstinate and shortsighted response. Instead, he says, "It's what we want."

"So, you'll just be together for another couple of weeks and then what? Long distance? Hyeri won't have as much time for phone calls and video chats as you might think. She's going to be busy on set."

"On set?" Minseok frowns. "What do you mean long distance? Where is she going?"

Hongjoo sighs. "So she didn't tell you."

Minseok feels a gnawing worry. A sensation that he hates acknowledging. "Tell me what?" His words are carefully flat.

The idea that Hyeri kept something from him doesn't sit well.

And the way Hongjoo gives him a sympathetic frown feels too parallel to the moment Hanbin had to explain to him that Jongdae and Sooyeon had been dating behind everyone's backs. To Minseok, it says, "Oh wow, they didn't tell you? How embarrassing."

"She was offered a role on a show in LA. She'll leave for the table read after the Hallyu Wave Awards."

"That's next week."

"Maybe she was waiting to tell you."

Or maybe she didn't intend to tell him at all. But if Minseok is good at anything, it's hiding his true emotions. So, he nods and gives a small smile to Hongjoo. "Thanks for letting me know. I'll see you at the awards show?"

But when he turns to go, Hongjoo says, "Minseok-ah?" Her face is set in a serious frown. "This is a big opportunity for her. She's taking a while to accept it, and I suspect it's because she doesn't want to leave you. But I don't know if she'll get a chance like this again."

Minseok doesn't like where this seems to be going. "What are you trying to say, Noona?"

"I'm saying when she does tell you, you should tell her to go."

"We can still . . ." He trails off, already hearing the desperation in his voice. Already knowing it's impossible to have it all in this industry.

Isn't this what he was pissed at Jongdae for? That his friend had tried to have it all and just made things worse. He can hear JD's voice now, calling him a hypocrite.

And he just nods. "Okay, I'll tell her to go."

Hongjoo gives him a pat on the shoulder, her eyes sad with the knowledge of what she's asking. "Thank you, Minseok-ah."

K-Pop Fan Attic article:
"Shin Hyeri Rumored to Be Cast in Hit
US Show *Musical Dreams*."

Rumors are circulating that producers of *Musical Dreams*, last year's breakout teen drama, have reached out to Bright Star Entertainment to cast rising rookie actress Shin Hyeri. If cast, this would be Shin's second acting role, and this time it's a big step up to Hollywood.

Sources say that Shin Hyeri might relocate to LA, where she grew up. This seems in line with rumors that Bright Star is looking to open an LA branch to both recruit and train new talent in the United States. If true, Shin Hyeri would be their first big name based out of that branch.

Shin stole hearts with her turn as the mean girl with a dark past in *Youthful Exchange*, one of the biggest dramas of the year. And she is currently one half of the beloved Shin-Moon couple on *Our Celebrity Marriage* with global K-pop star Moonster of WDB.

Fans are excited to see Shin in a breakout American role. Shin truly seems to be a bright new star.

FORTY-FOUR
HYERI

hurry across the hall, knocking on Minseok's door frantically instead of using the doorbell.

How did this information get leaked? I haven't even said yes yet. I need to tell Minseok before he sees this.

When he opens the door, I try to scan his face. Try to see if he looks upset. But Minseok's expression is neutral. Maybe he hasn't read the articles.

"Are you okay? You look upset." Is his voice more distant? Colder? Or am I just being paranoid?

"I needed to tell you something important."

"Sure." He opens the door to let me in.

When I do, I hurry to toe off my shoes while he walks into the kitchen.

I find him at the fridge, pulling out a Coke before offering me the brand of iced Americano I like.

I start to say I'm fine, but then I take it, needing something to do with my hands.

"Did you read the article?" I blurt out. I can't take the anxiety of not knowing.

"I did," he says, before taking a long sip of his Coke. Why isn't he reacting—being surprised or upset or anything? He's just blank.

The thing that scares me the most is that I've known him long enough to know that when Minseok gets really, truly angry, it's not intense or hot. It's cold like frost. I've been watching him icing out his own best friend— I know he's capable of doing it to me, too.

"I wasn't keeping it from you," I start to say frantically.

He holds up a hand. "You're not the first person to keep secrets, Hyeri. You won't be the last."

I can't tell if he sounds angry or not, and it's playing havoc with my nerves. "I just needed time to think."

"Well, you've had a week now, have you made up your mind?"

I start to list out my excuses when I finally catch what he said. "How do you know it's been a week?"

"It doesn't matter," he says. "I think you should take the role."

"What?" I'm still reeling that he knew this whole time.

"It's a good opportunity. It means what we did with *OCM* worked. You can't let this chance go."

"But we said that we were going to—"

"You didn't want this to be serious between us. Isn't something like this the reason? So we could be free to take a big opportunity without having to worry about the other person?"

"No." I shake my head. That wasn't my intention. That makes it all sound so cold, so calculating. "It was because I didn't know what I wanted us to be."

"Now you don't have to decide," Minseok points out, drinking the last of his Coke before turning to rinse the can in the sink.

"Are you angry at me?" I can't help but ask.

He sighs, pressing his hands into the counter to lean on them a moment. As if the effort to hold up his own weight is suddenly too taxing. "There's a reason you didn't tell me about the role, isn't there?"

"I'm sorry—" I start to say, but Minseok stops me.

"I think you didn't tell me because you didn't want me to talk you out of it."

It feels like he's putting words in my mouth, but I can't find the right way to dispute it.

Minseok nods, like he's taking my silence as confirmation. "I'm just trying to keep this uncomplicated. I messed up once with you when I pushed you away for my career. I'm telling you that I'm okay if you choose yours now."

This past week, I'd been avoiding even thinking about the role. Or what I was going to do about it. But suddenly, hearing Minseok tell me to take it, to leave him, I feel a cold flash of fear. I don't think I can do this. "What if I stay? Can't we—"

"What?" He does turn now, incredulity flashing across his handsome features. "Are you seriously talking about giving up something so big? For what? A non-relationship?"

My breath gets caught in my throat at the surprise of seeing his anger. "That's how you saw us?" I gasp out. Great, it sounds like I'm about to cry. Embarrassment weaves through me.

"Hyeri, you've worked too hard to get where you are. Didn't you tell me that you wanted to show the antis they couldn't push you down? This is your chance."

"But there can be other chances. You and I—"

He shakes his head, cutting me off. "No, I can't be responsible for you passing this up. You'll end up resenting me for it. I don't want that responsibility."

I need to take a minute to gather myself before I respond. "You don't want the *responsibility*? I'm not a child."

"Then stop acting like one," he bites out. "Make the adult decision here, Hyeri. For once in your life stop making your choices based on everyone else around you!"

This feels so eerily like four years ago, when Minseok yelled at me to stop being immature. When he said that my crush was selfish. He apologized for doing it, but now it's happening again. I guess he was never sorry after all. I close my eyes, because it's the only way to stop myself from crying. I don't need that right now.

I take deep breaths, relaxing my body one zone at a time until I am calm enough to look him in the eyes without breaking down.

"You're right, this is a huge opportunity," I say coldly. I feel so numb right now. "Maybe LA is the change I need to get away from all the baggage I have here."

With my chin high, I turn to leave, trying to hold on to what little dignity I have left in front of him. My shoes refuse to slide on easily. The more I struggle with them, the more they refuse to fit. It ruins the facade of calm, but I don't care anymore as I just flatten the heels, shuffling out quickly to escape back into the hallway. I can't be here anymore. I can't look at him right now.

When I enter my apartment, the door closes with a low beep. I turn and kick my shoes off, hitting the wall. Imagining that it's Minseok's body instead.

I hate him so much right now, and not because he was cruel. But because he was right.

K-Pop Fan Attic article: "Kim Ana Brought in for Questioning by Police in Drug Case"

It has been reported that K-pop idol Kim Ana was brought in by Gangnam police for questioning regarding allegations that she smuggled benzodiazepines into the country.

According to reports, officials were given evidence that Kim had brought an unknown amount of benzodiazepines into the country after visiting family in the United States this spring. Benzodiazepines (along with opiates and amphetamines) are strictly prohibited from import into South Korea, even with a doctor's prescription. Kim admitted she was prescribed the drugs by her childhood doctor in the United States before becoming a trainee. Kim was later released without charge.

According to Han Jongyul, the CEO of Fantazee Entertainment, Kim had taken the medication as a child due to anxiety over the death of a close relative. When she moved to Seoul to become a trainee, she had not been made aware that the drug was illegal in South Korea. She received a refill of her old prescription on her recent trip back to the States before beginning filming of her drama. Nerves over her first drama caused a relapse of her anxiety.

Though many fans are supportive of Kim, some seem disillusioned with the idol once deemed the "nation's princess."

Kim is currently starring in her first drama, *Idol Academy*, which has been struggling in the ratings.

FORTY-FIVE
HYERI

The Hallyu Wave Awards were once a bucket list goal of mine.

My stylist dressed me in a gorgeous ocean-blue dress with lace over-lay that sparkles as I walk. I should feel like a princess attending a ball. Instead, I'm too numb to enjoy it.

I'm late getting ready because David was double-booked. And by the time I walk the red carpet, I'm the last to arrive.

An assistant hurries me inside and points me toward my table. I thank them, trying to sneak to my seat without causing any distractions. But a few feet from my assigned table, I freeze.

I knew who I'd be seated with. Since I'm nominated for my work on *OCM*, it makes sense that I'd be with Minseok. I thought I'd mentally prepared for seeing him again. But the mere sight of the back of his head makes me start to hyperventilate.

I try to do my breathing exercise, relaxing myself by zones. But it's not working. Minseok shifts in his seat, starting to turn as if he senses my presence.

And, freaking out, I hurry away. I can't talk to him right now, not in this state. I rush to the back and dip into the bathroom.

I hide away in one of the stalls, wondering how long I can wait here until my absence is noted. I pull out my phone, texting Hongjoo to tell me when I have to be in my seat for my award nominations. Then I close the top lid of the toilet and sit.

I make it over half an hour before my butt starts to become numb. I'm wondering if I should just give in and go to my seat when two women come into the bathroom, gossiping about the outfits.

"I didn't realize poof sleeves were back," one of them declares. "I wonder if I should talk to my stylist before the next awards show."

"Did you see Kim Ana's?"

"Yea, she looks gorgeous as usual."

"Can you believe she'd even come tonight? Isn't there a rule against criminals coming to these kinds of things?"

"Omo, do you think she really did it?"

"Who cares? She's always been so high-and-mighty, thinking she's better than everyone when she's just a rookie. Serves her right."

I flinch at the words. It's a tone I'm too used to overhearing when people talk about my own scandals. It's way too triggering, even if it's not directed at me.

"Did you hear that some sasaeng is selling Ana's trash online? People think it's the same person who anonymously tipped off the police."

The other girl laughs. "Maybe Ana's company can buy the evidence back to keep her out of jail."

This isn't right; I should speak up. But something holds me back. A fear of getting involved and becoming the new target. So, instead, I take the coward's way and flush the toilet to let them know they're not alone. And immediately the gossip stops. When I push out of the stall, the two women are gone.

I feel a weird stab of guilt that I didn't say anything. Haven't I wished in the past that at least one person would stick up for me when false rumors were being spread? And now here I am overhearing gossip about one of my peers and I'm doing nothing about it too.

I wash my hands just to give myself a bit more time to collect myself.

When I get to my table, Minseok is gone. I can't help but look around for him.

One of the sunbaes leans toward me. "He was taken backstage for the Best Couple category. They want all of you to stand onstage for it."

That's right. I close my eyes in frustration. Hongjoo did mention an interview, but I've been too busy stressing about seeing Minseok here to remember.

"Shin Hyeri-ssi." An assistant PD hurries over. "I'm glad you're back. We need you backstage, please."

"Yes, of course. I'm sorry." I hurry after him, feeling bad that I caused any sense of a rush.

Minseok is alone next to the other three couples who are nominated. I can tell, even from this distance, that his suit is perfectly tailored to fit his frame.

Standing there, backlit by the stage lights, he looks so handsome. And goose bumps rise on my arms despite myself. It hurts to see him waiting for me like that. Because a part of me can imagine his smile spread as I run up to him. I can even feel the ghost of his arms coming around me.

Instead, when he turns to look at me, his face is blank. It's not until I'm only a few feet away that I see how turbulent his eyes are.

"Hyeri," he says softly.

"Minseok," I reply tightly; just getting his name out takes so much effort.

An assistant comes over to line us up and I welcome the distraction. Minseok and I are last. I feel like he's too close; his arm is just centimeters away from brushing mine. I take a small side step away just as the music for the show swells, signaling that the commercial break is over.

The other couples enter the stage as they're announced. And when our names are called, Minseok offers his arm. The other couples walked onstage arm in arm, and I know it's probably expected of us too. But I'm scared to touch him. Scared of how it will make me feel to be that close. Reluctantly, I rest my hand on his arm, ignoring the electricity that rushes down my skin at the touch.

It's just a few minutes. And you don't even have to look at him.

The host, a well-known and beloved comedian, walks down the line to interview the couples. Minseok and I are the last in line, but I'm already anxious just waiting for our turn.

His free hand comes up to cover mine in the crook of his elbow. I tense slightly, and he lets his hand drop again.

"And finally, our youngest couple, Moonster and Shin Hyeri!"

There's a huge cheer from the balcony where the fans are seated. Banners wave and I notice that some of them say *Go ShinMoon couple!* I'm surprised; I didn't realize that we have fans like that.

It takes a while for the cheering to fade and the interviewer chuckles. "Looks like you're one of our hottest couples and I'm not surprised. Your relationship on *Our Celebrity Marriage* is very heartwarming. Tell us, did you expect to be nominated for an award like this?"

Minseok leans in to answer. "Honestly, it feels like the first time WDB was a contender for first place on a music show. Except, I might cry more if we win this one." He grins at the crowd as they burst into laughter.

"Hyeri-ssi?"

"I'm just really grateful that a show that's been so fun to film has been received so well." It's a perfect reply, and not even one I needed pre-written for me. I know that Hongjoo would approve.

"We actually have a request for you, Hyeri-ssi."

"Oh?" My nerves flare. The other couples weren't asked to do anything. Is this because we're the youngest? Like some kind of hazing thing? I force myself to smile.

"We're wondering if you could finally call Moonster Oppa?"

I can't help stiffening, my hand flexing involuntarily on Minseok's arm. His hand comes up again to cover mine and this time I don't do anything to stop him. The camera's red-light focus is too glaring to do anything that wouldn't be caught live.

I hope my smile doesn't waver and I reply. "Of course. Anything for the fans."

I turn to Minseok, and he loosens his grip to let me face him.

His expression is carefully blank.

The host holds the mic by my face. That's probably for the best. My palms feel sweaty and if I try to hold the mic, it might go flying out of my grip.

Just the thought of saying it reminds me of the last time I called him Oppa. How happy we were together. I close my eyes and force away the memory.

I take a deep breath, clear my throat. "Opp—"

My throat constricts on the word, making the end an awkward squeak.

"Oh, I don't know if that should count," the host teases. "What do you guys think?"

"Again, again, again!" chants the crowd in the balcony.

I nod and take another deep breath. I can't quite look Minseok in the eyes as I do this, so I stare at the tip of his nose as I force a smile, and blurt out, "Oppa!"

The cheers from the balcony are wild, and the host has to speak louder to be heard over them. "I think they're happy with that one!"

I don't even hear the rest of his words as he introduces the short snippets from each of our shows.

But I can feel my whole body tingling. My breath comes in shallow gasps. I'm about to start hyperventilating, and I need to get out of here. What will I do if we win? Can I get through an entire speech like this?

Minseok's arm comes around my shoulders. I want to shrug it off, but I know I can't. He leans down, whispers in my ear. "Just take a deep breath, Hyeri, it's almost over."

I want to say something pithy. To tell him that I don't need his help. But in this moment, I don't have the ability to do that. Instead, I obey, pulling in a deep breath. It helps. The world stops spinning.

"You okay?" Minseok asks.

I can see the worry in his eyes. It makes me want to cry. It makes me want to just wrap my arms around him and beg him to erase the last week so we can go back to being happy together.

"And the winner is . . ."

We don't win. But I'm relieved—it would have been agony to accept an award for Best Couple when my relationship with Minseok is in shambles. After the other couple's names are announced, I pull away from Minseok so his arm drops from my shoulders. I use the excuse of congratulating the winners as a reason to separate from him.

And then I rush off the stage with the others.

All I can think is I need to get out of here. I feel like I'm completely losing my composure, and I can't let it happen in front of all these people. I hurry off the stage, to the darkness in the wings.

I'm sure I'm about to burst into tears or start hyperventilating. Either option is not optimal right now.

Someone calls my name and I scurry away. I can't talk to anyone in this state. I yank open the first door I find.

It turns out to be a storage closet, filled with lighting equipment.

But before the door fully swings shut, Minseok grabs it, stepping into the doorframe.

"Hyeri, are you okay?"

"Why do you care?" The angry words spill out before I realize they're living inside me.

He steps into the closet, letting the door close. Darkness envelops us. I hear Minseok's muttered cursing. He searches the walls, finally finding the switch on the one behind me.

When the low light blinks on, he's leaning into me. His arm is snaked around my back, still pressing the switch.

I nudge him away. "What do you want, Minseok?"

He sighs, running an agitated hand over the back of his neck. The movement makes my heart spark in reaction before it fades into even deeper depression. It sucks that I'm still so attracted to him when just being around him makes me want to cry.

"I don't want this to be how it ends between us," he says softly.

"We still have a few more things to shoot for *OCM*," I point out stiffly.

He scowls and the bare bulb overhead casts the expression into even angrier shadows. "That's not what I mean."

"I don't know what you want from me," I say, exhausted. "You told me to go to LA, so I am."

"I just—" He bites off the word, his arms coming up in frustration. He bumps his elbow against a shelf in the cramped space and lets out a curse.

"Can I go?" I ask.

"This all feels so messed up." He is still rubbing at his arm. "This isn't how I wanted this to play out."

"Then tell me how you imagined it? What perfect breakup scenario can I give you?"

"Hyeri." He growls out my name like a warning, but I'm incensed. How dare he lay his stress at my feet like I'm the guilty party.

"You know, I've been going over that last conversation again and again. And I call bullshit," I say.

"Bullshit?"

"Yeah. You told me to make my own choices, while at the same time making a decision for me."

Minseok scowls. "That's not what I was doing."

"Yes it is. You did it four years ago too. If you don't want to be with me, fine. But stop pretending like you're doing it for my own good." I feel too claustrophobic in here now. I push past him, opening the door and bursting out into the hall.

"Hyeri," he calls after me.

I hurry away, the tears I held in so successfully now on the verge of falling.

I know I can't cry. It'll ruin my makeup and we still have half of the awards show to go.

"Hyeri, please." He grabs my hand and turns me to face him.

We're close enough to the stage now that I can hear the announcers. "And now to present the award for Best Newcomer ..."

"I'm such an idiot," Minseok starts to say, his hand coming up to cup my cheek. And all my resolve starts melting away. I want to just lean into him, take in the smell and feel of him.

"I have to get back to my seat," I say, but I don't pull away.

"Maybe you're right. Maybe I have regrets about how I handled all of it." He's leaning down, eyes aligning with mine. Lips aligning with mine.

I have to stop him. If this happens it'll definitely mess me up.

"And the winner is ... Shin Hyeri!"

I turn at the call of my name, but Minseok still grips my hand. Holding me beside him.

A stagehand hurries over. "Hyeri-ssi, that's you! You have to go onstage!"

She must be harried because she doesn't even blink at Minseok and me standing here together, hands still clasped.

"Oh yes." I pull away from him as I'm ushered to the stage. But I can't help one last backward glance. Minseok is already walking away, though. And so I turn toward the bright lights of the stage to accept my award.

FORTY-SEVEN
HYERI

f anyone asked me, I could not tell them what I said in my acceptance speech. I'm not sure if I looked poised or harried or what. I just know that I blurted out some words and thanked my parents and my company. And then I numbly followed the presenters off the stage, gripping the little award shaped like a golden wave.

People are patting my back, congratulating me. I force a smile, though my brain isn't processing any of their faces.

Once the crowd around me thins, an assistant PD asks me if I'd like to be escorted back to my seat. My seat? Next to Minseok. I shake my head quickly. "No, I need to . . . use the restroom."

Before they can reply, I escape into the same corridor I went down with Minseok. Except it's completely empty now.

I walk until I come to the exit for the back stairwell. There are crates of sound equipment stacked, and I just lean against one.

I need to let my heart settle. I need to make sure I won't burst into tears.

They'll understand. I'll just say I was overwhelmed from winning the award.

I stare down at the shiny metal plaque. It says my name. It really does. But the joy I know I should feel in this moment doesn't come. It's buried under layers and layers of confusion.

The door to the stairwell opens, and I jump up to move out of the way.

It shouldn't shock me at this point that the person who comes through is Kim Ana. She's the last person I'd want to see right now, so of course it's her. She is gorgeous in an asymmetrical black satin dress. But despite her perfect hair and outfit, she looks frazzled.

She stares at me in stunned silence. Her eyes are rimmed in red. I can see a smudge of her mascara across her temple. She was crying.

"Excuse me," she says with a quick bow.

"Wait!" I call out.

She hesitates but doesn't turn right away. Finally, with a sigh, she does. "What? Do you also have an unsolicited opinion about my apparent rampant drug use?"

"What?" I frown. "No, you just have a smudge right here." I reach out and wipe at the mascara.

Ana gawks at me. "Are you serious? That's it? You wanted to help fix my makeup?"

"There's still an hour left of the show." I state the obvious, not sure what else to say. "You probably didn't want to go back out there with your makeup smudged."

Ana shakes her head in bewilderment. "Of all people, don't you want to throw my scandal in my face the most?"

I pause at the obvious implication. She thinks I'm some kind of petty witch. And maybe, some part of me did feel satisfaction at seeing the article at first. But now I shake my head slowly. "No, because of all people I know how much it sucks to have everyone gossip about you like they have a right to judge everything you do."

Ana's eyes widen before they fill with tears.

"Oh, um . . ." I'm not sure what to do. So, I pat her shoulder awkwardly in a not-quite-hug. "It's going to be okay. You'll overcome this."

She sniffles and mutters, "This is so embarrassing."

I almost laugh, because I truly understand the feeling. "I swear, it's not as bad as it feels in this moment."

She sighs. "I'm sorry, I shouldn't have done that. You shouldn't have to be the one who comforts me."

That takes me by surprise. Is she really acknowledging the messed-up relationship between us?

I'm about to ask when I hear someone approaching. I start to turn to block their view of Ana, knowing she wouldn't want someone to see her with mascara running down her face.

"Kim Ana!" Kwak Dongha hurries forward, a wide smile spreading across his face. "I have a gift for you!"

I start to lift my hands in defense, instinctively expecting an attack.

But when he thrusts his hand out it's not to strike but to offer. In his hand is a prescription bottle.

FORTY-EIGHT
HYERI

"Why do you have that?" I ask, staring at the label. It's partially ripped but *Anna Kim* is written clear as day at the top. The bottle is the orange kind that you get in the States, and while I don't recognize the drug name, it's clearly the same one that the gossip articles are referencing.

Dongha glowers at me. "What are you doing with Ana? Are you harassing her?"

I can't hold back a laugh. Unfortunately, it makes Dongha's frown deepen. "You're really accusing me of harassment when you have that?"

"It's a gift for Ana!" Dongha insists.

"Dongha, right?" Ana says quietly behind me. "Can you please just tell us why you have that? It was stolen from my trash." Ana is using all of her sweet-girl charm on him right now and from the way his eyes widen and his lips waver, it's working. I would be annoyed and jealous if I weren't more worried about making sure Dongha doesn't make any sudden moves at us.

"This?" He holds up the prescription pill bottle.

"Yes, that thing that's being used by a sasaeng fan to spread rumors about Ana," I say.

"I didn't steal it, I bought it. And I'm not a sasaeng fan. It's not stalking to support your bias. That's what being a fan is about!" He's practically yelling at me now, like he's lecturing me on the dos and don'ts of toxic fandom.

"Well, what else are we supposed to think? Ana says that was stolen. It's being used to create actual legal charges against her. And now you have it."

"What? No! I didn't steal anything. I wasn't even in Seoul last week. I was in Gyeonggi-do for Pink Petal's performance at Suwon; there are videos on my social media."

He reaches into his pocket, and I push Ana back to safety. But he just pulls his phone out and scrolls through it quickly. He holds it up to a clip of him in the crowd clear as day with his fan sign, screaming his head off for Mika.

"Fine," I admit, though I don't let my guard down. He might not be the sasaeng fan that stole the bottle, but he still feels dangerous. "You said you bought it? Who sold it to you?"

He glares at me, and I realize I'm the wrong person to ask this question. I turn to Ana and she nods, picking up the silent signal. "Please can you tell us who sold it to you?"

His face softens and he looks apologetic. "I don't know who it was, just an account in our Kim Ana Über Fan forum."

I glance at Ana for her reaction to that. But ever the professional, she keeps a blank face.

"What's the account?" she asks.

Dongha's eyes slide to me. "HyeriTopAnti."

"Of course it was," I mutter, and Dongha's face pinches defensively.

"How did they get the package to you?" Ana asks.

"They just said I could pick it up in a public locker and gave me the code. That's it. I swear I would never do anything to hurt you; you're my princess."

I shudder—the intense adoration on his face borders on dangerous obsession. I see Ana's lips thin. Seems she's not completely oblivious to it either.

"How did they send you the code for the locker?" I ask.

"They DM'd it with the verification photo."

"Verification photo?"

He sighs and pulls out his phone. "It's how we verify we actually have the thing we're selling in the forums."

He shows a picture of the medicine bottle next to a piece of paper with the handle "HyeriTopAnti" and a recent date scribbled on it.

I stare at the handwriting. A part of me hoped I'd recognize it. That I'd be able to identify who it was somehow, but there's no recognition.

"Fine, thanks," I say.

"Wait." Ana reaches out and grabs the phone. Dongha looks elated as her hand brushes his. She zooms into the note at a logo at the top of the pad. "Isn't that . . ."

She trails off as I lean in to see too. And all the air slams out of my lungs. It's David's salon logo.

FORTY-NINE
HYERI

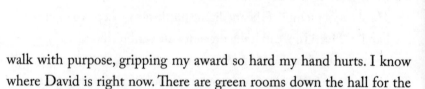

walk with purpose, gripping my award so hard my hand hurts. I know where David is right now. There are green rooms down the hall for the musical acts to change and freshen up during the show.

He's supposed to be doing hair for Kastor's performance.

HyeriTopAnti can't be David. He's always been there for me, comforted me when things are really bad. He's one of the few people I've let see me at my lowest.

That whole time, was he just pretending? Was he actually happy to see me so depressed? Did he collect secrets about me to warp into twisted versions of the truth and post for the world to see?

"It's not him," I whisper.

"It could be anyone," Ana replies even though I wasn't talking to her.

"When you're in the public eye like us, anyone around us could have an agenda."

I close my eyes because they're starting to burn. She's right, I know she is. But still, it can't be David. I don't know what I'd do if it was him.

I find the dressing room with Kastor's group name on the outside.

Their performance was in the first half of the show, but some of them might still be inside. I wonder if I could still confront David with witnesses.

They're not there. And neither is David. The room is empty except for Jeongho, who is packing away the supplies.

A part of me is relieved David isn't here. But a part of me flares with anxiety. Where is he? Is he sneaking around to find more dirt on me?

"Have you seen David?" I ask.

"Nope." Jeongho glances up, then does a double take, eyes widening. And I realize he's not looking at me but behind me. At Ana.

"You're here," he breathes out. The expression on his face looks a bit too bright, a bit too manic. It's an expression I've seen before. A look of obsession.

"Ah, yes, are you a fan?" Ana says politely. She's still glancing around the room. Like maybe there will be a clue.

But I'm focused on Jeongho now. He steps forward, still clutching a curling iron.

I instinctively put myself between him and Ana. And when his lips twist into anger, I'm sure I'm right.

"It was you, wasn't it?" I say. "HyeriTopAnti. You're the one who stole the pill bottle."

I hear Ana's sharp intake behind me.

Jeongho sighs, his eyes narrowing as he glares at me. He's wielding the curling iron like a weapon now. "So what? You can't prove it."

"Wait, I'm confused, I thought it was David," Ana says behind me.

"This is his assistant," I explain. "He'd have access to the same letterhead at the salon."

"Letterhead?" Jeongho sounds almost bored.

"The proof photo you sent Kwak Dongha when you sold him the bottle." I watch his face for the shock that comes with being caught. But there is none. Instead, he looks slightly annoyed.

"So, what do you want?" he says.

I'm taken aback by his reaction. Any normal person would at least show some guilt or apprehension at being confronted like this. But from the way he glares at us, he doesn't seem to think he did anything wrong.

"Why did you do it?" I ask, confused. It's me he hates, not Ana.

"You mean why did I take the pill bottles? Or why did I give one to the police?"

"Both." Ana is the one who answers, a small frown on her pretty face.

"Because I loved you," Jeongho spits out.

It's enough to have Ana hunching away from him. I find her hand with mine. She squeezes hard enough to rub bone against bone.

"I did everything for you. I knew you were special the moment I saw your introduction in *CiPro*. I made dozens of accounts to vote for you. I sent you gifts. I even tried to protect you from anyone who wanted to hurt you." He scowls at me now.

"You mean me?" I ask.

"You tried to sabotage Ana in *CiPro*; you were jealous of her!" I want to protest, but I'm too scared that it will set him off further. Instead, I take a small step away, pulling Ana with me. I'm still gripping my award and I lift it slightly. It's heavy enough to use as a weapon if I have to.

"I started HyeriTopAnti to make sure you were punished for what you did to Ana on the show. But it wasn't enough. People were forgetting. So, I leaked the story about the bullying to make sure they remembered."

"You didn't need to do that. I'm not in competition with Ana, I'm not even an idol anymore."

Anger twists his features as he flings the curling iron at us. It slams into the dressing room door, denting the metal. I barely manage to pull Ana out of the way, dropping my award with a loud clatter.

"Because you still needed to pay! You don't deserve your career after the way you treated Ana. I was going to make sure no one forgot what a bully you were, but you got in my way at the midsummer festival."

"The midsummer festival?" I say, confused. "Wait, was that you backstage? You were the one who stole Ana's flower pin? What were you going to do, plant it in my dressing room?" When I see his eyes flare, I know I'm right. I'm realizing how deep his delusions run. I glance toward the door. We can't be in here. We need to get help.

But Ana leans into me; it feels like she's too overcome to run. I don't know if I'll be able to drag her with me fast enough to escape Jeongho.

He's returned to the tray of tools now, his fingers running over the straightening iron. "I thought that by leaking the video of you and Moonster it would be just as bad. And it worked, Ana got the role in the drama over you."

I close my eyes. Of course the video leak was Jeongho. He was there that night, he had access. And apparently, he hates my guts. I suspected it the first moment I met him, but I talked myself out of it because I thought I was being paranoid.

"But then Moonster took pity on you and let you leech off his popularity in that stupid marriage show. And now people have forgotten all over again!" His bright eyes move to Ana. "You noticed, right? All the things I did for you?"

She shakes her head, a sob escaping. "I never asked for you to hurt people for me. I never asked for you to start bullying rumors or any of that." There's a frustrated pain in her voice that sounds so familiar to me. It's a feeling that's lived deep inside me for over a year too.

"If you love Ana so much, why did you steal those prescription bottles?" I ask. "Why did you give them to the police?"

"I wanted a keepsake. Sometimes I just want to touch something Ana has touched." His gaze fills with longing. "You don't even want it anymore. And the others in the Kim Ana forum sometimes like to buy your things from me. They love you almost as much as I do."

I shudder at the infatuation I see on his face. Then it falls into a disturbed frown. "And then I saw the pills. And I realized my perfect princess took illegal drugs. I didn't *want* to give one of the bottles to the police, but I needed to teach you a lesson. Why couldn't you have stayed beautiful and perfect like you promised?" His eyes are wild, but also hazy like he's not looking at Ana, but some illusion he wishes she was.

"I-I'm sorry," she stutters, still quietly crying. She's shaking beside me, and I wrap an arm around her shoulders.

"It's not wrong to need help," I say, pulling her closer to the door inch by careful inch. If I can just get it open, then we can at least get the attention of someone in the hallway. We can get help. "There's a lot of stress and anxiety in this industry. It doesn't make her less worthy."

It was the wrong thing to say. Jeongho's eyes sharpen, no longer glazed over. "No, she enticed me on purpose. She promised to be our nation's princess, and she broke that promise!"

His hand grips a pair of shears, knocking the cart over in the process.

"Don't," I blurt out. "You love her. You can't hurt her."

"I do love you, Ana. And you broke my heart. So, now I have to punish you for it." He grips the scissors tighter as he lunges forward.

FIFTY-ONE
MINSEOK

Minseok is getting antsy. Where is Hyeri? She hasn't come back since she accepted her award.

His fingers tap on the table impatiently as he checks his watch again. Usually he doesn't wear one, but this was sent to his stylist by a designer, requesting he wear it to the awards show. An unofficial kind of sponsorship that he's gotten used to. And he is grateful for it right now. Because it would be too obvious for him to check his phone. If a wayward wide shot were shown at the wrong time, avid fans might be able to zoom in and claim that WDB's Moonster was fooling around on his phone during the show instead of paying attention to his sunbaes.

Hyeri has been gone for almost twenty minutes now. That's too long. She'd never let her anger at Minseok make her look unprofessional.

The music for the commercial break starts, and he pushes back from the table. He mutters an excuse about the bathroom and hurries off.

Is she really just hiding somewhere because she doesn't want to see him? Or is something wrong?

He made a mistake trying to kiss her earlier. No, actually, the mistake had been breaking up with her to begin with—or the non-breakup, because the original mistake had been letting her convince him to keep things undefined. He wants to define them. He wants to tell her that she can go to LA and have him too. That he'll wait for her.

Minseok steps into the backstage area and almost collides with a tall gangly man wearing a low baseball cap. No, wait, not a man, or barely one at least. It's that antifan that keeps bothering Hyeri. What was his name again? Kwang Donghwa? Kwak Dongeun?

"Kwak Dongha." Minseok snaps out the name, and the boy's head jerks up before he dashes away. But Minseok is fast enough to grab the other guy by the shoulder, trapping him against the wall.

"Where's Hyeri?"

"How should I know?" Dongha struggles against Minseok's hold.

"Security!" Minseok shouts.

"Fine, fine! She and Kim Ana went to go talk to some hairdresser guy. Dave or something."

"Why?" Minseok scowls.

"They think he's HyeriTopAnti."

"What?" The surprise is enough to make Minseok's grip loosen. Dongha pushes away, causing Minseok to slam into the opposite wall.

When Dongha races out of an emergency exit Minseok doesn't try to go after him. He has to find Hyeri.

FIFTY-TWO

HYERI

"But you already punished her, didn't you?" I blurt out, and it's enough to distract Jeongho. He stops mid-stride, his angry glare turning to me.

Ana is fully sobbing now.

"The pill bottle," I clarify even though my own voice is shaking. "You gave it to the police to punish Ana, right?"

"The police?" he says, frowning like he's trying to recall the details. "Yes, there were two, so I gave one to the police and the other . . ."

"You sold it, right? To another fan," I provide. I'm inching closer to the door. Ana is clinging so tight to me that I'm practically dragging her along the floor.

"It was compensation!" Jeongho shouts so loud that I flinch as I reach for the handle. "I've spent thousands on Ana. Going to concerts, bulk buying albums, traveling to international events. I deserved compensation for that after Ana failed to keep up her part of the deal."

"The deal that she would be perfect?" I prompt, hoping it'll distract him into another tirade. Now that I feel the cold metal of the handle in my hand, I'm terrified. What if I'm not fast enough?

I take a deep breath, readying myself to yank it open. My hand is so slick with sweat that the knob seems slippery beneath it. But I grip it tighter, counting to three in my head. One. Two.

I start to twist the knob, but the gesture turns my arm and my elbow nudges at Ana.

She lets out a terrified scream.

It pulls Jeongho's attention back to us. His eyes flare with rage as he lunges forward.

I pull on the door, but Ana is pushed too hard against me. I can't move her back and the door swings into us. We both go tumbling to the floor.

Jeongho plows into the open door, slamming it shut again.

I pull Ana to her feet, dragging her after me to the other end of the room, where there's another door. If I can get to it in time . . .

But Ana lets out a scream a second before she's yanked out of my arms. Jeongho pulls her back by the hair.

I pitch myself at him, using nails, teeth, anything to make him let go.

The two of us tumble to the ground together.

I land the wrong way. Something in my shoulder pops, and my vision goes searing white for just a second.

It's long enough for Jeongho to get the upper hand. He's perched over me, knee on my chest.

I faintly hear Ana crying. She's begging him to stop.

I try to tell her to get out, to get help, but I can't breathe, let alone speak.

"You two are the same. Two lying, manipulative gijibes." Jeongho lifts the shears. I grab his wrist, but the movement causes a stab of pain in my shoulder.

The sound of the door slamming open is quickly followed by someone shouting my name.

Jeongho and I look over at the same time. Just as Minseok launches himself at Jeongho.

Even with his weight removed, it hurts to move, but I have to get up. I see my discarded trophy and grab it with my good arm.

Minseok and Jeongho are tumbling across the floor, bumping into Ana, who lets out a scream. The sound has Jeongho glancing back, and I take my chance, pitching the trophy at him. It catches Jeongho in the temple. With a scream of pain, he pitches backward.

Surprised, Minseok turns to me, calling my name. But Jeongho rears up behind him, gripping the discarded pair of scissors.

"No!" I shout, but the warning is too late.

I watch Jeongho plunge the shears into Minseok's back.

FIFTY-THREE
HYERI

I let out a strangled scream as I hurry to Minseok, shielding him with my body. But it's not necessary. Jeongho is staring at the bloody shears in his hand.

"Bl-blood," he stutters out. "I didn't mean it. I didn't do it!" He drops the scissors with a clatter. The moment they hit the ground I kick them out of reach.

Jeongho crumples into a ball, gripping his hair with his bloody hands, wailing that he did nothing wrong.

I turn to Minseok.

He's holding his injured shoulder. Blood soaks through his jacket, dripping off the end of his sleeve.

I press my hands to the wound, and he grunts in pain.

"What do we do?" Ana asks with a whimper.

"Get help," I say. "Find someone and call one-one-nine."

She nods before racing out of the room.

"Should we tie him up or something?" Minseok nods his head at Jeongho, who's still curled up in a ball, crying.

"No, he's in too much shock right now to do anything." I grab someone's jacket and press it against Minseok's shoulder as hard as I can, hoping it'll stop the bleeding.

"Hey, maybe be a little gentler? I've kind of been stabbed," he grits out.

I ignore him, pressing harder. "I have to put pressure on the wound. Just take deep breaths and try not to pass out or anything."

"Sure," he says weakly with a pained smile. "Anyone ever tell you you're really pretty when you're bossy?"

I'm surprised that he can still annoy me and make me laugh in a moment like this. But he does both. "Stop making jokes, it'll just tire you out."

"Impossible," he quips. "I'm never too tired for a good joke."

The jacket is now soaked through, and Minseok looks too pale, his eyes half-lidded like he can barely keep them open.

"Don't go to sleep, okay?"

"I'll try, but no promises."

I press the wound harder. His weight is now leaning almost completely onto me. I wrap my arm around his shoulder to hold him steady. Or maybe it's to hold me steady. I let my cheek rest gently on the top of his head. Where is Ana? Why isn't anyone coming to help?

"How did you know?" I ask.

"You were gone too long. Shin Hyeri would never shirk her responsibilities."

I laugh. "So, my good manners alerted you?"

"Maybe I'm a little bit psychic too."

I laugh again, but it turns into a bit of a sob. "Sure, let's go with that."

"Hyeri?" Minseok asks, his voice slurred. "Earlier, you were right, I never should have made that decision for you. I never should have done a lot of things to you. . . ."

"Oppa, I didn't—"

The door bursts open with a flood of people and shouting voices.

Medics enter, carefully taking Minseok from me and lifting him onto a gurney. They carry him away before I can protest.

I fall to the floor, staring at the crumpled jacket in my hands, covered in his blood.

"Hyeri!" Hongjoo hurries into the room, and her eyes widen as she sees me. She practically slides across the floor, her arms coming around me.

"Eonni!" The word comes out as a sob and finally, the tears I held back start to fall.

FIFTY-FOUR
HYERI

t's been twelve hours and no one will tell me how Minseok is doing.

I've been kept in the hospital overnight for observation. Even though the worst of my injuries was a dislocated shoulder and a few bruises.

I haven't seen anyone except my nurses and Hongjoo all night.

If no one gives me an update on Minseok soon, I'm just going to go find him myself.

In fact, I start to climb out of my bed and slip on the little disposable slippers the hospital provides. I have no idea where Hongjoo put my shoes or my clothes. But I don't care.

I'm trying to put my IV on the portable pole when the door opens. I freeze guiltily, assuming it's probably Hongjoo. But it's not. It's Kim Ana.

She's also attached to an IV, but she's wearing normal clothes. Not her dress from the awards, but a set of sweats. I guess her manager brought them for her.

"Ana, are you okay?"

She stops a foot away from me, frowning, like she's not sure what to say.

"What is it? Is it Minseok?" My chest constricts with fear.

"No, I don't know anything about his status," she clarifies quickly. "But I wanted to see you."

"Okay" is all I say, waiting for her to continue.

"I guess I just wanted to say thank you."

I laugh. "I don't even remember half the things I said or did. I just wanted to get away from him."

"So, do you remember what he said about all the things he did to you? The rumors? Leaking your information?"

I nod. "Yeah, I remember."

"When they were taking him away, he was rambling about a pool. How he didn't know you couldn't swim. Does that mean anything to you?"

I didn't think I could be shocked by anything else, but I nod numbly. So there *was* someone at the pool with me. I wasn't just seeing things.

"He did all of that to you because of me," she says, tears glistening in her eyes. "I don't know how . . . I'm not sure what I can do to fix . . ."

"It's not your responsibility, Ana," I tell her, oddly calm. "You can't control people like Jeongho."

"I knew you'd had it hard since *CiPro* because of me," Ana admits, head hanging low. "I never asked people to say those things about you, but somehow it still felt like my fault. It made it hard for me to be around you. I figured you were probably pretty pissed at me. I wouldn't have blamed you."

It's weird to hear things from Ana's perspective, but it also somehow helps. "You didn't start this fake rivalry between us. The producers of *CiPro* and the media did it."

She nods, taking a deep breath. "There were moments where I knew I could speak up. But I was so scared that if I did, they'd target me next." She flinches at her own words. "I'm sorry."

I remember that moment in the bathroom, where I chose to hide instead of confronting the gossipers. "It's okay, I understand." I realize now that anytime I blamed Ana for what I was going through, it was misplaced. It was easy to make her the villain of my story, but she was just another victim of the machine that made us both.

We were just trying to survive in this industry the best we knew how.

"It's all right if we're never friends," I say. "But I hope that maybe we can move past all of this."

Ana nods and holds out her hand.

I take her offered palm. Instead of a shake, we just let our clasped hands hang between us, like a tentative bridge.

FIFTY-FIVE

HYERI

My mom arrives at the hospital in the afternoon. She's a flurry of energy. But under it all, I can see that she's worried. She actually tears up when she sees me, wrapping me in a hug that makes my sore shoulder throb. But I don't pull away. It's nice to see that she's a real mom at least when her daughter is put into physical danger.

I have a small but steady stream of visitors. Sohee and Bomi bring me a care package of face masks and fuzzy socks. They tell me that all the Kastor girls wanted to come, but they thought it might be too overwhelming.

"There are so many fans out front sitting vigil with signs," Bomi tells me.

"You should look out the window when you get a chance," Sohee adds. "There's so many people who love you, Eonni."

David comes with a giant bouquet covering half his face, like he's hiding from me. He looks like he hasn't slept.

"I'll understand if you want to request a different stylist for your upcoming schedules," he says. He hasn't been able to look me in the eyes the whole time he's been here.

"What? No!" I blurt out. "I don't want to work with anyone else but you. I won't let that asshole take anything else from me!"

David lets out a surprised laugh and steps forward to hug me. "I'm happy to see you haven't lost any of that spirit I always knew you had."

When Robbie and Jaehyung come with Hyejun, they bear gifts of contraband bags of Honey Butter Chips.

I know it must be Hyejun's idea, but he just shrugs like it's no big deal.

"Have you been to see Minseok?" I ask, trying to sound casual as I pop some chips into my mouth. I pretend I'm focusing on the snack even though I'm waiting anxiously for an answer.

"He got stitches," Robbie says. "But the doctors say he'll be fine in a couple of weeks."

I'm relieved to hear it, but at the same time disappointed. Why hasn't he come to see me, then?

I'm about to ask if he's said anything about me when my mom bursts into the room. "I have good news! Oh, Hyejun-ah, boys, it's good to see you."

She sends Robbie and Jaehyung one of her bright smiles as they give polite bows of greeting.

"Oh, Hyeri, honey, you shouldn't be eating processed food right now." She plucks the bag of chips from my hands and shoves them at Hyejun. "Boys, you should probably get going, Hyeri is about to be discharged. You can see her when she gets back from LA."

"Oh, sure," Jaehyung says. "See you later, Noona."

"Yeah," I say as they leave. I want to ask them to have Minseok call me, but I'm scared it'll make me sound too desperate.

"Wait." I turn to my mother. "What do you mean 'back from LA'?"

"We're going there for the table reading," my mom says. "I was worried you might miss it. But you'll just make it! This actually works out. I can escort my daughter back home now."

I frown. "Me getting attacked is good timing."

"Oh, Hyeri, you know I didn't mean it like that." My mom shakes her head. "I don't even want to think about what that man tried to do to my daughter." She shudders, closing her eyes and rubbing at her temples.

I realize now that my mom doesn't do well with difficult things. She's not trying to ignore painful stuff. She just truly doesn't know how to deal with it.

In a weird way, it makes me feel better to know that.

"I don't know if I can travel," I start to say, but she waves her hand.

"I already asked your doctors, and they said it should be fine."

I'm still unsure about this. But I tell myself it's okay. Maybe even good. It would suck if I had to put my life on pause because of what happened.

"You're going to stay with me in my hotel tonight and then we'll fly out tomorrow."

I try to think of a dozen reasons why this is too soon. But I keep quiet as my mom bustles about packing up the few things I have with me. Because the biggest reason I want to stay is Minseok, and I can't admit that out loud.

FIFTY-SIX

HYERI

The next morning, Hongjoo takes me to my apartment to pack a bag for my trip. My mom told me to just let my manager do it, but I use the excuse that I want to pick out my own clothes. The reality is that I don't care about what I wear in LA. I wanted to come home to see Minseok. I need to see him in person before I go.

I tell myself that he probably got whisked away from the hospital by his own team like I did. That they didn't give him a chance to come see me. But a part of me is worried that he doesn't want to see me. He got hurt because of me. Would he be mad at me for that?

I knock on the apartment door, picking anxiously at my cuticles while I wait for someone to answer.

It's not Minseok but Jongdae who opens the door.

"Oh sorry," I say quickly. "Can I come in?"

Jongdae nods and opens the door to let me inside.

I look around the apartment. It's as messy as it was the last time I was here. "Where are the others?"

"Around somewhere," Jongdae says. "Sit. You want something to drink?"

I do sit, but I reply, "I'm fine. I have to meet my mom soon."

"How are you feeling?" he asks, pointing to my sling.

"Crappy. You?" I point to his brace.

He smiles. "Same."

"Um, so, where's Minseok?" I finally force myself to ask.

Jongdae nods like he was expecting this. "He's not here. He's at the hospital."

"Still?" I blurt out, worried that maybe his injury is worse than I was told.

"Not still, again. He reached for something without thinking and popped one of his stitches. Hanbin-hyeong took him to get it checked out."

"Oh, okay." I sigh, but I can't help biting my lip in worry. Is he not taking care of himself? "I was just hoping to talk to him before I left."

"You're going to LA today?" Jongdae says it with the lift of a question, but it's clear he knows the answer already.

"Yeah, but I'll be back." I don't know why I feel a need to explain it. Like I don't want him to think I'm just leaving a mess here for other people to clean up. But the messiest thing, it seems, is my relationship with Minseok.

"I'll tell Minseok you came to say goodbye," Jongdae says.

"Thanks." I stand to go, feeling dissatisfied with the unresolved status of things.

"Don't be too mad at him, Hyeri-yah," Jongdae says behind me.

"Minseok acts like nothing bothers him. But he takes a lot of things to heart. He just buries it away to make things easier for everyone else. It's built up over the years, I think. And none of us realized how bad it was until now. I'm probably one of the biggest culprits."

"Have you talked to him?" I ask, even though it's none of my business. Not anymore.

"I will," he says with a heavy sigh. "I didn't want to burden him right after the attack. And before." He shakes his head, rubbing anxiously at the back of his neck. A gesture Minseok does too. I wonder who adopted it from whom. "Listen, if I'm the reason you and Minseok broke up, then I was wrong. I said some stupid crap because I knew it would mess with him, and I was pissed at the time."

He must be talking about whatever fight caused the bruise on Minseok's chin. But I shake my head. "It wasn't because of you. I don't think we're on the same page about a lot of things. Maybe we'll never be."

Jongdae nods. "Minseok doesn't really talk to me about stuff these days. But I can tell you that sometimes you need to really push to get him to admit what's bothering him. He's really good at bottling stuff up."

"Maybe," I say. "It would be good if we can be friends again, eventually."

"So, you're really doing it?" Jongdae asks. "You're really relocating to LA?"

"Yeah, I guess so." I shrug, forgetting my injured shoulder. It throbs, but I breathe past the pain. For some reason it feels dulled right now, like I'm experiencing everything through a filter. "Tell Minseok I'll call him when I'm back, okay?"

"Yeah, sure," Jongdae says, a small frown on his face. "Have a good trip, Hyeri."

FIFTY-SEVEN
HYERI

'm surprised when it's Hyejun who comes to pick up my mom and me at the hotel.

"It'll give me a chance to finally use my license," he quips, and I make sure my seat belt is buckled securely before we take off.

Hyejun borrowed a company car to drive us. It's one of the nicer models—the back seat is plush, with an armrest in the middle.

"My manager says they can come pick you up when you return to Seoul," Hyejun says.

"That's okay, Hongjoo will come get us," I tell him.

"Shouldn't she get reassigned?" Mom says. "She's not coming with you to LA. I'm sure the company will want someone who can actually speak English."

I close my eyes and remind myself that Mom doesn't really get how close I am to Hongjoo.

"Hongjoo can speak English, Eomma."

"But she sounds very foreign when she does," Mom says. "I don't know if the Hollywood execs will like that."

I force my lips together, practically biting them to keep myself from blurting out a frustrated reply.

"So, are you really going to relocate to LA?" Hyejun asks, glancing in the mirror.

"I'm not sure," I say at the same time my mother says, "Of course."

Mom turns in her seat to give me a stern look. "Hyeri, you're moving to LA for the show."

"Yes, but that's just for a few months. I can come back to Seoul after that."

Mom shakes her head with a dismissive laugh. "Don't be ridiculous, you can't just come back. What if they promote you to series regular? What if you get more auditions? You have to capitalize on this momentum, Hyeri. Hollywood is a whole new market you're breaking into."

Just hearing her say that makes my stomach turn. The idea of auditioning in a whole new market, trying to convince people I'm worthy all over again, makes me feel a little sick.

"The show itself will be a lot of work," I try to say weakly. I roll down the window to help settle my stomach.

"Hyeri, no, the wind is going to ruin my hair," Mom says.

I obediently roll the window back up.

"You good?" Hyejun asks, looking in the rearview mirror. "You're looking pale. Is your arm hurting?"

"She's just excited to get to LA," Mom answers for me. "Can you drive any faster? I want to go to the first-class lounge before our flight and fix my makeup."

Maybe she's right, I think. Maybe I'm just nervous. I reach for my phone, needing something to distract myself, and come up empty.

"I left my phone," I say, trying desperately to remember where I last saw it. "Hyejun, turn around, I left my phone at the apartment."

"We don't have time to go back," Mom says. "I'll buy you another phone in the States. You'll need one with a US number anyway."

I frown. Does that mean I'll lose all of my contacts too? What if someone tries to call me? What if Minseok tries to call me?

"Mom, I think Hyejun's right, my shoulder hurts a bit," I try. "Maybe I should take another day before we fly?"

"The tickets are nonrefundable. It's not like you broke anything. You should be fine."

"I'm not feeling well." I can taste the beginning of bile rising in my throat.

"We're almost at the bridge," Mom says.

"Oppa, pull over," I call out.

"Don't be dramatic—"

"I said pull over!" I scream.

Hyejun pulls the car off the road into the parking lot of a high rise.

As soon as the brakes are on, I burst out of the car. I feel like I'm going to throw up.

FIFTY-EIGHT
MINSEOK

Minseok is in a horrible mood. He hates having his arm in a sling, but Hanbin-hyeong insists after he pulled his stitches this morning.

As Minseok passes Hyeri's door he pauses to knock. But just like last night, she doesn't answer. She's either not home or not answering. And he doesn't know which explanation frustrates him more.

He automatically reaches for his phone and then remembers it got crushed in the fight with Jeongho. Hanbin promised he'd get a replacement but has yet to do so. Another reason to be frustrated.

When Minseok steps into his room, Jongdae is waiting for him.

Yet one more thing testing his patience.

"What are you doing in here?" He doesn't even try to hide his annoyance.

"I want to check on you."

Minseok lets out a bitter laugh. "Oh really? Why? You feel bad that I got stabbed?"

Jongdae flinches a bit at that, but he doesn't leave. "Yes, I do actually."

Minseok rolls his eyes. He used to like how blunt Jongdae was, but today, like most things, it's just getting on his nerves. "I'm tired from all the pain meds, I can't talk."

He flops onto his bed, then curses as his shoulder lands a bit too hard.

"You okay?" Jongdae starts forward.

"I said get out!"

Jongdae freezes and so does his expression. Then it drops into a scowl. He's finally had enough. He's been trying to talk to Minseok for months, but his friend has brushed him off. So, he accepted it, stayed out of Minseok's way. Partly because of his guilt. But partly because he took the excuse not to confront the broken parts of their friendship. Now it's getting ridiculous. Screw being careful. They'll have it out now and if the rift between them can't be fixed, he'll deal with it.

"You're using being hurt as an excuse to be an asshole," Jongdae says.

Minseok looks astonished. "Are you serious right now?"

"Not just your injury, but whatever happened between you and Hyeri."

Minseok clams up at the mention of her name. He doesn't want to hear it, especially not coming from Jongdae. "I'm tired." He turns on his good side, facing the wall.

"She came to see you."

It's the only thing that could get his attention. Minseok turns slightly, eyeing JD to see if he's making it up to get under his skin. But Jongdae just stands there expectantly.

"Did she really?" Minseok asks, finally sitting up. "When? Where is she now?"

"She wanted to say goodbye before she left for LA."

"What? But she's hurt. She can't travel." Minseok is on his feet now.

"It's just for the table read, she says she'll be back," Jongdae reminds him. But it doesn't calm Minseok.

Instead, he storms out of the room with purpose, intent on leaving to go after Hyeri. "How long ago was she here?"

"Minseok-ah." Jongdae captures his friend's arm to stop him. "She's probably halfway to the airport by now."

Minseok shakes his head, his shoulders deflating with the realization of defeat. "I didn't get a chance to tell her that I regret—" His voice cracks.

Jongdae isn't sure what to do. It's a complicated thing, wanting to console his friend but unsure if his comfort will be accepted. So, Jongdae merely lays a hand on Minseok's good shoulder.

"I shouldn't have told you that you were being selfish with her," he says softly, the fight gone from him. He no longer wants to lash out with his anger. His friend is hurting.

"I *was* being selfish." Minseok sighs. "I pretended like I was okay with keeping things casual. And then the offer came up and I kept pretending like I was okay until I ended up pushing her away."

"Is that what you want to tell her now?" Jongdae asks. "That you want her to stay?"

Minseok shakes his head. "No, I can't do that. I can't make her give up something this big for me."

"You didn't want to be the reason she'd have regrets." Jongdae nods. "I get it. I feel that way with Sooyeon sometimes. She lost her contract because of me. Some days I'm scared she'll look at me and realize that it wasn't worth it."

"Yeah, well, it's because of that ugly face of yours. Of course, she's going to regret it."

Jongdae cracks a smile at the familiar ribbing he's more used to from his friend.

"I should have told you about Sooyeon to begin with. And I should have apologized better when it came out."

"Why didn't you tell me? Did you really think I couldn't be trusted?"

"No." Jongdae looks genuinely shocked, and it goes a long way to soothe the festering wound that Minseok has been nursing. "I was just scared because I wasn't sure how to protect Sooyeon. I guess I didn't end up doing a good job of it."

Minseok nods. In a strange way, he can understand that fear so much better now than he would have a few months ago. With everything that happened with Hyeri, he's well aware how complicated these things can get. "I shouldn't have let my anger at you sit so long. I'm too used to being the easygoing one. I didn't want to disappoint anyone by taking things too seriously."

"I know you better than that, though. You should have been able to tell me."

Minseok grins. "Are we going to kiss and make up now?"

"You wish." Jongdae recoils slightly.

And just for that, Minseok leans in and smacks his lips hard against his friend's.

"Oh wow, what did we miss?" Jaehyung asks, walking into the apartment with Jun and Robbie. They're carrying takeout bags.

"Our love-line has been restored," Minseok says, throwing his good arm around his friend's stiff shoulders. JD tries to push away, but it only makes Minseok hold on tighter. The more Jongdae resists, the more fun he is having.

"Ya, stop that!" Jongdae shoves him and accidentally smacks Minseok's bad shoulder.

He winces at the stab of pain that radiates down his arm. Everyone immediately crowds around him.

"Hey, Seok-ah, you okay?" Jongdae asks as Minseok clings to him for support. "You need to go back to the hospital?"

Minseok gasps out. "I think . . ."

"Yeah?" Jongdae asks, leaning closer to hear his friend's request.

"I think that if you kiss it, it'll feel better."

"Ya!" Jongdae drops Minseok, who stumbles back, doubled over with laughter.

"Do you guys want to eat?" Jun asks, pulling out fried chicken from one of the bags.

"Yes!" Jaehyung says immediately, eyes widening with delight.

Minseok smiles, knowing that things are already feeling lighter in the apartment. But he hesitates, glancing at the door again. Because as much as he knows he should let her go, he can't stop wondering if he can catch up with Hyeri before she takes off.

"Call her," Jongdae says, holding out his phone.

Minseok takes it, dialing Hyeri's number. But just as his phone rings, so does another in the room. The others all check their pockets, but none of them are the culprit. Robbie, who's leaning against the back of the couch, reaches between the cushions and pulls out Hyeri's phone.

"She must have accidentally left it," Jongdae says as Minseok takes it, the screen now declaring a missed call.

He looks back and forth between the phone and his friends.

"Go after her," Jaehyung says.

"What?" Minseok frowns.

"You'll regret it if you don't," Robbie says with a knowing grin.

Minseok looks at Jongdae, who nods encouragingly. "Take my phone, call a taxi."

"Thanks," Minseok says, racing out of the apartment.

FIFTY-NINE
HYERI

"Hyeri!" Mom calls after me, slamming out of the car. "Get back here right now. We're going to miss our flight."

"I can't," I gasp out, starting to hyperventilate.

"Okay, just breathe." Mom leads me to the curb and sits me down, pushing my head between my knees.

I take in deep gulps of air until I don't feel like I'm going to pass out anymore.

"Better?" Mom is rubbing circles on my back. It feels good and I don't want her to stop. It reminds me of when I was seven and I'd stay home sick. Mom would lie next to me in bed and rub circles on my back until I fell asleep.

"I can't," I say again.

"Yes, you can, just breathe in slow and then out slow."

I lift my head to look at her now. "No, I can't go to LA."

She blinks at me like she doesn't understand what I'm saying. "Of course you can go. We're not even late; we'll still make the flight."

"No, Eomma, please listen to me," I say. "I don't *want* to go to LA."

"That's ridiculous. This is what you've dreamed of. It's what you've been working toward."

I hear Minseok's voice in my head, telling me to stop making decisions just to please everyone around me, and I find the courage to shake my head. "No, it's what *you've* dreamed of. What *you've* wanted me to work toward. I'm only nineteen. I want to have a life, not a career."

Mom laughs and shakes her head. "Don't be silly. Anyone would kill for the life you have. You're a celebrity, Hyeri. The world is obsessed with you."

"Yeah, and they're obsessed with catching every single mistake I make. It's too much. I feel like I'm suffocating." I pound my fist against my still-tight chest. "Please, don't make me go."

Mom looks horrified. Then she shakes her head, her face becoming stern. "Shin Hyeri, you will listen to your mother. I know what's best for you. Hyejun-ah, start the car, we have a flight to catch."

"No."

We both look up in shock at Hyejun's reply.

"What did you just say to me?" Mom says slowly.

"You heard Hyeri, she doesn't want to go. Can't you just listen to her for once?" He doesn't sound angry, but he sounds firm.

"Oppa," I rasp out before my throat tightens and I can't get more words free.

"Fine, I'll just call a taxi. I will not let you make the biggest mistake of your career," Mom says pulling out her phone. "You are going to LA with me."

SIXTY
MINSEOK

The airport was swarming with fans. Minseok asked the taxi to drop him off at the far end, but within minutes someone recognized him and shouted his name, which called the other fans' attention to him.

Though they were all holding signs for Hyeri, they quickly converted to chasing him down. And without managers or security, he was overwhelmed. He had to escape back into the taxi while dozens of screaming fans surrounded the vehicle.

He could barely hear Jaehyung's voice when he called.

"We got ahold of Hongjoo-noona! Her flight took off already. I'm sorry, Hyeong."

Minseok knew it had been a long shot, but still, he was disappointed.

Back at the apartment, Minseok curses quietly as he climbs into the elevator. He wanted to see Hyeri before she left. Even if she's coming back, he doesn't want her going all the way to LA without resolving their fight.

But maybe this is for the best. He knows that despite what he told Jongdae, if he saw her, he would've broken down and begged her not to go. Not to take the role. Not to move away and leave him.

If this is what she wants, then Minseok wants it for her, even though it hurts to think that he lost his chance with her.

He's punching the code into his door when the lock behind him beeps open. He doesn't even register it until he hears that familiar voice say his name.

"Hyeri?" He turns to stare at her, somehow standing in her apartment doorway. "What are you doing here? Your flight."

She steps out into the hallway, letting the door close behind her. "I didn't go."

He hurries to her, then stops awkwardly a foot away. What he wants is to take her into his arms and thank her for staying. But he hesitates. "Why not?"

She lifts a brow and says, "I didn't stay for you, if that's what you're thinking."

SIXTY-ONE

HYERI

watch as Minseok's face falls. Then I take pity on him. "I stayed for me. I don't think that role is what I want. Not right now, at least."

"Really?" he says slowly with a dubious frown.

"Really," I confirm. I thought about how to tell him this a dozen times as Hyejun drove me home. We finally convinced Mom to let me stay and sent her to the airport in the taxi with kisses and apologies. She claimed she did not accept them, but I'm certain she'll get over it. I realize that for all of Mom's blustering, she always gets over it. "I felt pressured to take this role because everyone was saying what a huge opportunity it was. But to me, I felt just like I did before I was told I was cast in *CiPro*. The company told me instead of asking. I never had a choice. This time I do, so I said no."

"And you don't regret it?"

"No," I say, and I mean it. Mostly.

Minseok nods. "Good, I'm glad you did what you actually wanted."

"So, yeah, I guess that's what I wanted to tell you." I don't really know what to say now, but I feel like I don't have the closure I was hoping for either.

"I'm sorry I wasn't here. . . . I was at the airport actually," Minseok says.

Now it's my turn to be shocked. "You followed me to the airport?"

"Followed? No, I mean, kind of. Yes, I guess I did." He looks flustered all of a sudden. "You left your phone; I thought you'd want it with you." He pulls it out of his pocket, shoving it into my chest.

I take it, frowning as I rub where he jabbed me. "Thanks, I guess. You didn't need to go all the way to the airport for this. I'm sure it was crowded."

"Yeah, I realized after I was mobbed that it wasn't the best idea I've ever had. I'm sure Hanbin is going to be pissed."

I feel a strange clenching in my stomach. He went to the airport, alone, for me. He wanted to see me that badly.

No, I can't be swayed. There's more we need to talk about. We can't just continue doing what we were doing. It's not fair to either of us.

"Is this really the only reason you went?" I hold up the returned phone, trying to keep my voice calm, measured.

He sighs and shakes his head.

"No, it's not the only reason. I also had something to tell you."

My heart rate picks up, but I ignore it. The last few weeks with Minseok have taught me a lot of control when it comes to being around him. Now, even though my hands are itching to grab ahold of him, I ball them into fists around the phone instead.

"What is it?" I ask carefully.

"I was stupid for pretending that it didn't kill me that you were leaving. And you were right, I lectured you about letting other people control your choices when that's exactly what I was doing. I was just trying to avoid confrontation, which is obviously an issue I have. Oh, I talked to Jongdae, by the way. Which I might not have done if I hadn't felt totally shitty about how I mishandled everything with you."

He's rambling. Minseok isn't really a rambler, but I find this new side of him endearing.

"So, you and JD are better?" I ask when he finally stops for a breath.

"Mostly. We'll figure it out. You're right; family figures it out."

I nod. "Good."

"I'd like to figure things out with you too. I don't want to lose my chance at this." He points a finger between us. "So, I guess the first step is to be honest. I want it to be a real thing, not just fun or pretend or undefined. I want to be with you, Hyeri, officially."

I suck in a deep shuddering breath. My heart is now going haywire. It's literally the kind of stuff I've dreamed of hearing from Minseok since I was thirteen years old. But I have to make sure I have my say first. "I want to be with you too, but we have to be better about talking about the hard stuff."

Minseok nods. "I know."

"And I don't want to tell anyone."

His face falls. "What?"

"I mean, the public. Or the media. I don't think they should have a right to every part of my life."

He nods with a grin. "I agree. But I have to tell the guys and Hanbin."

"And I probably have to tell Hongjoo-eonni."

"Doesn't she already know?"

"Yeah, but I should tell her it's official." I am dreading that conversation. I'm sure Hongjoo is dealing with enough having to explain why I'm not on a plane to LA right now.

Minseok reaches out now to take my hand. "Is it, then? Official, I mean."

"Yeah, sure," I say. "Today can be our day one."

He cringes. "Oh wow, who knew you could be so corny."

"Ya!" I punch his good shoulder, but he catches my wrist and uses it to pull me into him.

My hand is twined with his, the other stuck in my sling. So I can't do anything but lift my chin to meet his kiss.

His lips are warm and full. He tangles his fingers in my hair, pulling me forward.

My newly freed hand grabs his lapel, holding on.

He breaks the kiss, but doesn't move too far back. Instead he leans his forehead against mine. "Maybe let's not do this in the middle of the hallway."

"Your place?" I ask.

He shakes his head with a grin. "Let's go to yours. More privacy."

"You're so smart, Oppa," I say, pulling him to my door.

He laughs as he brings my hand up to kiss my knuckles. "That's why you love me."

K-Pop Newsfeed article: "Bright Star Entertainment Announces They're Going Public"

Bright Star Entertainment announced they are going public.

Recent successes highlighted in the announcement include the popularity of Robbie Choi's self-produced mixtape, which was released earlier this fall, with one of the songs even hitting the iTunes chart, despite not being an official album.

The announcement also included the success of Bright Star's breakout rookie group, Kastor. The girl group's first mini album broke debut records as the largest first day sales by a debut girl group. Kastor has already been nominated for multiple Rookie of the Year awards.

There is one mystery in Bright Star, however: Where is Shin Hyeri?

The rookie actress was a huge rising star earlier this year, even winning the Entertainment Newcomer of the Year award for her appearance on the variety show *Our Celebrity Marriage* with WDB's Moonster. There were rumors she would be cast in *Musical Dreams*, but Bright Star released a statement last month disputing it. Since then, Bright Star has not announced any future projects for the young star. And Shin Hyeri has not been seen in public since she finished her stint on *Our Celebrity Marriage* earlier this month.

Fans have taken to forums to share theories that perhaps she was more injured while defending Kim Ana from an attack by a sasaeng fan at the Hallyu Wave Awards at the end of the summer. Kim Ana—who is taking time off due to anxiety—did post a message of appreciation for Shin Hyeri after the ordeal, dispelling the longtime rumors of a rivalry between the girls.

Many fans are hoping for Shin Hyeri's good health and sending her encouraging messages to come back as soon as she's able!

In the meantime, most are waiting impatiently for WDB's comeback schedule. Many speculate that the comeback dates will be announced right before Bright Star Entertainment officially goes public later this month.

EPILOGUE

The heat of summer has left Seoul. Autumn has taken its place with changing leaves and cooling winds.

Korean universities have started up again. The campus of Chung-Ang University sits below the Han River and boasts beautiful greens, lovely trees, and state-of-the-art facilities.

A student named Jo Mikyoung races out of her class, almost bumping into a pretty girl with a face mask on. The girl's cap falls off, revealing long dark locks that fall in satin waves.

Mikyoung hurries to pick up the cap, bowing low in apology. She's still just a first-year and is horrified at the idea that she might have slammed into an upperclassman in her major.

"I'm sorry, I wasn't looking where I was going."

"It's okay. I was spacing out myself." The girl smiles at her, eyes crinkling above the black face mask. She accepts the cap with thanks.

"Oh my god," Mikyoung stammers. "You're Shin Hyeri."

"Oh." Hyeri's eyes widen with surprise.

"Sorry, I know we're not supposed to bother you here," Mikyoung says quickly. "I'm in the Department of Film Studies with you. We have some classes together and the professors made that announcement at the beginning of the semester."

Hyeri grimaces in embarrassment. "I wish they hadn't. By saying not to make it a big deal . . ."

"They made it a big deal," both girls say together. Then burst into laughter.

"Well, maybe I'll see you in our next class." Hyeri makes her way down the stairs.

Mikyoung stares after her, wondering if her friends will ever believe her if she tells them she just met the actress Shin Hyeri.

Hyeri hums under her breath as she makes her way off campus. Her life feels even more surreal these days than when she was on set every day. Sometimes she can't believe she's allowed to be a normal university student.

Bright Star seemed a little reluctant at the idea of not finding her an immediate project to follow up the success of *OCM*, but Hyeri stuck to her resolve. It helped that Minseok and Hongjoo were completely on her side.

Plus, Bright Star is in a flurry preparing for WDB's comeback.

Hyeri smiles up at the autumn sun as she makes her way to the subway station. Hongjoo didn't like the idea of Hyeri taking public transportation to school. But Hyeri doesn't think it's appropriate use of company vehicles to drive her to and from campus whenever she has a class. Plus, it's nice to have autonomy.

Still, she's always vigilant. Even though the antis have quieted down lately, Hyeri knows there are still some out there.

That's why she notices the dark sedan inching behind her. It seems to have been following her since she left campus. But she doesn't want to make any assumptions yet.

To test it, Hyeri picks up the pace and as she does, so does the car. Okay, so she's definitely not being paranoid. It's following her. She's about to break into a sprint for the subway entrance when the window rolls down and Minseok calls out, "Hey, pretty university student, you have a boyfriend?"

Hyeri hurries to the passenger side. "What are you doing here? Someone could see you."

"So? I'm just here to offer a ride to my good friend." He leans over the center console with a suggestive grin. "Want a ride, good friend?"

"Oh my god," Hyeri groans, but she climbs into the car, rolling up the tinted window.

Minseok laughs as he takes off.

"What are you actually doing here?" Hyeri asks, leaning into the supple leather of the car. She's pretty sure this is not a company vehicle; it's too nice. "Shouldn't you be in the recording studio?"

"Just finished a track today. Robbie's producing it; he's being really intense about it." Minseok pretends to complain, but he's actually proud of the group's maknae. Robbie made a total hit with his mixtape and fans are clamoring for more of his music. The company agreed to let Robbie write and produce three songs on the upcoming full-length album. One is even in contention for the title track.

Hyeri shrugs. "Robbie's got a good ear for music. He probably just wants it to be perfect."

"Well, I think I deserve to take a break with my girlfriend." He reaches over and laces his fingers through hers.

Hyeri laughs, blushing a bit at the phrase.

"Did you read those scripts Hongjoo gave you?"

"How did you know Hongjoo gave me scripts?" Hyeri eyes him.

"Because you left them all over the table. You know, you're kind of a slob, jagi-ya."

Hyeri scrunches up her nose. "Why do you still call me that? *OCM* has been done for a month."

"I like it. Jagi-ya. Jaaagiii-yaaa." He pulls out the vowels like a kid teasing another on the playground.

"Anyway," Hyeri says firmly to get him to stop. "I actually did find a script I liked. It's for an independent film."

"Oh yeah? I thought you were going to take your time picking your next role." Minseok stops at a red light, bringing her hand up to kiss her knuckles absentmindedly the way he likes to.

Hyeri nods. "I was going to, but I really love this script. Plus, Hongjoo-eonni doesn't think they're going to start production until November, so it still gives me some time off."

"Does it make you happy?" Minseok asks.

Hyeri grins; of course he'd ask that. "Yeah, it does."

"Then it sounds perfect."

The light turns green, and Minseok takes off. The sudden speed makes Hyeri laugh. Her heart dances in her chest, knowing that right now, she's choosing the direction she's going in. And Moon Minseok, the boy she's loved since she was thirteen, is right next to her.

ACKNOWLEDGMENTS

Thank you to all the readers who have embraced my chaotic K-Pop boys, I hope you love the K-Pop and K-Drama girls that I've introduced in this book!

Thank you to my amazing agent, Beth Phelan, and my wonderful editor, Rebecca Kuss! Two people who have helped me through many ups and downs in this industry.

Thank you to Velinxi for my gorgeous covers and jacket art. I am honored to have this art adorning my books and bringing my characters to such colorful life!

Thank you to the team at Hyperion who worked on this book. Thank you to the design, publicity, and marketing teams who worked on bringing this book to readers!

Thank you to g.o.d, 2NE1, BtoB, B.A.P, BTS, and Stray Kids. You've all helped me through different rough times in my life. I am forever grateful for the joy and entertainment that you created.

To my talented writing friends, though the process of writing might seem like a solo endeavor, you make it so that I am never alone on this journey! I would not have made it this far without your amazing support and counsel!

To my sister, Jennifer Magiera, your support means the world to me. This life wouldn't have as much meaning if I didn't have you to share it with. And I love you very much!

Lucy and Nora, thanks for being my K-pop dance buddies!

Mom & Dad, I love you. 보고싶어요.